MURDER
MOST COLD

A gripping and terribly twisty murder mystery

VICTORIA DOWD

Smart Woman's Mystery Series Book 5

JOFFE
BOOKS

Joffe Books, London

www.joffebooks.com

First published in Great Britain in 2023

Cover art by Dee Dee Book Covers

ISBN: 978-1-83526-231-3

For K, D, J & S

THE MÖKKI MURDER PAPERS

Containing a short record of the trials, travels, exploits and various deaths experienced by the Smart Women and their associates, compiled by Ursula Smart.

I have faced many trials so far with the Smart Women. As with most people, you don't really need to know how many deaths I've seen to understand me. But it might help. A few are mentioned below. Not all. There are many more, but I never find a body count very reassuring. Suffice to say, the number is higher than normal, but less than an undertaker. However, one thing I have learned, and one thing to remember in all that you are about to read, is that you can only ever die once.

The question I am asked more than any other is 'just exactly who are these Smart Women?' Sometimes it's a question asked in slightly more colourful language. I will attempt to answer this as honestly as I can.

Ursula Smart: I will be your guide through this particular circle of hell. Somehow, I still live with Mother. Dad died unexpectedly when I was thirteen and, occasionally, I see his ghost. I don't mention this too much due to the lack of judgement-free space in my world. I'm with Spear, a man I met on an expedition to the Outer Hebrides where he was the leader and many people were murdered.

Pandora Smart: aka Mother. Author of the blog and podcast *Death Smarts*, a forum where she relates in graphic detail our many near-death experiences and close encounters with killers. Often exposes intimate facts about her family, in particular, me. It is also a rather fanciful account and, therefore, the reason why I think it is vitally important for me to keep this more accurate, less salacious, record of what really happened.

Charlotte Smart: aka Aunt Charlotte. My mother's sister. Has no basic grasp of popular culture. Devoted to tweed. Has recently taken up residence in our house.

Bridget Gutteridge: Associate and one-time member of the Smart Woman's book club, which no longer meets due to the murder of a member at the last meeting. Self-professed Smart Woman, which is hotly disputed by Mother. Keeps various unusual pets, including Dupin, a monkey she adopted after both his original owners were killed.

Mirabelle: One-time member of the Smart Woman's book club. Deceased. No ghost, as yet.

Spear: Expedition leader until boat sank and various crew members, including his wife, were murdered. Widower. Slightly shady past, but that's all behind him now. Left me. Tried to rescue me. Now with me again.

Angela: Spear's mother. Widow.

Dupin: A monkey.

AT THE MÖKKIS (SOME COTTAGES IN NORTHERN LAPLAND)

Descriptions taken from Bridget's contemporaneous notebook. Errors and opinions Bridget's own.

Tapio: English owner and drunk. Unfaithful to wife. Inhospitable. Poor cleanliness.

Aino: Finnish wife of Tapio. Dissatisfied.

Helmi: Twenty-year-old, weed-smoking, feckless daughter of Tapio and Aino. Recovering from failed elopement with Matthias. Needs a strong talking to.

Matthias: General handyman and reindeer wrangler. Carries deep-seated belief in the old spirits and myths of Finland. Could be attractive with a lot more grooming.

Onni: Works at *mökkis* alongside Matthias. Weasel-faced. Ate Bambi.

As in all of our previous exploits, names have been changed to protect everyone's identities, including ours. No one really has a monkey called Dupin.

MÖKKI COTTAGE ALLOCATION
(AS ENFORCED BY MOTHER)

Mökki 1: Mother (Pandora) and me (Ursula)

Mökki 2: Aunt Charlotte and Bridget

Mökki 3: Angela and Spear

Main lodge: Tapio, Aino and Helmi. Matthias and Onni.

The name of the location has been changed. The venue is no longer taking bookings for reasons that will become obvious. There are, however, plans for a visitor centre for true crime fans.

CHAPTER ONE: DREAM A LITTLE DREAM OF ME

I should have noticed it wasn't a good start to the first day of the rest of my life. Right there at the very beginning, even the birds were singing out of tune. Irritating, feathery pests had been sitting outside my bedroom window with no respect for a decent hangover. It was the first thing I noticed when I woke up. It all had the wrong sound to it. And things just carried on that way.

Somehow, from that first moment, I must have known it was going to be one of those uneven days when it was all slightly off balance. The kind where you never feel fully awake. My mind was still in that muddy haze of sleep, bits and pieces of dreams seeping over like muffled voices from another room.

They were those odd kind of remnants of dreams — silvery scraps that should have known when to leave and slip away quietly at daybreak like any other unfaithful lover. It's not good for me to keep breathing them in, except perhaps the quick little smoke of memory. Maybe. Occasionally. But no more than that. Dreams are just fool's-gold thoughts, a glimpse of a world that's not meant to be. As the therapists tell me, I should remember they're guests in my head, not residents.

But there are always some guests that want to linger too long, clinging on to the next day, all in the wrong clothes, still smelling like last night. Those overstaying dreams make everything feel disjointed. They're the difficult ones who just don't know when to go. The perilous ones. Because, as I was about to learn, they're the kind of dreams that are liars, deceivers and cheats, and so are the people who peddle them.

Unfortunately, deception and betrayal were the furthest thoughts from my mind as the rest of that day rolled out.

'My lady, your carriage awaits.' Spear held open the door to the car and gave a flourish. He's not really a flourishing kind of guy so my suspicions should have been raised even then. But it was too late. I'd already let myself be carried away.

Spear and I traced a line through the shimmering countryside, blissfully unaware of where this dream would take us. There was a synchronicity to our movements, as if we were being guided by something else. The borrowed vintage Jag and our borrowed time lent an air of ageless nostalgia to our journey. It felt like we could borrow the future. I can still, even now after everything, look down on this dream, like a reflection in a pond, and enjoy that fleeting image, in spite of all the pain that rolled out from it.

I watch that image of myself, hair drawn back on the white air, Spear glancing over with a truthful smile. And in that little seed of time, right then, I can pinpoint that moment when I'm letting myself be reeled in by the dream. All neatly tied up. No loose ends. No frayed edges, nothing that might unravel.

Spear had been reborn from my past — a frightening place for anyone. We'd met when he'd been the leader of a fateful expedition I went on that ended in tragedy. We'd spent time together after that. But he disappeared and just didn't exist for a while. I don't like to linger on those shadowy days. When he came back, more death followed. Almost mine that time. With all this history of death in mind, an astute observer might suggest that perhaps he wasn't such a good idea, and that perhaps he carried tragedy and darkness in his back pocket as easily as his wallet.

But I was starting to fall under the spell of this particular dream. He'd convinced me it was light, *not* darkness he brought with him. A future. All those shallow concepts that use bland words to numb the mind. '*Leave it all behind,*' he'd said, like the past was just a parcel in a lost property office that could be abandoned. But there is all too often something ugly in those things we try to forget or hide from ourselves.

That was the day the sunlight had an unreal quality to it as well, as if those particular colours had been blended solely for the purpose of preserving that moment in my memory. It was a peculiar, coppery light gilding that picture. The air smelled different, a warm, heavy flavour that lulled me. It was all conspiring to make the next decision seem like a good idea.

We pulled up at the hotel, a quaint little building shrouded in ivy that might have been conjured up from a fairy tale, the kind with just a faint hint of eerie malice peeping out through every curtain. That's where Spear chose to do it, in a bedroom with faded chintz wallpaper, by the light of a flickering exit sign. Perhaps he thought that slightly dark, disturbing charm was somehow appropriate for what he was about to suggest.

'You're kidding?'

'I'll be honest, Ursula, that was not the response I'd imagined. And, trust me, I've imagined quite a few. Even some really out-there ones.' Spear fell back on to his heels, crouching at my feet as if he might break into prayer.

'Can I ask why you're kneeling on *both* knees?'

'Again, when I walked through this scenario this was not one of the questions I'd envisaged.'

'It's just that it's meant to be . . .'

He started to get up, putting his hands down to the floor and leaning forward. 'I know what it's meant to be, Ursula. I've got dodgy knees. I can't put pressure on just one knee. I thought I'd spread the load.'

3

'What every woman wants to hear.'

He paused and tilted his head to the side, as if trying to find a different view. 'I have just asked you to marry me.'

The air turned dense in my chest.

'Ursula?' He was still on all fours looking up at me.

I focused intently out of the window. The irritating birds were still out there. I watched the trees swaying, the clouds passing by. It was all just normal, as if nothing strange was happening in here. When I looked back at him, Spear was still analysing me like he was recording the results of this experiment.

'Right.' He'd curled his toes under and started to push his knees up. 'OK. Well, this obviously wasn't—'

'Stop!'

He was caught in a kind of semi-yoga pose, a half-downward-facing dog, looking up at me expectantly. 'I can't . . .'

'I know you can't understand but . . .'

'No, I can't hold this for much longer.' He was shaking. His arm gave way and he fell to the side. 'Christ.'

'Oh . . . Right. Shit. Sorry. Let me help you.'

'I'm fine, thank you.' He held out a hand to fend me off before slowly climbing to his feet.

Neither of us spoke until he was standing, trying to look a little more collected and stable.

'It's just . . .' I began.

He held up both hands and closed his eyes. 'It's fine.' His voice grew quieter. 'Call it a test run.'

'You've made us sound like we're crash test dummies.' I attempted a laugh. It didn't help to dispel any of that awkward atmosphere. My smile faded out.

He wiped his hands down his trousers as if brushing something away. Those were his best jeans and, if I wasn't mistaken, his favourite shirt too, the one with all its buttons.

'I need a drink.' He shoved his hands in his jacket pockets. Pulling his chin up in acceptance of defeat, he turned to go.

'Wait.' I put my hand on his sleeve and he looked at it as if he was inspecting it. 'I just haven't had time to take it in.'

'OK.' He breathed out slowly. 'That's fair. I'm sorry. I wasn't thinking. I just wanted to . . . to . . .' The words lost their sound.

'To what?'

'Well, I suppose I'd say . . . surprise you.' He nodded to confirm his own thoughts.

I couldn't keep the smile down. 'You certainly did that. Listen, I don't mind a bit of the spontaneous.'

He looked vaguely caught out. 'Actually, it's not quite that *spontaneous*.'

'How do you mean?' I let my hand fall from his arm.

'I've got a ring.'

'A ring?'

'Yes, a ring. It was my great-grandmother's. They say it was the colour of her eyes and, well, that . . . that's probably true given mine are the same but no one else . . . sorry, well, yes. I'm rambling. I'm sorry. That's about it really.'

I waited, letting it settle. 'You're serious about this? You want to get married? To me?'

He pulled back his head. 'Who else would I be marrying?'

It seemed a curious thing to say but there were a lot of questions here already.

'Why?'

'Why what?'

There was something uncomplicated about him. Neat. The blue-grey stubble was cropped a little closer than normal, his hair tidier. He'd prepared for this. But now all I could see was that lost, surprised look again, as if he'd got to the top of the stairs and forgotten there was another step.

'*Why* do you want to marry me?' I wasn't even sure that was the question I really wanted to ask, but it was the nearest to hand.

He looked so far adrift from where he'd imagined this conversation would go that I almost felt sorry for asking the question. But it remained.

'Because . . .' He sighed. 'Look, let's just forget it.'

'No. I want to know.' I really did.

His shoulders fell. 'Because . . .' He blew out, steadying himself. It was almost imperceptible, but the tips of his hair were trembling. His breath was moving the air a little faster. He fixed his eyes directly on me, and when he spoke his voice had almost dried up completely. 'Because I think it's the only way I'm going to survive.'

It was my turn to falter now. The silence lingered over us. I studied him doubtfully.

'You've made that sound faintly like you're in danger. If you're looking for someone to keep you alive, I'm probably the worst candidate.'

He placed his hands on my shoulders and stared keenly. 'Stop, Ursula. Don't make this a joke.' There was a strange concentration to him — an intensity I'd not seen before. 'That's not what I meant. I'm not in danger. No one's trying to kill me.' He paused. 'Anymore.' His eyes flickered, trying to refocus on where he wanted this to go. 'This is not about anyone else but you and me.'

It is very possible that some people might not see any of this as a good reason to tie yourself to another human being for the rest of however long they've got left. But somehow it was enough. And, let's face it, enough can be more than some people ever get in a lifetime. Enough is what sees us through those dark hours, it's what carries us home on a lonely journey. One foot in front of the other. It's the glue that outlasts all the other fiery extremes. It brings purpose. Enough is quiet. Peaceful. The solace I'd been reaching for all this time.

It is a dream.

CHAPTER TWO: TELLING MOTHER

Spear's mother flicked on the kettle and took down two mugs from the cupboard. We'd never had a kettle until Angela bought us one. Mother prefers coffee. We don't have a coffee machine either. Mother prefers takeout. She doesn't do homemade. She doesn't really do home anything. It's more a 3-D living embodiment of an interior's magazine.

'So, how did it go, you guys?' Angela dropped a tea bag into each mug for me and Spear. 'Pandora?' She glanced at Mother, who was trying to look distracted.

'Hmm?' Mother looked over the top of her laptop momentarily.

'Tea, dear?'

'Filthy stuff.' Mother went back to the screen. She spends a lot of time on her blog these days, and the new podcast. *Death Smarts* has admittedly gathered quite a large following, which grows exponentially with every murder we encounter. It's successful but it's not a business model that would suit everyone.

'Four sugars for me,' Aunt Charlotte called as she wandered in. 'Have to keep up my strength.' She readjusted her sporran. Aunt Charlotte had taken to wearing full Highland dress as she said it gave her a sense of freedom she didn't experience with other skirts. No one enquired about the exact mechanics of that.

'When are you moving out?' Mother had adopted her most disinterested voice, but I knew Aunt Charlotte's living arrangements were definitely an issue at the top of Mother's thoughts. She'd even instructed the local estate agents to message Aunt Charlotte every day. Unfortunately, Aunt Charlotte has been on airplane mode for two and a half years, both literally and figuratively. It's something which Mother remains unaware of due to the fact that none of her texts, or commands as I know them, require a response.

'We had a wonderful time, thank you.' I passed the milk, deeply aware Mother was listening to every word. Her mouth was working hard not to speak. 'It was just lovely for us to have some space,' I added.

Mother made a sharp little noise of disapproval.

Spear cleared his throat and picked up one of the biscuits. I'm sure Aunt Charlotte only meant to tap his hand playfully, but it was actually more of a hard slap she gave him. The biscuit fell into pieces on the plate and he pulled his hand back. 'Oh, you're a naughty boy, aren't you?' Aunt Charlotte giggled coquettishly and swung her sporran from side to side.

I grimaced apologetically at him and he smiled, rubbing the reddening hand.

Angela held out a mug of tea to him.

'Thanks, Mum.'

'It's good to see you two so happy,' Angela smiled. There was warmth in her face, a softness. She'd been so kind, so accepting, not just of me but also my now infamous family. Not everyone wants their son involved with the Smart Women, particularly when it often ends up with someone dying. It had almost been her own son on one occasion. His first wife was murdered and the killer had then shifted their aim on to him. Spear has a past, but then show me a widower with a murdered wife that doesn't. I'm in no position to criticise someone for having a bloodstained background. Mine began at thirteen and I haven't really looked back since.

I've made that sound a little like I'm a murderer. I'm not. Although, I could make an exception for Mother sometimes. Let's just say my dad was murdered when I was thirteen and ever since then the body count has been mounting. Some people just attract death, I suppose, each new one adding to the collection of little black iron filings following me around like I'm the magnet.

'Cooey!' It was Bridget, another possible exception to the no-murders-in-this-house rule.

'Get out.' Mother didn't even look up this time.

'Mother, please . . .'

'I don't know how she keeps getting in.'

'I had my own set of keys cut.' Bridget jangled the bunch in the air. The noise sparked a sudden, harsh scream from somewhere around her legs.

'She's got the bloody monkey with her again!' Mother's eyes were fixed on the creature like the double barrels of a gun.

Dupin danced around by Bridget's feet, grinning with his wide keyboard of teeth.

'She's one of us now.' Bridget adopted her prim, upright look, the one where you just know every single orifice has tightened simultaneously. 'She just reads my subtext so well.'

'She?' Aunt Charlotte frowned at the monkey and raised her monocle, wedging it into her eye socket and squinting. This was another recent addition that she thought was Scottish. I'd tried to explain it was actually called *Monarch* of the Glen, but it made no difference.

Bridget nodded with the kind of grave sincerity she might assume for meeting royalty or Alan Titchmarsh. 'It's been confirmed,' she said.

No one was about to explore that any further.

'We now have a new Smart Woman!'

Mother's fuse was lit. She slammed the laptop shut and rose with the slow, threatening presence of the undead from a coffin. 'Neither the organ grinder nor the monkey are Smarts,' she said with a flat, steel-edged voice.

'Oh, Pandora, you love us really.' Bridget bustled forward like she'd spent a lot of time perfecting the most irritating way to enter a room.

It worked. Certainly for Mother, who was bristling so much you could almost see the river of spines prickling down her back.

'What's wrong with her today?' I said quietly out the corner of my mouth.

'More of those nasty messages, I'm afraid,' Aunt Charlotte sighed.

I looked at her. 'How bad?'

She shrugged. 'They all look bad to me, but she persists with the blog nonsense. Won't report them, although I'm not sure that would get anywhere.'

Mother had been receiving unpleasant emails, tweets and DMs for a long time and from various accounts. In her view it came with the true crime territory, but just recently there'd been an increase, and from one account in particular. I'd taken to checking whenever I could, even deleting them sometimes before she saw them if they were too bad. These messages had a more personal tone than usual. A more threatening one.

'Tea?' Angela said in a light, airy voice. She always managed to keep a sense of delicate patience that Mother just . . . didn't.

But there was one overriding thing Angela, Mother and Spear did all have in common. Widowhood. And each of them dealt with it in very different ways.

Dad was killed many years ago but I still see him now and then. I won't go into that right now as it doesn't present me in the sanest light.

Spear's dad had died on an expedition before Spear was born. Unlike Spear, when his father's ship had gone down, he'd drowned. I'd seen the photograph of him proudly displayed at their home, staring out, just like the son.

Mother never admitted that she saw anything of Dad in me. She rarely speaks about him, but I catch her sometimes looking at their wedding photo as if she could step right back under the same church arch and recapture that lost smile. Mother doesn't really do smiling now. She says it leads to wrinkles. That would account for why her face is as smooth and featureless as a blank piece of paper. That, and the constant sea of Botox.

'Angela!' Bridget was trotting across the kitchen with Dupin beside her, mimicking her every movement. 'Oh my goodness, it's so good to see you!' Bridget had convinced herself that Angela was her new best friend. She'd always been on the lookout for someone to take on that role, and this time she was sure.

'Good to see you too.' Angela offered her the plate of biscuits. Bridget stared at her as if she were about to be knighted. She's been practising this look for years. I was half expecting her to curtsey but even Bridget has her limits.

'Oh, oh, surely not . . . for me?' Bridget held her hand to her chest. Dupin did too. It was hard to know if the monkey was copying her or mocking her, a perennial problem for Bridget.

'Thank you so much.' Bridget took one of the biscuits and handed it to Dupin, then reached out for one for herself.

Mother was close to detonation. 'They're *Tesco Finest*! Stop feeding them to the bloody animal.'

'Oh, sorry, Pandora.' Angela pulled the plate away from Bridget. Bridget's smile wilted.

'So.' Spear put his mug down and I knew now was the moment. I felt an insatiable urge to run. He must have sensed it as he put a proprietorial arm over my shoulder. I wanted to scream out, 'Forget it! Let's just elope.' I'm not sure that people over thirty do elope but I have good reasons.

'Ursula and I have an announcement . . .'

Mother's mouth cracked open.

The room was slowly closing in.

I heard Aunt Charlotte release a little gasp. She looked at me, then her eyes quickly landed on Mother.

'We are—'

'No!' The word shot out of Mother like a bullet.

Angela and Bridget were looking confused. Spear seemed utterly oblivious to the changing temperature of the room.

'Ursula and I,' he squeezed my shoulder, 'are going to get married.'

There was a very distinct moment when I thought Mother's eyeballs might actually drop out on to her laptop. But as the seconds passed, her reaction grew into something much worse. Her face fell into a grave, lost look that infected every part of her.

No one spoke. No one moved.

Even the monkey stood solemn faced, biscuit in hand.

If there hadn't been a clock to mark the seconds, I could have counted them out myself. Each one driving a little nail into my head. Tick tick tick, like the timer on a bomb. Everything had stalled to listen.

Then suddenly the room ignited. 'Oh, that's such fabulous news!' Angela was hugging Spear. And through my warped lens, that was the unusual thing to do — to congratulate us, to be excited, thrilled that her son was embarking on a new journey. The silent, stunned faces that looked like he'd just announced a death were somehow the ones I'd anticipated, the ones I understood.

There was one face among them all that I sought out.

Dad.

His grey spirit was there in the back corner of the room, his head slightly bowed, watching me with that mischievous look. The smile broke all over his face and his eyes crinkled at the edges. He was the very embodiment of a proud father. Although, as a ghost, he doesn't really have a body. But he just drifted above it all. That lonely soul had, for one brief moment, abandoned his lost look and happiness had taken its place. The joy couldn't wait to make its way on to his face. It settled in with an easy familiarity. He'd always been comfortable with happiness. He'd been the kind of man who was very at home with it.

I suppose I should explain that I see my father's ghost at moments of high stress and emotion. 'Continuing bonds' was

12

the theory. When a person dies, we lose them, not the relationship. We still have that dialogue. Well, that's how the counsellors mindsplained it to me. One even suggested I might consider 'death tech'. He showed me an app called Neverdead, where they would gather all the pictures, voice messages and videos they could find of him and create a kind of AI ghost. I prefer my analogue ghost though, to be honest. Bob the Therapist, who'd definitely earned his invite to our wedding, told me it was a *physical manifestation of trauma*. That was before he disappeared. He was last seen paddling away down the Congo with a tinfoil hat on his head, wearing no pants. The final words anyone heard from him were, 'Never open Pandora's box!'

As usual with all Dad's appearances, I was both pleased to see him and concerned that I might be sailing off down that river of insanity with Bob the Therapist.

'Oh, it's so amazing!' Angela seemed to be the only real person in the room who knew how to be pleased. 'I'm so happy for you. I'm going to have a daughter!'

Mother looked like she might have stopped breathing, her face stripped of emotion.

Angela hugged me. 'Oh, you are going to be so happy! Bless you.'

Spear pulled me in close and smiled. 'We haven't planned anything yet but, you know, she's got the ring.'

'The ring!' Bridget repeated with a sort of long, dramatic disbelief.

'Quiet, hobbit.' Aunt Charlotte drew closer and wedged the monocle in her eye socket again. She bunched up one side of her face in an effort to keep it in place.

'Yes.' I heard my voice pitched just a little too high. I held out my hand, working hard to stop it from shaking, and the stone caught the light.

'Look at that!' Bridget was mesmerised. The monkey beside her was up on the counter thief-fast too.

'It's a black opal,' I said quietly. 'It changes colour with the light. Sometimes it's kind of a deep blue, sometimes green.'

'My goodness.' Aunt Charlotte looked at it in wonder. 'That is magnificent.'

'It's a family heirloom.' Spear smiled at Angela, who nodded in confirmation.

Mother's eyes sharpened. 'So *she* knew about this before me?' There was a distinct edge to her voice.

The room ground to a silence as the words took effect.

'I . . . I . . . asked her if I should. I mean, if it was the right thing to do.' Spear's excitement was dissolving by the second.

Angela stepped in. 'I couldn't have been happier. I gave him the ring immediately.' She looked at me with an open smile, squeezing my hand. 'I couldn't imagine a better person to wear it.'

I turned the ring. The colours seamed through it, catching the light and rippling over the surface in trails of blue and green.

Mother remained in the same position, with a constant look of appalled confusion caught on her face. Dad was watching her, his head leaning to the side in concern.

'Dearest Ursula,' Aunt Charlotte whispered. She wrapped her big, comforting arms all around me until my thoughts just stopped. 'You be happy, girl,' she whispered into the top of my head. 'You just find that place.'

I buried my head into her chest until it felt like I was cheerfully drowning. But when I closed my eyes, Mother's face was still there, imprinted on the back of my eyes like an irate flame.

There were a lot of arms around me now. I was being passed around from smiling face to face, an ocean of noisy voices all clashing. I can't tell you what they said. It made no sense. Nothing did. I held on to Spear's hand so hard I could feel the bones. He didn't let go or flinch. He just held tight.

But Mother was still silent. Transfixed.

I could feel Spear guiding me through the room. I knew exactly where he was aiming. There was some laughing, some questions. I smiled and nodded, my head filling up with static.

Eventually, we were standing face to face with Mother. Spear looked so naively happy. I glanced at Dad, whose joy had been replaced with a solemn, contemplative look. To be fair, as a ghost, he's good at that one.

Mother's eyes were clear. Unblinking. She didn't break with mine for a second.

'I—'

Mother put a hand on both of my shoulders and stared. 'Ursula,' she whispered. 'My Ursula.'

I felt the warmth of every word fall across my face. She drew in a long breath, readying herself. Grounding herself.

Her arms fell and she lifted her shoulders, as rigid as a drill sergeant. 'Well, young man.' She turned to Spear.

He's thirty-two.

I heard him swallow. 'Mrs Smart.'

'Firstly, you *will* take care of my daughter.' She had an undeniable look on her face now. 'You will never put her in harm's way.'

He nodded.

'And you cannot marry my daughter—'

'Mother!'

She held up one finger and waited, locking eyes with Spear.

'You cannot marry my daughter without answering one thing.'

His face was so open but I felt his grip loosen.

'What—' Mother paused — 'is your first name?'

'I just . . . I'm happy with . . . with . . .'

His mother was giving a warm laugh. 'He has an old Irish name. It's a family tradition. It was his father's name.'

Mother raised an intrigued eyebrow.

'His name is Breffni,' Angela said proudly. 'It means trustworthy, strong, caring.'

It took a moment for it to percolate.

'Wait.' Aunt Charlotte was thinking out loud again. 'So your name is . . .'

'Breffni Spear,' Bridget announced in disbelief. 'His name is Breffni Spear.'

CHAPTER THREE: THE WEDDING PLANNERS

I would say it took a while for them to absorb the news, but I'm not sure Mother ever really did. She seemed in a distant dream for the first few weeks, impervious to the life that was just going on around her. She only spoke when she thought she should. The photograph of her and my father was regularly on the bed in the morning, alongside a half-drunk bottle of Gordon's. She'd even brought down the photo albums and some of my old baby clothes. I found her one morning clutching a small, white Babygro to her face. As she half-surfaced from her stupor and dreams, she smiled and said it smelled of her baby. She'd kept them all preserved in a Ziploc bag, and when I went to reseal it, she was right. There was the lingering scent of baby powder and milk.

I asked Mother repeatedly if she was OK, but she just gave a weak, resigned smile. She had a bland, diluted look about her. For a while, I thought she was sinking again. She was taking so much of the zolpidem to sleep. I always check on her meds. It was as though she was distancing herself from me. From all of us.

Aunt Charlotte was patient and just said to wait. She was right. She usually is.

Mother doesn't do defeated very well, and after the initial impact, she began to rally and gradually morph into someone new. Someone far more worrying. An insatiable creature.

The Wedding Planner.

Her first job was to place an engagement announcement in *The Times* without telling anyone in advance.

I protested. 'Mother, what possessed you? There's been more messages from that account, you know.'

She laughed. 'Oh, they're nothing. That's been happening for years. Every blogger gets them.'

'This could bring out a whole host of crazies from our past! Killers, people with a grudge—'

'Relatives,' Bridget added.

'Now, that is worrying!' Spear's mum smiled.

Aunt Charlotte shrugged. 'Not for us. We haven't got any.'

Mother was deaf to it all. She was embarking on an obsession that would cloud her mind to all reason.

She had no shortage of willing assistants. Aunt Charlotte wanted to help with organising the dress and ordered lots of samples of different tartans. Bridget indicated she'd be interested in doing a ballroom dancing display that she'd been practising with Dupin. With a ponderous look she informed us that her personal favourite was the tango but the monkey was verging more towards a cheeky Charleston.

There were some moments of consternation, such as when I said the guest list Mother had compiled, which included Gyles Brandreth and Clare Balding, needed to be whittled down to the people we knew rather than those she would like to know. But generally, it seemed like the wisest option to stay out of the organisation. I was happy to be no more than a guest at my own wedding.

Mother had set up mission control for the wedding in our spare bedroom and filled every wall with pin boards. She had Post-its, photographs, maps and a lot of red string. It looked a lot more like a police incident room than the joyous celebration she was supposed to be preparing.

But I have rarely seen her so focused, with so much conviction. It was a shame I had to break the news to her.

'Spear and I just want to keep it very simple. It's his second wedding . . .'

'That's not your fault!' Mother crossed her arms defiantly. 'This has taken weeks of preparation.'

'I know, Mother. And I'm very grateful.'

'Really.'

'I am! Truthfully. But I don't want all the publicity. You know there'll be intrusion.'

'Nonsense. I don't know what you mean.' Mother said it in that way she does when she knows exactly what I mean.

'It's already on your website.'

She didn't respond, letting the pause do the talking for her.

'Look.' I held up my phone and read out the headline. '"Love and Blood. Smart Woman to wed man she saved from savage knife attack. Full details to follow."'

Mother tried to look sheepish. It didn't suit her. 'I've had a lot of interest. Plenty of advertisers too. I've had a Japanese knife manufacturer, a stain-removing company who specialise in blood, and a natural funeral company all approach me about sponsoring the event. I mean, wedding.'

I pursed my lips to keep in all the things that had immediately sprung to my mind. I didn't want to have a row with anyone, least of all Mother, over the wedding. I took a breath and tried to find a pocket of calm.

'Mother, all this has nothing to do with us getting married. This is something else entirely. I just want immediate family. I want a private, quiet affair, not this circus!'

'Darling, you don't want to regret missing this *opportunity*.'

I wasn't getting through to her. So I was grateful someone else arrived who might be able to.

The knock at the door was unassuming.

'What is it?' Mother's frustration was rising.

The door opened and Angela came in, smiling and holding two steaming mugs of tea. 'Thought you could do with a break.'

'Oh.' Mother looked slightly irritated. 'I didn't realise it was you. Sorry. We're just thrashing out a few last details about the event . . . wedding.'

Angela put down the tea on the side. 'I wondered if I might make a suggestion.'

'Oh, please do.' I couldn't hide my relief.

Mother shot me *The Look*.

'Well, I was thinking, given that you met on a survivalist course . . .'

'I'll stop you there, Angela.' Mother stood firm. 'I am not, under any circumstances whatsoever, going on one of those lunatic death courses again. The one your son led nearly got me and my family killed.'

'Mother!'

Angela continued unperturbed. 'No. She's right. I wouldn't want any of you to go through that kind of trauma again. But this website was up on our computer at home when I came down this morning, so I thought I should mention it. Looks like he's been reading up all about it.' She held out her phone and showed us a website. 'You wouldn't call it a survival course, but it is a real off-grid kind of experience, without actually being too isolated. Perhaps he thinks it might be a little more private. I must say, it does sound amazing.'

'OK,' Mother sighed. 'Let's hear it.'

'It says it's their Winter Wilderness holiday.'

'Christ.' Mother slumped on to the sofa, which she'd covered in various swatches of ivory satin and tulle. I'd told her repeatedly I didn't want a big white wedding dress and she'd obviously ordered a new sample every time.

'It's in Finnish Lapland.' Angela continued to read. '"Enjoy a pre-Christmas break like no other."'

Clearly, whoever had written that had never had the joy of a Christmas in our house, which last year involved a charred turkey, three bottles of gin and a game of Cluedo that almost ended with a real victim.

Mother looked at her in astonishment. 'Have you gone out of your mind? Why would I want to visit Father bloody Christmas? What do I look like, an elf?'

I studied Mother for a moment.

In some ways there were similarities, with her long eyelashes and small, sharp pointed nose. It was more than a little disturbing.

Mother looked at me as if she could see every thought. I dropped the image quickly.

Angela, tactfully, did not acknowledge the elf comment.

'Well, we could always go a little earlier than Christmas to avoid the crowds. It actually looks quite wonderful. I was surprised. It's quite tasteful. It says it's a real sanctuary where you can relax, leave all the stresses of wedding planning behind.'

'There are no stresses!' Mother was digging the trenches already.

Angela seemed doubtful. 'They use the word "simplexity" but I think we can overlook that.'

'*You* might be able to.'

'They've got all sorts of activities.'

'Activities! This just gets worse.'

'Exploring, get out into the wild if you like. Husky rides, sledges, skiing,' she read.

'I can't ski.' Mother leaned back defiantly.

'Oh, it's easy enough to learn. You could have a few dry slope lessons before we go.' She read down further. 'It's got a lot of stuff about wellness.'

'So has the gym, but she's not getting married there!'

'What gym, Mother?'

'Hypothetically.'

Angela scrolled through. 'Scenery is beautiful. There's lots of animals.'

'Like?'

She looked at Mother. 'Bears. Reindeers, that sort of thing.'

'So, dangerous stuff.'

Angela frowned. 'Well, not all of it. They've got red squirrels. Now, you don't see those much in England, do you? Very pretty, with their—'

'Stop!' Mother closed her eyes. 'We don't want any squirrels at the wedding. Red, grey or purple!'

'I'm not sure there are pur—'

'I've got a strict no-rodent policy.'

Angela lowered the phone. 'OK, well, to be honest, I thought it was a bit left field myself, I must say. It's just he hasn't really got involved with anything about the planning, so when I saw this, I thought he might want a say.'

Mother's eyes narrowed. 'Everyone can have a say. They just don't necessarily have to have *the* say.' She picked up one of the satin swatches and ran it through her fingers.

Angela nodded. 'I know what you mean. Too many voices. Sorry. It's up to you. I think you might be right about missing opportunities to do things in a more memorable way.' She glanced at the phone again and looked doubtful. 'This might not be special enough. If it's not right for everyone, I'm not sure we should do it.' She shrugged. 'For what it's worth, it does sound peaceful. I think that might be why he's been looking at it. They've been through a lot of drama.'

It sounded so reasonable that even Mother had to admit there were distinct advantages to what Spear had been looking at. Angela had at least made an effort to let us know. I'm not sure Mother would have done the same for me. I'd not even dared to send Mother any ideas or even leave them around for her to see. To be fair though, that was probably more to do with the fact that I hadn't had any. It all still seemed like a distant concept to me that was keeping Mother occupied in the study, the same as when she planned for us to learn golf together and set up a mini putting green in there.

We didn't make any decisions right there and then, but it was enough for the idea to put down roots and grow over the next few weeks. It looked so tranquil that I was even beginning to welcome the thought of spending a week with my family. I should have known then that it was turning into a dream. When we talked, Spear was, as his mother had said, keen on the idea.

'Your mum saw this on the computer.' I showed him on my laptop, scrolling through every picture. 'We've been talking. To Mother,' I added, and widened my eyes.

He smiled. 'I know. She said she'd mentioned it. I think it's very beautiful. Very . . . calm.'

'I like it.'

He kissed the top of my forehead. 'Well, Miss Smart, if you like it, you must have it.'

I laughed and looked back at the idyllic wilds. It seemed somehow very appropriate for us.

And that's how we ended up heading into a strange wilderness to get married. Mother's objections died down as we all began to warm to the idea of a frozen paradise. It had seemed like such a good idea. We booked for the slightly less busy period a few weeks before Christmas when the winter wonderland would be even more untouched and with far fewer people. But as time rolled out towards it, Spear was less excited with every passing day. When I tried to talk to him about details, he seemed elusive.

He was becoming more distant, more closed off. I put it down to nerves. Back then. But there was a noticeable, growing sense of unease about him.

It all began to seem so unreal for me. Even when I was packing to go, it didn't feel like it was happening. Everything seemed unnatural and strange, even down to the clothing we had to take. So many thick, sweltering items, base layers, long thermal underwear, fleeces, snoods. And when Angela brought round the high-tech coats that had finally arrived, they were so bulky it would be a wedding night miracle if Spear ever found me under the vast quantity of technical clothing we were going to have to wear just to stay alive. I think we were all starting to question our decision by that point, but I suspected Spear was more than anyone else.

CHAPTER FOUR: VISITING SANTA

As soon as we stepped out of Rovaniemi Airport, my breath paused in a silvery white mist right in front of me. Everything was so still. So dry. The fierce glare from the frozen landscape burned my eyes. All the light seemed to emanate from the snow, not the sky that was low and as heavy as lead. The air was stiff with cold and a strong mineral salt smell of winter. There was a bitter astringency to it that I could almost taste. We were faced with a hardened world I'd never envisaged.

Spear squeezed my gloved hand. I could barely curl my fingers around his for the padding inside the gloves. He widened his eyes and leaned close. 'OK?' He'd been so agitated since we set off. In fact, he'd been at his most anxious for over a week now, as jittery as a thirty-a-day man on his first pack of Nicorette. Even for wedding nerves it was starting to be more than a little disconcerting.

I nodded once, the large clasp of my hat digging in under my chin. It was all so uncomfortable, so unfamiliar to me. I was instantly out of step with the place. Every action had to be considered and performed exactingly in these bloated layers of clothing. My movements were so constrained. The coat alone vastly constricted me. I couldn't even put my arms flat to my side, and then there were the fleece, jumper, T-shirt and thermal layers all adding up below. Yet still, the cold was seeping through to my skin already, finding its way in, all the way to the core of me. We'd been entranced by the photographs of snow-drenched forests and frozen landscapes. It had been an easy decision to plan a winter wedding, but no one could have prepared us for the severe reality. It seemed like every individual molecule of me was starting to freeze. Even my eyelashes were beginning to crystallise.

'Blimey.' Angela breathed out a huge plume of white air. She gave an encouraging smile but there was more than a hint of trepidation in her expression. 'This is definitely going to be an experience.' She pulled her thick scarf over her nose and shuddered into it.

'It's going to be good. Really good. I promise.' Spear was looking down at me, waiting for confirmation. He put his arm around me but I could barely feel it through the swathes of clothing.

'It will.' I smiled.

'Christ, look at this.' Mother had a distinctly turpentine look. She'd rejected the technical coat in favour of a giant faux fur with matching hat that created a bearlike impression. She called it her *Doctor Zhivago* ensemble. 'We're all going to freeze to death.' She glared at me as if it was somehow my fault. It was. The more I'd researched this ancient, frozen land, the more I wanted to go.

When I'd seen the photographs of roaring fires and isolated log houses, I'd imagined a timeless place where I could silence all the noise and close the door on the outside world. It promised placid solitude. All the articles I'd read had spoken of the simplicity, not just in the lack of ostentation, but in the whole attitude, delighting in peasant traditions. A 'noble poverty', they called it. Mother was utterly horrified by this stripped-back idea of life.

I glanced up at Spear — the apprehension was set deep in his face now too. Was it just concern for how it would all go? It seemed to be growing into something more. I couldn't escape the fact that every time I looked at him, a much more treacherous word had started to surface in my mind.

Doubt.

As much as I pushed it down, the sound of it whispered in my ear every time I saw that shadow pass over his face. I'd given him plenty of opportunity to tell me his fears or even to back out, but every time I mentioned it, he batted it away. I'd raised it so much that it had started to sound like I was the one looking for an exit. Or at least a pause. Perhaps this was natural. The onslaught of preparations and exposure of our relationship to such close scrutiny by everyone had to have some sort of an impact. Perhaps we just weren't robust enough for this. Secure enough.

I held his hand even tighter and it was beginning to feel more like I was clinging on to him.

'We need to find Charlotte.' Mother turned, swinging the vast coat out dramatically like she was determined to find those missing Dalmatians. She started making her way across the car park, her head bent low as if she were embarking on an expedition, her face shrink-wrap tight with determination and Botox. She'd had a lot of wedding treatments in the run up to this. Everything had to be in peak, fighting condition for leading her troops out into battle. We dutifully followed without question, each of us attempting to drag suitcases through the thick mounds of snow.

Aunt Charlotte and Bridget had insisted on going on ahead a few days before us. They wanted to explore Rovaniemi, which we all really knew was thinly veiled code for visit Santa. Even though we'd booked it to avoid being subsumed in the Christmas period, Santa was on hand all year round in his own small village for a modest fee. Aunt Charlotte and Bridget had been unable to curb their excitement. It helped to soften the blow of being made to leave Dupin behind. The monkey had gone to the specialist vet who also owned a monkey. Bridget felt it was good for Dupin to socialise more.

When we reached the car, the engine was already running to make sure the fuel didn't freeze. But the car wasn't much warmer inside than out. Spear and I sat in the back like we were still the kids. We quietly held hands. There hadn't been much time to be on our own recently. We'd become everyone's property, questioned in a way that neither of us was comfortable with. Will it be a religious service? What faith are you? Would Spear be wearing a wedding ring? One wedding magazine even asked the question *What does it say about a man who doesn't want to?* These intense questions followed ones such as chocolate cake or traditional fruit? Simple menu questions ran alongside deeper considerations such as what we should say in our vows. Vows — even the word itself was frighteningly serious, as if they would be carved into stone tablets for all eternity. It was a constant chaos of decisions that paralysed me.

The biggest of all was 'Where will you live?' Mother had looked puzzled when Bridget asked that one. Up until now, we'd half lived at mine, half at his and Angela's, in a kind of sleepover arrangement that seemed to suit everyone. Mother got the house to herself some nights, but I'd not actually moved out. We both knew we couldn't always live like that. It was a student-like existence with our mothers still doing our washing at weekends. Now, it was just another one of the uncertainties that I shoved away into that ever-expanding box of confusion and doubt.

The unbelievable nature of this place wasn't helping to settle anyone's unease. Mist hung low over the road, a thin, white spine carving a path between the towering pines. With their thick crusting of snow, the trees had a calcified look to them. There was no break as we drove out. They continued to line either side of the road in solid, impenetrable walls, the canopy forming a high, bleached skyline. The whole world had been stripped of any colour. It was both awe-inspiring and yet somehow disorientating. Maybe I'd have said it was unnerving even then.

It was a daunting passage through that deserted realm. The remains of any light had already fallen below the level of the trees, their shadows striping grey bands across the white road. The scale alone was intimidating. I felt exposed and insignificant beside the shape of this place. It was so overwhelming and alienating. I was beginning to regret the choice of somewhere this challenging for a wedding that already had its fair share of difficulties.

Spear was gazing out of the window, and I could sense that word lingering over him too. Regret. Was it just the place that he was starting to question or was it something more? Did he *regret* asking me at all? If he could go back to the quiet, pottering-along way we had before, would he? I don't know why I was questioning this so much. But every single insecurity button was being pushed. It had been his idea to marry, to come here. Had he been dissatisfied before? Did he need this change? There were so many questions spinning around in my head now that there was no room for any answers.

Ahead on the road, the large, illuminated name board surfaced out of the frozen fog with the words *Santa Claus Holiday Village*. Aunt Charlotte and Bridget had said they'd meet us there. I'd assumed it was because it was an easy local landmark to find, but as we drove closer it became very obvious there was a much bigger reason.

The Smart Woman's Grotto was a makeshift shed by the side of the road just before the turning for the actual genuine attraction. I couldn't see Mother's face. Only her eyes were visible in the rearview mirror. That was enough. If she could have burned the little hut to the ground with a look, that was the one she would have used.

The sign was roughly hand-painted and surrounded with a string of fairy lights where most of the bulbs had blown. There was a smaller notice by the side of it stating that gifts were extra but it was free to sit on Santa's knee.

'It seems like they've been very industrious since their arrival here.' Angela turned and gave us an encouraging look.

Mother remained glacially silent.

Just as we turned off the road and stopped, a large reindeer appeared from the side of the shed and started walking towards the car.

'Good God!' Mother locked the doors. She turned round to me and glared. 'Did you know about this?'

'No, of course not.' Even though I had no idea about it, I managed to sound guilty. I always do when faced with Mother's cross-examination. Aunt Charlotte had mentioned spreading a little seasonal cheer, but I'd imagined she meant in more normal ways than this. Like so many suggestions surrounding *the wedding*, I'd just let it slide away with a smile.

'It's kind of sweet, don't you think?' Spear nudged me.

Mother sighed. 'No, I do not. You will come to realise that my sister's ideas are where the trouble usually starts.'

Bridget appeared from a side door dressed in full costume. From the top of her pointed hat, right down to her curled-up little boots, she was dressed entirely as an elf. She'd even got cherry-red cheeks painted on. At least, I thought they were painted on, but it was so brutally cold they might well have been real. She didn't seem to have many layers on and there were holes in her stripy stockings where the puckered pink skin was showing through. I could only imagine how freezing she must have been.

In spite of this, Bridget waved and smiled. The excessively keen face, coupled with the oversized elf outfit, gave her the look of a slightly bewildered gnome. As she shuffled over, it was very clear that the elf shoes were not made for snow and ice. She slid from side to side like a large green penguin attempting to shimmy along, her feet slipping out to the sides with every step.

'What the hell does she think she looks like?' Mother shook her head.

'She's an elf, I think,' Spear offered.

Mother raised an eyebrow. 'Yes, thank you, Attenborough.'

Angela leaned closer to Mother. 'I don't think Sir David deals with magical creatures — just the real ones.'

Bridget had finally reached the car. She started knocking on the window and tugging at the door handle. 'You're here!'

'Not for long,' Mother shouted.

It wasn't clear whether Bridget could hear or not but she continued without acknowledging Mother's comment. 'Come and visit Santa!' She peered in closer at the window, leaving a circle of breath on the glass.

'Not a chance,' Mother mouthed.

'You might even get to sit on Father Christmas's knee.' Bridget's face was giddy with excitement. She turned her head towards the dilapidated shack behind her, still grinning manically with the cold, and shouted, 'Quick, Charlotte, they're here! Get your beard on.'

CHAPTER FIVE: HO HO NO

There are moments when even my family surprises me. Sitting in a shed in Finland looking at Aunt Charlotte dressed as Father Christmas, with Bridget as her elf, was one of them.

It was viciously cold in the hut. A bare concrete floor and the thin wooden slats of the cheap shed were doing nothing to insulate us from the Arctic air. Apart from being a fairly basic construction, there was very little furniture or decoration. A sad branch from a pine tree had been leaned up in the corner. Wilting excessively, it was creating a large pool of pine needles below it. There were a few pieces of what looked like some of Aunt Charlotte's more elaborate costume jewellery festooned around it like a tragic magpie's nest.

Aunt Charlotte's Father Christmas costume had more than a hint of the budget about it as well. The tattered old fur had formed into little spikes with dirty brown tips and it was riddled with bald patches. The red velvet suit was shiny with wear and threadbare in places. The beard seemed to move independently even when Aunt Charlotte was sitting still, suggesting that it could very easily have been harbouring any number of minor pests from moths to mice. Looking at her now, in the dim light cast by a small lantern, there was a worn look about Aunt Charlotte herself too.

She took a moment to gather her composure, like an actor inhabiting the role. Finally, she began, adopting a strange, deep voice. 'Well now, children, what would you like for—'

'Stop!' Mother held up her hand. 'Absolutely not.'

'Oh, come on, Pandora, even you must like Father Christmas.'

We all looked at Mother for any trace of agreement. She remained unmoved.

'There's a little gift if you're a good girl . . .' Aunt Charlotte said teasingly, before blowing out the stray hairs from her beard that had drifted into her mouth.

Mother stiffened. 'I remember the last time you gave me a gift, Charlotte. I have no wish to repeat the experience.'

That was the Christmas Aunt Charlotte decided to give handmade presents. She'd been on a taxidermy course. In some ways, I wish we could have preserved Mother's expression as she unwrapped the stuffed squirrel that sported acorns for eyes and the distinct tortured look of roadkill.

I looked around the small, ramshackle shed and the thought struck me that this wasn't a very usual wedding party and bore no resemblance to the magazines I'd secretly leafed through when I'd dreamed of having a typical wedding with typical guests.

Instead, here we were with Charlotte and Bridget in the pound-shop grotto, with Mother dressed as Rasputin. I don't think anyone expects the journey into marriage to be smooth but, so far, this had not gone in a direction I had anticipated.

The press had already had a field day imagining what a Smart Woman wedding would look like. One even speculated 'Will they all survive this time?' They'd started to refer to me as Ursula Smart, the Queen of Death, which Mother advised me to copyright. She'd helpfully run an online poll as to what our celeb name should be. Smart-Spear was the most popular. But there were some outliers. Smear, following the usual celeb mashup formula, was particularly unsavoury. The whole thing was starting to look like a bizarre farce. The biggest question of all was who the hell would want to marry into this?

I glanced at Spear. If there were any doubts smouldering away at the back of his mind, this was definitely feeding them a lot of oxygen. He smiled at me as if he might actually be enjoying something about this pantomime.

But as he looked away, there was that uncertainty about him, waiting just below the surface. I'd searched those blue-green eyes so many times. Just like the ring he'd given me, they were constantly changing. They say the pupils dilate if you feel overwhelming love. I was still waiting to see that.

I watched the smile fall too quickly from his face.

'Charlotte.' Mother was finding it hard to contain her anger. 'What on earth do you think you're doing? I thought you were coming on ahead to do a little sightseeing and *scope out the area*.'

Bridget let a small laugh escape. 'You must recognise us! Surely even a Grinch like you has heard of Father Christmas, Pandora.'

I don't think Mother really appreciated being compared to a misanthropic, wizened creature, but I made no comment on that score.

'I'm thoroughly aware of who Santa Claus is but I can assure you this is a million miles away from it.'

'No, he's just down the road, actually.' Aunt Charlotte pulled down her beard and whispered, 'I'm not the real one. Don't tell!'

Mother's singular approach to revealing the truth about Father Christmas to me as a young girl was for me to find her on Christmas morning among the presents, with the mince pie I'd left out hanging from her mouth and gripping a bottle of brandy.

At this very moment though, we were facing an even more disturbing Santa scenario.

I began slowly. 'I think what everyone wants to know is why you are doing this?'

Aunt Charlotte gave me a weak smile. 'Who wouldn't want to take the opportunity to actually *be* Father Christmas in Lapland?'

'*Meet*, Aunt Charlotte. The word is "meet". You're supposed to meet Father Christmas in Lapland. You're not supposed to *be* him.'

She laughed. 'I know that, dear. I just thought it might be a bit of fun, that's all.'

'And we're skint,' Bridget added.

Mother narrowed her eyes and frowned. 'Why?'

Aunt Charlotte looked at me, then Spear. 'Well . . . not so much skint as . . .'

'We couldn't really afford all this, so we devised a cunning money-making scheme.' Bridget leaned in and lowered her voice. 'I've also adopted a reindeer and called it Mr Jingle-All-the-Slay, in honour of our numerous brushes with death. It's just Mr Jingle for short, of course.'

'Oh, of course!' Mother arched her eyebrow. 'Who on earth names a reindeer in honour of the near-death experiences she's been through?'

The simple answer to that was, of course, Bridget.

So far, she'd owned an extensive menagerie of pets. The location of some of the animals was no longer known and nobody dared ask. Except for Aunt Charlotte when she was on the taxidermy course.

There'd been Mr Bojangles — a small dog, the original and worst. Then Mr Bojingles, a dog so similar to the first one that it occurred to me it might actually be Mr Bojangles in disguise. That was around the time I realised I was spending way too much time thinking about Bridget's dogs. She then moved on to cats — a bald Sphinx known as Dingaling, short for Schrodinger. There then followed a giant python called Magic Mike, which in turn ate Nelson the not-so-micro pig. Finally, there was Dupin, the devilish monkey she'd adopted from a dead lord.

Suffice to say, Bridget had a kind of pathological need to have animals that were difficult or routinely dangerous. It had, at points, led to her house turning into a no-stay zone, which meant she had to live at ours. A more naturally suspicious person might start to suspect she was harbouring these creatures to give her an excuse to come and live with us. Suspicion is always riding shotgun in my family.

'Reindeers can also be a very useful form of transport,' Bridget nodded to herself.

'You can't ride a reindeer,' Spear said flatly.

There was a silence while we all considered this statement for a moment. I wondered if he had actual knowledge of reindeer riding or if he was specifically referring to Bridget. We all took out our phones to google whether you can ride a reindeer. Thankfully, there was no signal and Santa's shambles of a shed certainly didn't have Wi-Fi.

'Not unless it's a really big one,' Spear added.

Bridget looked confused as to whether she should be insulted or not.

I cleared my throat. 'Why didn't you tell us you couldn't afford this, Aunt Charlotte? We'd all have chipped in.'

'I wouldn't,' Mother said.

Angela looked concerned. 'We can all help out, I'm sure.'

I walked over to Aunt Charlotte and put my arms around her. She smelled of mothballs and animal hair. 'I'm so sorry.'

'Nonsense, darling. I've loved every minute of it!'

'Have you even had much custom?'

She let out a heavy breath through her beard. 'Not really, dear.'

I held Aunt Charlotte out from me and looked into her soft face. 'I think it's time to hang up your beard, Aunt Charlotte.'

'Until next year!' Bridget announced. 'We could even take the concept back to England with us.'

I had a picture of them setting up a grotto in southwest London every year with these moth-eaten, decaying robes in a sort of *With Santa and I* kind of way. From the look of dis-may on Mother's face, she'd also imagined the same prospect appearing on a street near her.

There was a minor tearful farewell for Mr Jingle-All-the-Slay, who looked more excited by the carrot than any of Bridget's emotional outpourings. But she held the beast close and spoke softly into its ear.

Mother was growing impatient. 'Come on, reindeer whisperer, get in the car.'

'Time to go and get these two married!' Angela was the only one with any trace of excitement left on her face.

The rest of us gave wary, uncomfortable smiles. As we climbed back into our car with Santa and an elf, the idea of our sophisticated, intimate ceremony seemed very much in doubt.

There it was again. That word floating to the top with increasing regularity. It just refused to drown.

CHAPTER SIX: INTO THE WILDERNESS

The drive out to our cabins was daunting. We were heading for Arkijarvi, a lakeside area about four hours north of Rovaniemi. Mother made the point more than once that if we hadn't had to go via Santaland we might have been able to fly in closer, but Aunt Charlotte and Bridget were oblivious behind us in their boot seats.

We took the border highway from Pello alongside the Tornio River. The waters were completely frozen, forming a wide border of ice stretching out to what I could see from the map was Sweden. It felt isolating, as though we were on the other side of a frontier from the rest of the world. This was borderland, a crossing point that had been frozen solid. The vast expanse of the rapids had been brought to a sudden stop, the peaks of water from its current caught in solid waves, suspended mid-flow. It seemed so unnatural to see such a vast quantity of water unable to move, utterly still as if time itself had been locked. It had the feel of a liminal place, where everything was paused on the edge, set into the moment. The slate-grey sky cast only a slim light across its dark, glistening surface. In that instant, there was a strange quality of glowing blue to the light, reflecting from the snow and ice. I'd read about this point of the Kaamos, the Polar Night, when the sky was in fact not completely dark, a twilight world but one where the sun would not fully rise. The small moment had a peculiar clarity before it disappeared into darkness.

For the hours after that, we followed this petrified river until what little light there had been was completely lost.

The further we journeyed, the more colossal the scale of the landscape became, as if we were heading away from any normal realm. There was an undeniable grandeur to its vastness. The bone-white trees formed thick ribs along each side of the long, relentless road. The hire vehicle was large enough to accommodate all six of us but treacherous in the extreme conditions. As usual, Mother looked confident at the wheel, but she'd have been confident driving Jeremy Clarkson into hell for a meeting with the Devil.

The reading on the dashboard showed it was minus fifteen degrees and the temperature was still dropping with every hour that passed. When the website said it was a distant wilderness, I'd not imagined it as utterly removed from civilisation. We were warm enough in the car with the heater working overtime, but the bleak world outside was increasingly raw. The thin window between me and the severe land beyond seemed like a very fragile barrier. The day had vanished, snow glittering like coal against the dead sky. The road grew more hostile with every mile. I tried not to imagine all that might be waking and emerging out there in the night air as we journeyed on through the wild. What kind of creature could survive such a freezing wasteland? Not any from the world I knew. I looked around the silent, empty faces in our car. I could only hope all of us would.

By the time we finally arrived, our headlights were no more than two single searchlights cutting through the darkness, the weak beams barely making an impact on that ocean of snow. There was a small log cabin ahead, its lights suspended in the frozen air.

Mother brought the car slowly to a standstill. She didn't turn off the engine but sat tensed, her hands fixed on the wheel. It had been a gruelling drive.

'. . . OK?' Angela was hesitant.

Mother nodded once but didn't speak. Her shoulders finally lowered and she let out one long breath. It had been a remorseless journey. She'd given up communicating with anything other than the road many miles back, her eyes fixed ahead. She was clearly exhausted.

I leaned forward and put my hand on her shoulder. 'Thank you, Mother.'

She unfurled her gloved fingers from the wheel.

'Everyone all right up front?' Aunt Charlotte, still in full Father Christmas outfit, called from the boot.

'We're good,' I answered.

We all looked out at the unprepossessing cabin that stood alone in bleak shadow. No one had come out to greet us, but the outline of a figure passed momentarily through one of the glowing windows. A thin curl of smoke rose up from the chimney.

This was such an unsettling place, so hidden and inhospitable it felt as if we'd travelled into some uncharted world, that we'd just stumbled off the edge of the map to a place where those ill-defined creatures of imagination could so easily be real. I peered out from behind the condensation fogging my window. Cat's-eye drops of light reflected through the mist then disappeared. Stiff branches shifted, creating small flurries of snow as if some hidden presence was following alongside us, just beyond the thick line of trees. Watching.

We climbed out of the car warily into a taut atmosphere, as though the air itself was too thin. The stillness brought a sudden unexpected feeling of disquiet.

There was an undeniable rarity to this space but at the same time it was unnerving, like a clear-cut diamond crafted into a weapon. Each of us stood hesitant, our eyes scanning nervously, looking to one another for approval.

The unreal darkness looked back.

I turned to Spear. There was a heightened look to him, a keenness to his eyes.

'Right.' Bridget was the first to break. She turned her face towards the lodge. 'Let's see if Norman Bates is still awake, shall we?'

'That's the owner?' Aunt Charlotte asked.

We were too exhausted, our minds too overstretched to explain.

I glanced at Spear again and he pulled his mouth into a reluctant smile. The journey had done nothing to ease that anxious look.

I hooked an arm around him and pressed my face into his neck. 'This is going to work,' I whispered. 'Trust me.'

He closed his eyes and took a nervous breath. 'Let's do it.'

The air was sharp and raw in my chest. The cold instantly settled in a brittle layer over my skin, covering every bare piece of flesh. My mouth was dry from the ice, my eyes cold in the sockets, even the inside of my nose formed crystals in seconds. Anything with any moisture content was dried and frozen. As soon as I stepped forward, I could hear the solid snow breaking beneath me. The air was frigid and every movement I made seemed to disturb it.

I trod carefully in distinct steps, learning how to walk in an alien, new way. I didn't dare take my eyes from my feet for more than a moment. When I did, I saw Spear still looking up in apprehension at the log cabin. He was so mesmerised by it that it seemed as if it might somehow be familiar.

'You OK?' I spoke quietly, as though someone else might be listening.

He nodded. 'We've come this far, Ursula. We might as well finish what we started.' It wasn't the most romantic thing a groom has ever said.

The others were already hurrying towards the light regardless of what was waiting in it.

Spear looked at me with a face utterly devoid of any expression. 'Are you all right?'

'I'm fine. Yes, I'm fine.' I could hear my own uncertainty and cupped my hands around my mouth to hide it. 'Shall we go inside? It's time to do this.'

He turned his mouth down at the edges, as if considering whether there were any other options.

Was I seeing things that weren't there? We'd had a long journey. None of us were prepared for the sparseness of this place. I felt so exposed. The extreme conditions alone were overwhelming, let alone the thought of committing myself to a scheme that would unbreakably bind me to this one person for the rest of my life. When I thought about it like that, it seemed like one of the most ludicrous ideas I'd ever had.

Only I hadn't had it. This had been Spear's idea from the very beginning.

Regret is such an ugly, ill-conceived word but it was writing its way across his face right there in front of me in that unthinkable cold and dark.

Inside, the house was bigger than it had first seemed. It smelled of damp wood and charcoal cinders. There was a flinty edge to the air. The remains of a fire grizzled in a mean grate and a large elk head looked down sombrely from above it. There were various unrecognisable pieces of sporting equipment hanging from the walls, most of which looked like strange versions of oversized tennis rackets or javelins. Hunting equipment was displayed among them. Savage knives, crossbows and traps seemed rather ill-placed for a wedding party. Though they were probably more appropriate for us than most parties.

A small desk lit by a pool of weak light stood unattended. The whole place was struggling under a morbid gloom, watched over by many dead, stuffed animals. Aunt Charlotte's taxidermy class would have had a field day. There was a little bell on the side of the desk that Mother showed no hesitation in ringing.

'Well, this is very nice.' Aunt Charlotte had pulled the beard down underneath her chin. Her face was chapped red with cold.

'No, it's not.' Mother was scanning the room with the disdainful air of someone who had found themselves on a tour of a particularly unpleasant prison facility. She rang the bell again, more insistently.

'Hold your horses! I'm coming, love.' The distant voice was definitely not Finnish. More a distinct east London.

A flurry of cold air circled us and a door slammed. The man walked from a small room behind reception. He took laboured, shambling steps, rubbing his face and sniffing. The smell of whisky and cigarettes clung to the cold air around him like the end of a night outside a downbeat club. It was only six o'clock in the evening, but the lack of any real daylight seemed to make the actual time an irrelevance here.

He had the kind of liquorice-black hair that spoke of a desperation to look young, but the rest of him disagreed. The thick jowls were encrusted with a rash of dirty stubble. The skin a sickly, tallow colour. His eyes were almost overwhelmed by the swollen rolls of their lids and he was making very little effort to see us through the tiny slits they left.

He paused with his hand still on his rough chin. 'Are you another bloody Santa? We haven't booked one this year, not after last year's disaster. Surely the agency told you.' He drew his hand over the stubble, releasing a rough, sandpaper sound, and stood analysing Aunt Charlotte.

'We have a reservation.' Mother used her best checking-in-to-a-hotel voice. Acerbic yet unchallengeable authority is how she describes it.

He frowned at Bridget. 'Is that an elf as well? We never have an elf. Creepy little fuckers.'

'Thank you.' Mother continued, 'However, we are not paid employees or any form of travelling entertainment.'

He looked sceptical about that.

'We are guests, some of whom have chosen to dress in festive outfits. That is none of your concern. We are the Smarts and the Spears.'

He looked at Mother as if she'd announced a circus troupe.

'And a Gutteridge,' Bridget added.

Mother continued. 'We simply wish to be shown to our rooms. We'll be ready to go through the wedding itinerary after that.'

'Ite . . . itin . . .'

'The itinerary.' A brusque-looking woman was making her way across to the reception area. She did have a Finnish

41

accent. 'You must excuse my husband, he has some intelligence issues. I'm Aino.'

'How are you spelling that?'

The woman ignored Aunt Charlotte. 'Your *mökkis* are all ready.' She saw our confusion. '*Mökki*. Your cabins, basically. There are three, as discussed. Tapio, keys please, these people have had a long journey.'

'Yes, your majesty.' He bowed and gave her a surly look. The grease on his hair shone like a beetle's back in the dim light. 'Right, let's see.' He licked a grubby-looking finger and went down the register before pulling a key from the wall behind. 'Mrs Spear, looks like you're in with your son . . . eh . . . Breffni.' He handed her the key, which had a faint trace of spit on it now. He tilted his head, looking around her, and gave her a lewd smile before winking. 'So, no Mr S—'

'No. Thank you.' She took the key and looked down self-consciously.

'Disgusting,' Bridget murmured.

Tapio frowned before looking back to the register. 'Wait, Breffni? You're called Breffni Spear?'

Spear sighed. 'Every time. OK. It's Irish.'

The man looked confused for a moment. He analysed Spear through half-open eyes as if he was trying to place him. He gave a slow, indulgent smile, revealing an untidy row of discoloured teeth stuck in his gums like old wooden pegs on a washing line. 'I recognise the name, I'm sure. Have I met you before somewhere?' He gave another supposedly playful wink but there was a different kind of edge to it this time.

'Never seen you in my life.' Spear didn't offer any more.

'My son was in the tourism industry too. He used to have a boat and run expeditions,' Angela said with a sense of pride. She'd missed the rising tension.

'That was a while ago,' Spear added.

'Oh, while ago, was it?' Tapio leered.

'That's all done with now,' Mother said, shutting it down.

But Tapio looked even more intrigued.

Bridget cleared her throat to announce herself. 'He doesn't run those things around any longer. He's cleaned up his act.'

'Bridget!' I almost shouted her name.

'Oh.' Tapio clicked his fingers. 'That'll be where I know you from! If you used to *run those things around* for people, I mean. Ha!' He gave a vicious laugh. 'Fancy someone like you being all the way out here.'

My eyes went to Spear. He had a new evasiveness about him. 'Like I say, that was a long time ago. I'm running expeditions now.'

I knew that wasn't exactly true. He'd not run any tours for quite a long time and the one we went on sank. Some pretty unpleasant guys had some stuff on that boat and, at one time, they'd been looking for him. But he'd promised it was all sorted now. And I'd believed him when he said that. We all have a past.

Tapio was still smirking. 'If you say so, mate.' He leaned over the desk. 'Pay all your debts, did you? Don't want any funny business with the bill.'

'There's no concern there.' Mother gave a skin-tight smile. 'It's already been paid in full.'

It sounded a little like Mother was taking the credit for this when, in fact, we'd all chipped in. But Mother does like to advertise her generosity.

'My business is none of your concern.' Spear had an impenetrable, glazed expression.

The two men locked eyes as if there was another, silent conversation being passed under the table.

I reached for Spear's hand and looked questioningly up at him. For a moment, he didn't respond, and then he glanced at me before easing down a little.

'I think that's enough dissecting your guests, Mr Tapio.' There was a decisiveness about Mother now. 'Perhaps I might have my key. I'm Mrs Smart, and no, there's no Mr Smart before you ask. I'll be sharing with my daughter, Ursula.'

'Hang on, Mother. Why am I in with you?'

She attempted to look scandalised. 'You can't possibly sleep with the groom the night before your wedding. It's bad luck.'

I gave a resigned sigh. Some battles are not worth fighting with Mother and things would all be very different in twenty-four hours anyway. I only had to hang on until then. 'Well, it'll all change after tomorrow, make no mistake.'

Mother shrugged. 'As they say, *tomorrow is another day*. You never know what might happen between now and then.' She gave me a meaningful stare and took the key. She turned to the rest of them. 'The *mökki* allocations are, I'm with Ursula . . .'

I rolled my eyes. Spear gave me a forced smile and squeezed my hand.

'Spear, you're with Angela. And Santa is with the elf. Right.' She turned to Aino. Mother was getting very efficient, which is always a sign of mounting stress. As yet, I wasn't sure just how high that could reach but anything was possible. We were in unknown territory.

'We'd like to be escorted to our cabins, immediately.'

Tapio rang the small bell. He waited. Nothing happened. He rang it again, his face sinking into resigned frustration. 'Why can she never come first time?'

'She can't hear through the haze.' Aino said it in a pointed, almost accusatory way.

Tapio sighed before bellowing so loud that the walls rang with the sound of his voice. 'Helmi!' It sounded like some sort of call to arms. 'Helmi, get your lazy arse down here.' He looked around his guests. 'Sorry, ladies.'

'We've all got one,' Aunt Charlotte tapped her red velvet backside. 'Even Santa.'

He frowned before opening his mouth to release another call, but paused at the sound of a distant door slamming.

The footsteps were lumbering without any urgency to them. The young woman who appeared was predictably feckless. She was as curved over and thin as a leaf. Tall, with lank brown hair that hung over one eye, she had a sullen expression which looked fairly permanent.

'What the hell have you been doing?'

'Weed.'

Tapio clenched his jaw and stared intently at her.

'Helmi!' Aino frowned. 'These are our guests.'

'Well, I didn't think they were your friends, did I?' The girl's laugh had a spiteful edge to it. 'Unless they were some new little waitresses for you, *Dad*,' she sneered.

'That's enough!' Tapio glanced at Aino.

'Ha! Like she doesn't know, Dad.'

'Oh, I know.' Aino was unmoved.

The atmosphere had quickly descended into hostile and that seemed like familiar territory to them.

'Just take the guests out to the *mökkis*, if you can manage that, Helmi.' Tapio's eyes were fixed on her. 'And you can keep away from Matthias as well.'

Helmi raised her eyebrows defiantly. 'Oh really. One rule for one, eh?'

'You're twenty. He's the wrong side of thirty. It's disgusting.'

'And how old was *Lily*? That little maid wasn't much older than me, was she? She's gone as well now too. Like all the others.'

'Enough, please.' Aino seemed to visibly deflate in front of us. 'Can we just be grateful we've got some willing guests here?'

'Do you have many unwilling ones?' Bridget's interruption seemed remarkably ill-judged.

They fell into silence and turned to look at her en masse, like a pack that had been disturbed.

The girl flicked her hair back before taking a long view of Bridget in her elf costume. 'What's it to you, Dobby?'

The smile died on Bridget's face.

'She was just being friendly, young lady.' Aunt Charlotte adjusted her Santa trousers.

Helmi snorted out a laugh.

'I've had enough of this.' Mother pulled down her furry hat. 'We need to get to our lodgings right now. You can go back to playing happy families on your own time. Is there transportation to these cabins?'

'We have our wonderful reindeers,' Aino said.

'My family's pathetic attempt at Scandification.' Everything about Helmi's surly tone seemed almost purposefully designed to be repellent, as if she'd spent a lot of time perfecting it.

'I knew it! You *can* ride them!' A satisfied smile lifted Bridget's mouth.

Confusion crossed Aino's face. 'No, no. It's a reindeer ride. They're pulling a sleigh.'

'Oh, I see.' Bridget was momentarily wistful but then a fresh thought arrived. 'A sleigh ride dressed as an elf! I've always dreamed of this!'

'Right,' Tapio attempted to sound decisive. 'Get these people over there. I've got things to do.'

'Such as what, smoking out the back there?' Helmi said sulkily.

'It's no business of yours.'

I peered round him to see a grubby little office with a small exit at the far end.

Tapio looked at me with a sharp, cautioning face and pulled the door shut. 'Says *Private*, miss.'

'Look, I don't care if we're being transported in a bloody TARDIS.' Mother was growing impatient. 'We need to get there now.'

'That's Dr Who's vehicle. The TARDIS, I mean,' Aunt Charlotte said with certainty. 'Not Father Christmas.'

Mother gave her *The Look*. 'I am aware, thank you.'

Aunt Charlotte leaned closer to her. 'No reindeers pulling it, you see.' She looked doubtful. 'At least, I don't think so, anyway.'

Mother spoke through clenched teeth, grinding out the words. 'We've got a lot to do.'

I felt my heart sink. How much more could there be to do other than actually just getting married? Surely getting hitched, spliced, wedded or diced, whatever you wanted to call it, couldn't be this difficult for everyone.

But this wasn't difficult. So far, this had been a gentle nursery slope in comparison to how far this was about to go off piste. And when I looked into Spear's eyes it wasn't excitement or anticipation I saw there, but that ever-increasing murmur of apprehension. If I was entirely honest, when I started to contemplate the enormity of what Spear and I were about to do and all that we had planned, my anxiety started gaining a new urgency too. Perhaps it was even fear. But it was no time for examining our levels of honesty. It was time to get this done.

I glanced at Mother. What I really should have been asking myself right then was whether she was ever going to forgive me for what I was about to do. But I already knew one thing. Mother is not the forgiving kind.

CHAPTER SEVEN: TO THE ENDS OF THE EARTH

Outside, there was an eerie stillness to the frost-bound air. A clarifying, unyielding purity. Deep within that velvet grey landscape, the point where the ice met the sky had grown so indistinct, so blurred that it was all one disorientating, blank illusion. With only the memory of light now, there was still a harsh edge to this world that cut right through all those layers of clothing. We were immediately vulnerable, the cold finding a route in any way it could, burrowing through a thousand tiny veins to settle down in my core. I breathed deep and the air, blade sharp, stuck in my chest. The cordite smell of winter ran through it, a dry rawness that I hadn't expected. Even my hair was crisp, as if it could snap in two, my eyes so hardened they could shatter.

A sturdy man appeared from the corner of the cabin holding reins in his hands and leading out a reindeer. With the sleigh dragging along behind, it was as close as we'd come to the romantic Lapland scene I had imagined. The dream was starting to look less distant, less fanciful than before.

'Matthias.' Helmi nodded to the man and for the first time she seemed to thaw. But a sour note hung behind her voice.

'Helmi.' It was a cordial response. With his grizzled beard and hard-bitten face, there was something primitive about the man. He didn't seem to have any use for conversation. With a gloved hand, he stroked down the animal's muzzle.

He guided the sleigh up beside us and nodded in simple acknowledgement. Helmi climbed up front and took the reins without speaking. There was a sombre, unspoken atmosphere between them. A regret hanging in the air.

I tried to inject some lightness. 'Shall we?'

'Just let me help Mum with her bag, hang on.' Spear turned and bent to where her bag was on the snow beside her.

'I'm fine, love. You just get in with Ursula. I can look after myself.'

'Are you sure? These people aren't going to lift it in.' Spear gave a quick glance towards Helmi, who was staring resolutely ahead.

Matthias stepped forward. 'Don't worry. We will sort them all out. I will bring the other guests along with Onni.' He spoke with a lilting Finnish accent that had a song-like nature. He called towards the cabin. 'Onni?'

A furtive, rat-faced man slipped round the corner of the building. His quick little eyes sparkled in the darkness, darting from one of us to the next before sliding over towards where Spear was standing. A sly smile crept over his lips. 'Well, hello again.'

Before anyone could speak, Bridget started laughing and turned to Spear. 'Well, we've come to the middle of nowhere and you seem to know everyone.'

Spear's face clouded over. 'He must have worked with someone I knew.' He was struggling to sound nonchalant.

He stepped in among the furs, the cowbell ringing low as the reindeer shook its head. Holding out his hand, Spear watched me with that familiar look of resigned apology. I'd started to dread it. It was one I knew so well and that I would have done anything to be able to erase. It was the face that said he didn't think he was good enough, that he was convinced he was letting me down. He'd often said how I could do so much better than him. However much I'd told him he was all that I'd ever need, he would not be persuaded. I'd thought the

49

proposal was a turning point, a sign he could believe in himself, believe he could do this. But I could see now that it was going to take an awful lot more than that to set us free from the demons. Those thoughts were surfacing again. People knew him here. Those voices from the past seemed to be resurrecting all that doubt. We had to find a way of silencing them once and for all. There was no turning back now.

I climbed into the sleigh next to him, watching him closely. But, as I sat down, he only half acknowledged me. He was so distracted, staring into the darkness as if he was expecting to see someone else waiting out there.

'It's OK, you know.' I leaned into him. 'I do know. I know your past. It's not important. That's all gone.'

He turned to look at me, studying me with a confused, troubled expression. 'Has it?' He shook his head. 'Sometimes it doesn't feel like that.'

I smiled and tried to seem reassuring. 'Of course it has. Everything you owed has been paid. They called off the dogs a long time ago. This is just a coincidence, these guys here thinking they know you.'

'Is it?'

As we began to pull away, I looked to where Mother was standing next to our sleigh. She was watching as if she knew what was happening, knew where this was going. In the dark halo of mist lit by the cabin, I thought I might have seen the glimmer of a sheen appear on her eyes. She pressed her lips together, a look of strange nostalgia passing over her. I don't know which memory she landed on in that moment as we drew away, but it felt like somehow time was getting away from us.

The sleigh moved out slowly and, down by the side of the cabin, I could see a small telltale curl of smoke followed by the circle of glowing amber light from Tapio's cigarette floating in the frozen mist. Was he watching us?

Spear put his arm over my shoulders and pulled me in. 'Hey.' He looked at me so intently, as if he was trying to memorise every part of my face.

'Hey,' I whispered back.

He lifted my chin. 'I want you to remember one thing, Ursula.' There was a new, unrelenting look in those blue-green eyes. They'd changed somehow. Darkened. 'I would never intentionally hurt you. Never.'

'I *know* that.' It sounded like I was almost pleading with him. I could hear the desperate, anxious undertone in my own voice but there was nothing I could do to stop it.

He blew out a sigh and the white cloud of his breath hung on the air. I felt him lightly kiss the top of my head. 'This time tomorrow it'll all be over,' he said softly by my ear. The words sank through me like warm balm, and I closed my eyes.

'This time tomorrow,' I repeated, and made a small, anxious sound.

He pulled the furs and blankets up higher around me. I leaned my head back to look up, sinking into the vault of the sky.

A shock of stars fell down towards me like snow. I was drifting as easily as floating down a river towards an uncertain destination with no thought to save myself or anyone else. I wanted this. I was willing to be washed away by all of it, no matter where I ended up. I was willing to do anything.

'Linnunrata. You call it the Milky Way.' Matthias was sitting up in front of us holding an arm up to the sky. 'It leads to Lintukoto. It is an imaginary place, warm and peaceful like paradise.' He swivelled a little in his seat and glanced back. 'Now, we go out to where guardian spirits and the ghosts wait for us.' He turned and faced forward, jerking the reins in his hands.

I looked out into the darkness, a thin grey mist gathering, forming shapes on the icy air. The trailing wind tugged at my hair like fingers winding through the strands. As we journeyed out, a crawling sensation prickled over my skin. I told myself it was just the cold. But I rarely listen to the reasonable voice when there is a far more compelling one underneath.

Helmi called out to the reindeers, her sharp voice cutting the air. My heart thumped hard in response. Their sleigh was just behind us, the reindeer's bell tolling in rhythmic time, half muffled by the sound of the sledge runners slipping through the snow. We were heading out there to that place where the sky fell into the black ice, to where it felt like we could just fall off the edge of the world and disappear. Perhaps we would. Perhaps that was the answer. To disappear. For some of us at least. The further we were dragged out into that wilderness, the further it felt from reality. We were being slowly detached from the world we knew.

As we arrived at the cabins, we let the unnerving silence roll over us for a moment. Hidden beneath the dominant line of trees, three small log cabins crouched by the side of the frozen lake. The whole scene was becoming less a romantic private hideaway and more reminiscent of the start of a horror film. If we weren't going to freeze to death, the mad axe murderer in the woods would definitely finish us off, that is if the ghosts and goblins didn't scare us to death first. I was starting to forget why we'd chosen this decidedly isolated, difficult location as the best place to begin the next chapter of our lives. But solitude has its uses.

The clear, dark night was suddenly shot through with an acid-green streak that reflected out across the frozen lake. It shimmered in and out in livid skeins of yellow-fringed light through the darkness before falling away. It flickered again in a vivid electric pulse.

Matthias looked back at us. 'Northern Lights. Aurora borealis. People love it. Out here we call it fox fires.'

'It's beautiful,' I murmured, and felt Spear's grip tighten.

'Ursula?' he said. There was barely any sound to the word, as if it was more of an escaped thought.

I watched the colours whorl across the sky and settle before dying into the darkness. It seemed almost as if we were being given a glimpse of something that wasn't intended for us, some celestial event that was happening far out there, much bigger and more important than any of this insignificant event. We were simply witnessing the tail end of greater lives.

But Spear wasn't looking at the sky. He was still watching me, with an anguished look as if a thousand thoughts were breaking on his eyes.

'I . . .'

His face was lit by the flaring sky. He looked different. Changed. It was a new light opening something I hadn't seen in him for quite a while. But I knew it straight away.

Fear.

'Ursula, I . . .'

The bells from the other sleighs were drawing in closer behind. Helmi was driving. Her face had the same tired, cynical look.

'Everyone's here!' I said with the pretence of excitement. I turned away to deflect anything else Spear wanted to say. I moved to get out but felt him drag on my sleeve.

'I *need* to say something to you. Wait.'

I wanted to say, 'Don't. Please, don't say anything.' But the words dried up in my mouth when I saw his expression.

'Ursula, you know I'd never hurt you, don't you?'

'I know! You don't need to keep telling me that.'

The ethereal lights were burning in and out across his face, then fading. Everything about him was altered. The way he moved. His eyes. His face. Changing. In this cascade of new light, he seemed darker. Somehow hidden.

We both paused. If I could have driven us away right then, I would. Far away, where we could just be who we were, not some invention. Not bent into these new shapes I didn't recognise anymore.

He let his hand fall and looked down. I climbed out of the sleigh and greeted the others with a forced air of joviality, waving to them as if I didn't have a single care.

I was grateful for Aunt Charlotte's unmistakable singing drifting on the icy air.

Spear's footsteps on the snow crunched behind me and I felt his arm around my shoulders again. It had a more possessive feel to it this time, as if he did not intend to let go.

'Hey, you two.' Aunt Charlotte was standing up waving, dressed as Father Christmas with her beard flowing behind her and her voice echoing out. *'Ding Dong Merrily on High!'*

Sitting beside her, Mother was a perfect fairy-tale witch, in her fur hat and long, flowing coat.

The sharp-faced Onni was driving the last sleigh that had Bridget the elf and Angela in it. They were smiling and waving, a happy little crew. And I'd never been more pleased to see them as they emerged from the frozen darkness in all their bizarre, unbridled glory, their faces glowing in the curious light. I wanted to seal that moment away in a little envelope and bury it inside me so that I could unfold it whenever I needed to. I had that strange after-Christmas feeling of forewarning about certain cards that should not be thrown away. Ones that should be kept and cherished as there might be a moment all too soon when the need to look at them again with more poignant eyes would come.

The sleighs drew up like graceful boats alongside us.

'Well, well, you lovebirds. Look at this!' Aunt Charlotte was still standing, holding out her arms, embracing it all.

'We should get to our cabins.' Mother was being slightly more practically minded.

'Come on then, you'll have plenty of time for *mischief* tomorrow.' Aunt Charlotte winked at Spear, who didn't really know what to do with that. 'My little motto, always make sure your pants are clean even if your thoughts aren't.'

Spear didn't answer.

Bridget was starting to look like a very weary elf. 'And I'm the one who's got to share a room with Bad Santa here.'

'Come on, come on. Enough of this. Charlotte's got a motto for everything. I'm freezing and God knows what it's doing to my skin.' Mother's patience was burning thin now.

'I thought you liked that frozen-face look, Mother.'

She let the remark bounce off her.

'God, it really is just like bloody *Frozen* isn't it, eh, lad?' Aunt Charlotte elbowed Spear.

Bridget was trying her best to get out of the sleigh in her curly-toed elf shoes.

Angela smiled, rubbing her hands together. 'Isn't it gorgeous? Look at the lights!'

'Bloody freezing,' Mother murmured. 'Are our bags going to be taken in?'

Helmi had already turned the sleigh around and was leaving. Our luggage was in an untidy pile on the snow. She didn't respond.

'That'll be a no, then,' Mother sighed.

'I'll meet you back there, Matthias,' Helmi called.

Matthias simply nodded.

He glanced over at us as he threw out the last bag. 'There's some provisions for you inside. I think reindeer burgers or maybe steaks.'

'What the hell?' Bridget balked. 'I'm not eating . . .' she lowered her voice and cast a look towards the reindeer. '. . . *them*.'

'You were willing to ride them,' I offered.

'Well.' Aunt Charlotte looked contemplative. 'There are many things I'd ride that I wouldn't eat.' Her eyes lingered on the sturdy frame of Matthias.

'If you need anything, telephone reception. I can be over on the snowmobile. Otherwise, you have an *ahkio* if you need to come back quickly.' He saw our blank faces and pointed to the side of one of the cabins. 'Basic small sled. Good for dragging over snow. There's snowshoes and skis inside with lots more equipment in the large cupboard. You'll have everything you need.'

'I can't ski!' Bridget announced.

'It's fairly easy on the flat,' Spear said.

Angela started picking up the bags and handing them to people. 'Let's get a drink first and get this celebration started!'

Matthias paused before lowering his voice. 'Be careful of the *menninkäinen*.' He saw our confusion. 'Like your small goblin.' His eyes rested on Bridget. 'Mostly harmless but some of the impish ones have been known to trick children into following them into the forest.' He looked entirely serious about this. 'And be watchful. There are spirits in the ice.'

'I prefer ice in my spirits, to be honest,' Aunt Charlotte laughed to herself.

There was an intense conviction to Matthias now. 'This place is different. A thin place where things . . .' He paused and glared at her. 'Cross over.'

'Things?' Bridget scowled.

'Souls are gathered here, and those that seek them stalk the darkness.'

The air seemed to contract and close in around us.

'People have seen creatures, monsters made of ice and shadow, *weaving* through trees out here.'

I could feel my heart tapping faster behind my ribs, a nausea rising in the back of my throat.

'This is nonsense!' Mother declared. 'My daughter is getting married tomorrow. We have no time for spooks and ghouls invented to keep children out of the woods.'

Matthias looked at her with dismay. There was a hint of pity there for someone who clearly did not understand the true ways of this place. 'You have no idea what surfaces in the Arctic night. The darkness comes alive and there is no escaping those spirits and demons.' A purposeful element of mystery drifted under the surface of his voice.

He glowered into each of our faces, his jaw so tight the tendons stood proud in his neck. 'You'll regret not listening. People go missing out here.'

I noticeably shuddered and Angela gave me a reassuring glance.

But Matthias wasn't slowing down. It was almost as if he was enjoying frightening us. 'Only this autumn—'

'Right.' Angela saw my fear and held up her hands. 'Thank you for the local colour but I think that's quite enough Stephen King.'

'Who?'

'Quiet, Charlotte,' Mother broke out in frustration.

They gave each other that familiar look of sororicidal love.

'Well,' Aunt Charlotte blustered. 'I should have known you'd appreciate extra material for your *podcast*. If you'll excuse me, I've got some other local customs I'd like to investigate.

Starting with getting naked in the sauna with a bit of that local hooch.' She winked at Matthias. '*Pontikka*, eh? Heard it's rather *stimulating*.'

Matthias looked bemused but asked no more. He settled into his seat and jerked the reins.

As the sleighs pulled away into the darkness, they left behind a very real sense of abandonment to this wilderness.

I looked towards the close-packed trees forming a thick fortress around our small clearing. That thin finger of ice still traced along my spine. Slight tremors amongst the snow-covered branches caused flurries to fall. It was impenetrable. Or perhaps it might have been more appropriate to say inescapable. A flat, grey light lifted from the trees as if some remnant of life was rising into the night. Among the icy mist, I thought I caught the tail end of some movement, something turning back into the fog. I couldn't stop all those fluttering thoughts.

A hand grabbed mine and I flinched.

'It's OK,' Spear said quickly. 'I'm here.'

But for the first time in a long time, those words did not bring reassurance.

'Come on.' Angela picked up a bag and started walking towards one of the cabins. 'I've got some of that terrible *jaloviina* from the airport. Filthy but it'll keep us warm.'

'I'm your woman!' Aunt Charlotte called after her. She grabbed her bag.

'Ursula, can you take my suitcase?' Mother has never been very good with luggage.

Spear let his hand drop. 'I'll maybe see you later?' he said quietly.

'Yes,' I smiled. 'That would be nice.' It all had a strange formality to it, courteous but somehow cold.

He leaned forward and kissed my cheek, like a relative might, before he picked up his bag and walked away. I watched him walking with his head bent low, a new weight slowly being lowered on to him.

'Come over when you're settled,' Aunt Charlotte called out. 'I've got a few surprises!'

Surely, there couldn't be any more surprises beyond the thought of Father Christmas getting naked in a sauna with a bottle of Finnish hooch. I was wrong about that.

Thin whines and barks drifted out from the trees.

'Wolves,' Bridget said authoritatively and readjusted her elf hat.

Mother looked aghast. 'Actual wolves?'

'As opposed to . . . ?'

Bridget paused for a moment, holding out her arms. 'It's just so wonderful!' I could see her mind getting to work on another pet name already. 'I hope we see a bear as well.'

'Right, that's it!' Mother flared. 'Get in the cabins.'

'Which one?' Aunt Charlotte looked blank.

'How the hell should I know? I need to find out which is the best one first.'

Mother spent the next ten minutes running between the cabins working out which key fit which one, which had the biggest bed, the best shower and the hottest sauna.

She only decided to call a halt to it all when Aunt Charlotte started stripping off the Father Christmas outfit to go for her au naturel sauna.

'Join me, Pandora?' she said with a look of mischief. 'We can take the *jaloviina* in with us. It's exhilarating!'

Mother had the hostile look of someone distinctly opposed to exhilaration, especially naked with Aunt Charlotte and some filthy local spirits. But that didn't deter Aunt Charlotte. She entered the sauna wearing nothing more than her sporran and singing 'Let It Go' at the top of her voice.

CHAPTER EIGHT: THERE'S NO ACCOUNTING

Eventually, I was sitting on the edge of the bed, unpacked in a fashion, the white velvet trouser suit hanging up in front of me. It had been a welcome compromise for both me and Mother. I sat looking at it like it was another person standing in the room. Intricate pearl buttons ran down the long sleeves. There were small embroidered white roses and lily of the valley twining through them, a concession to Mother's disappointment that it wasn't the full snowstorm of a dress. She'd still cried when it had arrived though. She'd said it was perfect. That was all. That was enough. Nothing has ever been perfect for Mother before and I doubt it ever will be again.

But now, it was overwhelming to think I would be wearing that garment in a few hours' time to make one of the biggest commitments of my life. It was almost like I had to dress as someone else who wasn't anything like me to do this.

'Oh, Dad. Why can't you be here now?'

'I'm always here.' His dark outline was lingering in the corner. He'd felt no need to dress any differently for the cold.

'I know,' I sighed, 'I didn't mean like that.'

'You didn't think I'd miss my daughter's wedding, did you?'

No, I never thought he'd miss that, or my graduation, or all those birthdays and Christmases. I didn't think I'd be sitting on the edge of a bed talking to the air and imagining in some way that it might answer when I asked what happened to all the lost days.

I'd found Dad's diary after he died and I studied it over and over until I would never forget all the things he had done with me. But the biggest day of all was the first one that was blank. The first of all those empty entries.

The average human lives for twenty-seven thousand three hundred and seventy-five days. I like to collect facts about death. It reminds me I'm supposed to keep on living. I've lived for eleven thousand six hundred and ninety of those allotted days. That leaves me fifteen thousand six hundred and eighty-five to live. I like to make sure I know what I'm dealing with, that it's all set out there and catalogued. But death has managed to take me by surprise too many times. Dad's was the first but by no means the last life that didn't come close to the average.

I'm not sure setting my own personal Doomsday Clock is entirely healthy, but in some ways I see it as an attempt to make the most of it all, to 'live my best life', as all the well-being podcasts tell me I should. Or maybe I just need to know what to expect. I've had too much unexpected. Also, if I can't hide from death, I might as well know when it's due to arrive. Roughly.

I looked at the white suit and then back at Dad's hazy outline. 'Am I doing the right thing? Is this how I should spend those next fifteen thousand six hundred and eighty-five days?' I asked it of him like it was my bank balance, and I was checking on the right way to invest it.

He shrugged. 'No one knows the answer to that.'

I pulled out the Bible, Dad's Bible, as if the answer might be in there. I opened the cover. It was an answer of sorts. Inside was the hollowed-out area with the same old hip flask he'd always used. It had been refilled too many times to remember now. But remembering wasn't the idea of it. I took a big mouthful and held it there, before finally letting its warmth trail down my throat.

My thoughts were starting to clarify. If that's all it was, a set of decreasing numbers, then what had I got to lose? Those days would be spent anyway, so why not spend them with someone I love?

I paused for a moment, turning those last three words over again and again like they were playing cards and I was just deciding whether to go all in. They were three such simple words that blew everything else away. All the doubt, the worries just ceased to exist when I focused on them.

In the end, there was nothing more to think about beyond those words. I just had to keep them at the front when the queue of troubles muscled in. It was happening. Tomorrow. It was the beginning of the next fifteen thousand six hundred and eighty-five days, or however long we had left. Because for all my accountancy of life and death, I had no idea how quickly it could all end. It could quite easily all be over in a matter of hours.

Right then, though, I was expected in the living room for Aunt Charlotte's 'surprise'. That was definitely the right word.

'Come on, Ursula!' I could hear the impatience in her voice. 'We need a bride,' she shouted.

I smiled and opened the door. This could be fun. It didn't need to be all darkness and concern. I could actually *enjoy* this. But when I looked down over the banister into the sitting room, it was very clear that the next hour was going to challenge that idea a lot.

I walked down the stairs in astonishment. They were all standing in a circle. Aunt Charlotte was beaming. The rest of them wore the guilty, embarrassed look of humiliated MPs, some of whom I'm sure would have been familiar with the items that were now in that room.

Aunt Charlotte had dimmed the lights and lit some candles, but it didn't quite create the cosy evening atmosphere she'd obviously intended. More a disturbing basement feel. I caught Spear's eye and he instantly looked away. Mother was standing bolt upright in the manner of a Victorian lady who'd just been shown something compromising. Angela and Bridget were looking anywhere except at other people.

'There was one thing we overlooked in all that planning.' Aunt Charlotte raised her glass. 'A hen party!' She glanced over at Spear. 'And a stag, of course!'

I paused on the stairs, the shocking details of what she'd prepared becoming clearer with every minute.

'We've only got one night, so I've combined the two. But don't worry, there'll be plenty of fun for everyone!'

My knees were giving way.

'Come on,' she beckoned. 'Don't be shy. We haven't got all night and there's a lot to get through.'

I took each step at a time, noticing new additions to the room with every moment. All over the floor were large floating shapes that had a distinctly fleshy colour to them. As I reached the bottom step, one turned over and smiled up at me. I recoiled into the wall behind me. It was a man-balloon. A grinning-faced inflatable doll of a man. One that was strangely familiar.

I peered closer and Aunt Charlotte could see me inspecting the face.

'It's Richard Madeley.'

I looked closer. In a strange latex way, it was. She was right.

She shrugged. 'I was pushed for time so I had to get what was to hand.'

I looked in awe around the room. There must have been about ten of the things, drifting aimlessly across the floor. Thankfully, they were clothed. All of them were grinning. It was like being trapped in a morning television-based nightmare.

Aunt Charlotte came over and hooked her arm through mine, leading me through the room as they bobbed in and out. 'I read people like blow-up dolls on stags and hens. And I remembered that Bridget got these to train Mr Bojangles when he was considering being an emotional support dog for

Richard Madeley. Mr B didn't take to them but thankfully I kept them under your mother's stairs.'

'What?' Mother's face fell. 'Those . . . those . . . *things* have been in my house all this time?'

'They couldn't hurt you,' Aunt Charlotte said. 'They were deflated.' She turned to me. 'It's taken me ages to blow them all up. They didn't have a pump at reception. Do you know how long I've spent with my mouth on Richard Madeley?'

Spear choked on his beer.

She looked over at him. 'Don't worry, there's some for you too.' She turned two dolls to face the room as if she was introducing new guests. 'I've got Theresa May or one of the Loose Women. I wasn't sure which one you'd prefer.'

She let them both drift towards a dumbfounded Spear before rubbing her hands together.

Stepping towards the table, Aunt Charlotte held out a hand to display the items she'd set out there.

'Now, I've got squirty cream, plenty of cling film, penis or breast pasta, depending on your tastes . . .' She paused. 'But I think they're both the same flavour though. The man at the shop—'

'Shop?' I said in astonishment.

'Yes, we got a flyer through the door about something called an *adult* shop. I asked your neighbours about it, Pandora, but they hadn't heard of it.' She shrugged.

At this point, Mother might have had a seizure. It was hard to tell.

'Anyway, he suggested these handcuffs, the man in the adult shop, that is, not your neighbour.' She pointed to the items among the lineup of indescribable objects she'd placed there. It was like an indecent *Generation Game*.

'Some edible knickers.' She leaned closer towards me and lowered her voice. 'I've tried to get them on, dear, and there's no chance.'

Spear stifled a laugh. I looked at him and covered my smile.

63

'And, best of all, we've got . . . games!' She grinned through the darkness at us all.

I noticed Mother hadn't blinked for a while.

Bridget looked horrified and confused.

Angela was quietly smiling to herself behind her glass.

'I decided on an escape room game.'

I held up my hand like a bewildered schoolgirl. 'Is that a good idea, given our track record?'

Aunt Charlotte nodded enthusiastically. 'Oh yes! This one is! It's set in a country house, and we have to escape from the unknown killer.'

'Jesus,' Mother whispered.

'Well, if you prefer, we can start with these cards.' She held up a pack of fairly normal-looking playing cards and pulled out the top one. 'What's this?' She squinted at it and began reading. 'Yes, it says, "Shout out if you're going commando!"' She laughed. 'Well, I am!'

I stared and she winked at me. 'Can't beat it with tweed.'

It took her a moment of persuading but Aunt Charlotte gently encouraged us all to take our seats around the coffee table of smut. I glanced tentatively at Spear and he smiled. It was the most relaxed he'd looked in weeks, which was good, if not a little disconcerting given the items in front of us.

The rest of them moved slowly towards their chairs. Mother was last, sitting straight-backed and looking resolutely ahead, avoiding the smorgasbord of props arrayed before her.

'Now then,' Aunt Charlotte began with enthusiasm. 'Let's get you all a drink to loosen up. Because you all, especially you Pandora, will definitely need to.'

Mother's eyeballs looked like they might burst.

Aunt Charlotte was right, though. The fizz did help to ease us into the evening, and after the initial heart-stopping nature of the revelations, we actually started to have fun. There was laughter, embarrassment and quite a bit of Mother shouting, 'Quiet, Charlotte!' Particularly when revelations from Mother's past were hinted at. Apart from the blow-up Richard Madeleys occasionally drifting across our games, we had a great time.

There was a moment when it could have been derailed during the escape room game when no one could agree how to evade the killer. Eventually, Mother insisted on a course of action and there was a death. Aunt Charlotte ensured there was no more interference from Mother by putting the pink fluffy handcuffs on her before realising she'd misplaced the key.

It was fun. I forgot the worries. I forgot we were getting married. And somehow that felt better.

CHAPTER NINE: THE NIGHT BEFORE

After the laughter died down and the games had ended, they all sat round the fire, a perfect scene of bliss, drinking, giggling, reminiscing. Even Mother was having a good time, after she'd been freed from the handcuffs by Bridget's use of a hairpin.

'Little trick I learned,' Bridget said with a dry grin on her face. She'd had one too many glasses of the prosecco.

'Where?' Mother raised an eyebrow. 'In prison?'

But I watched Mother finally loosen the ties on all that pent-up anxiety. She'd been coiled pretty tight in the last few weeks. We all had.

I sat with Spear in the small kitchen diner off to the side of the *mökki*'s living area. For once, they'd all realised it might be quite nice if we had a little time on our own. We'd been everyone else's property since we'd told them all. It seemed that every moment had to be devoted to the wedding.

I sat looking out through the long window, watching the tapers of those spectral lights chase across the black sky. Through the glint of smeary glass, the trees were outlined in a hazy rime. It was so still, so quiet out there. I imagined I could hear the ice cracking and shifting in the air, those ghosts Matthias had spoken of waking to our sound, whatever lived out there suddenly aware of these new intruders. Watching.

'It's very beautiful here.' I was doing most of the talking again.

'Hmm.' That same distraction was there in his voice. An absence. Spear turned his glass, focusing hard on the liquid swilling around. He wasn't looking out there, or at the snow, or the heavenly display of lights. He wasn't looking at me. He was far away, drowning in his own thoughts.

Thick candles had been lit in some of the windows, weeping down on to the ledges below, their light reflecting on the black glass. To anyone else, the night before their wedding, this would have been the most perfect romantic dream, hidden away from the world in candlelit icy seclusion. But I could only feel that insistent rising hum of anxiety prowling round the back of my mind.

'Spear?'

'Yep.' It sounded curt.

I put my hand across his. He didn't move. 'If there's something . . . If you're having . . .'

He was resolutely not going to help me out. But we could both sense that unspoken word still lingering above us.

'Please . . .'

'It's just—' He stopped abruptly, snatching the rest of the words back. He slipped his hand from under mine.

'Yes?'

He waited, finally making the decision to speak. 'It's just that I've done this before and it didn't go well.'

It took a moment for what he'd said to make sense. 'You mean . . .' I knew what he meant. A wife. An unfaithful wife. A murdered wife. 'None of that was your fault.' Perhaps he had his ghosts too. 'I'm not like that.' I leaned closer. 'I would never do anything like that. You know I wouldn't.' I gripped his hand tighter and this time his fingers curled around mine.

'You mean die? I'm sorry. I think . . . I think I need to just rest a little. It'll be clearer in the morning, I'm sure. I'm just so tired.'

'Of what?'

He didn't answer that. He shook his head. 'Ursula, I'm very tired. That's all.' He must have seen the disappointment instantly spooling out across my face. He frowned and cupped my face in his hands, inspecting it as if there was something that he didn't quite understand. 'It's just all so different now. I didn't expect . . .'

He leaned across and kissed me but drew back quickly as if he regretted it. He looked puzzled. 'You know, you even taste different to me now.'

The words stung me and I pulled away. 'I don't understand, Spear. If you don't want this. If you don't want any of this, then why are we here? I thought this was what you wanted.'

His hands fell to his sides and he looked down. 'I don't know. I don't know. It's not you. Everything just tastes foul tonight.' He took a long breath. 'Listen, do me a favour. Keep the doors locked.'

I frowned, then gave a half-laugh. 'To keep the monsters out?'

'I'm serious, Ursula.'

I folded my arms. 'Did you not notice the array of hunting weapons they're using for decoration on the walls here? We've got knives, mantraps, a crossbow . . .'

'Well, doesn't that seem odd for a start? All the cabins have them, like they're armed and ready for some sort of siege. Look, I'm going to turn in. Big day tomorrow.' He gave a weak smile but for some reason I thought I heard something else in his voice, as if it was an ironic thing he'd just said. It didn't sound like excitement for the beginning of all those days we had left.

When I thought back over it, through the rest of those long night hours, he didn't walk out of that room with the spring in his step of a man about to face the most memorable day of his life.

'Goodnight, Mr Spear,' I called. If I'm honest, part of me was still holding out for a rom-com-style reply, reflecting my words back at me — *Goodnight, Mrs Spear*. I'd seen a lot of that sort of thing — *Mr and Mrs* scrawled on wine glasses, T-shirts, even pants, but none of it seemed made for us. I was painfully aware that this was definitely not a rom-com.

'Goodnight,' was all he said without looking back. Perhaps I'd been looking for too much drama from a man who'd faced all this before. I was even starting to think of this in terms of a campaign now, that I just needed to see through to the end.

When he'd gone, it wasn't long before their tentative faces peered round the doorframe. One after the other. Mother was first, closely followed by Aunt Charlotte.

'How's the blushing bride?' Aunt Charlotte said, wide-eyed. She'd forsaken her Father Christmas outfit in favour of a tweed ensemble which she called her Margaret Rutherford.

Mother wasn't quite as diplomatic. 'Quiet, Charlotte, she's having doubts. You wouldn't know anything about it.'

'Is everything OK?' Angela looked between them, then back at me, her face etched with concern. 'I know he can be a little undemonstrative at times but he utterly worships you, you know. He's devoted to you, Ursula.'

That was enough to start the tears. I couldn't stop them.

'Oh, come on, girl. It's not that bad. Nothing is ever that bad.' Aunt Charlotte sat next to me and put her large arm around me. She smelled of a comfortable blend of soap and face powder. There was a warmth to her that was so immediate, I could have fallen into her great barrel chest and stayed there without having to think about tomorrow at all.

Mother gripped my hand and looked up into my tear-streaked face. 'Ursula, let's get those wiped away.' She stroked a finger efficiently under each eye. 'No one likes a weeping bride. Makes everyone uncomfortable. They start thinking about their own misfortunes. You have to be the perfect one of us tomorrow. The one who got it right.'

I laughed at that.

'Just while we're on the subject of the wedding.' Bridget was at the door, still wearing the elf suit. 'I was meaning to ask if you'd had any thoughts about a ring bearer?' She liked to pick her moments.

It was very easy for Mother to turn her frustration on Bridget. 'Look, Frodo, we don't need your—'

'Wait.' I held up a hand. 'If that's what Bridget would like to do . . .'

'Hang on, dear.' Aunt Charlotte look stunned. 'You can't just have people baring rings. I realise it's not a church, but even so.'

I sighed. 'Bridget, I would be honoured for you to bear the ring.'

Aunt Charlotte looked appalled.

Bridget could not have been more honoured if she'd been told she was about to be awarded an OBE. She probably will be one day. She should be.

I tried to wipe away the tears with my sleeve.

'Oh, Ursula.' Angela looked so anguished. 'Do you want me to speak to him? I can suggest he perhaps puts a little more effort into *telling* you how he feels.'

I laughed and finished wiping my face. 'No, no, I don't think that will be necessary.'

'He utterly adores you, you know. I've never known a man feel so deeply about someone. He talks about you all the time and I know he's nervous. He just wants to get it right. He can't stand the thought of upsetting you.'

'Well, he's making a good job of it!' Mother shot.

I shook my head. 'It's fine. Really. I'm being over-dramatic.'

'You? Over-dramatic?' Mother sent up a little ironic eyebrow.

'OK. OK. I can take that.'

I leaned back and closed my eyes. 'I just want tomorrow to work out. That's all.'

'And it will.' Aunt Charlotte held up the bottle of fierce-looking Finnish spirit. 'Especially if we have a little bit more of this.' She gave me that familiar wink and her face lit up with a smile. Just in that moment, she made me believe that it truly would all be all right.

CHAPTER TEN: LISTENING AT WINDOWS

Announcing an engagement always sounded to me like there should be a herald in the town square followed by some sort of elaborate costume ball, rather than a trip to the pub and a takeaway. But ever since the *announcement of our engagement*, I'd been expected to look happy every waking moment. It was exhausting, all this joyous celebratory time. There just didn't seem to be one single moment that was my own, where I could sit down and do all the things I was far more comfortable with. Being quiet, being on my own, contemplating life and death.

So, in some ways, I should have embraced a night of no sleep in the quietest place I could imagine. Only it wasn't. Mother couldn't sleep either. And when Mother can't sleep, the world should be awake. She'd been on the zolpidem for so long now that I was beginning to wonder if she might be starting to develop an immunity to tranquilisers and just never sleep again, like some kind of living undead. That was a very disturbing thought. We all need our breaks from Mother.

Finally, after what seemed like hours of her turning and murmuring, she seemed to be giving up the fight, working her way down through the layers of sleep. The tablets still allowed her to mumble incoherent words though. Bob the Therapist had said that was to be expected and that marked the moment when we should increase the dose. It had gone so high that she was macrodosing now and I was starting to worry we'd run out. I'm not sure Bob had been in the right frame of mind though when he was giving Mother the kind of advice that basically implied we should keep her sedated at all times. The last time Mother saw him he was running away shouting, 'God, release me from this curse!' The receptionist at the practice said he'd tried a number of religions and had even attempted a DIY exorcism. They were still finding the name Pandora scrawled on burned pieces of newspaper weeks after his disappearance. The thought had crossed my mind even then that his insistence that she keep upping the dose of her tranquilisers might have been motivated by something other than Mother's insomnia. Perhaps even, eventually, something much darker indeed. But I don't like to dwell on the people who could cheerfully murder Mother.

Bob the Therapist had predictably ignored the wedding invitation but Mother remained hopeful for his return and continued to leave little messages on his mobile. She was determined not to abandon him as her therapist as that would in some way be disloyal. In the meantime though, that left me covering the cracks, which seemed to grow wider with every passing month.

I'm not sure it was really fair to blame Mother for my inability to switch off that night. Even if she'd been sleeping the sleep of the heavily medicated, I still wouldn't have been able to free my mind from the merry-go-round of doubts and fear. In the darkness, all those worries were brighter than ever, turning on a great carousel, one then the next, repeating. Would it all go well? Could I remember what I was supposed to do and my role? What if I forgot the details of everything we had planned? Why was I doing this? The last thought was needle-sharp in my head.

I stared at the empty air. This was ridiculous. I'd been happy, or thereabouts. Why were we doing any of this? Spear clearly wasn't over the moon about it. But when was he ever ecstatic? He'd never been an ecstatic sort of man. Did I want to spend the rest of my life with an unecstatic man? Is unecstatic even a thing?

The long reel of night was playing out slowly, torturing out thoughts I just wanted to bury. As the hours wore on steadily, those ghosts rose up and began to circle. I even started to wonder if Matthias's spirits were wending their way through the trees towards us now.

A faint cry travelled over the ice. The wolves had been growing increasingly vocal since our arrival. Perhaps all those creatures and spirits out there, real or not, were becoming more alive to our presence. More interested. Well, at least someone was *ecstatic* about our being here.

And it just grew worse as the night drew on. Initially, it had seemed like such a quiet place of solitude, but as hour followed hour, I listened more closely. The night seemed laced with half-caught noises. Strangled cries and ill-defined howls circled the frozen air. I sat keenly, my eyes wide in the darkness. A distant creak from the wood sounded like someone was on the stairs. Perhaps they couldn't sleep either. Perhaps Aunt Charlotte had come over. A louder creak seemed closer. It was so easy to start picturing a foot above those steps, a figure moving up the staircase.

I thought of Matthias's warnings about the spirits that roamed these lands. What kind of ghosts were forming now from the frozen air outside? Were they outside? Were they even ghosts or something more substantial? More real. Matthias had said there'd been disappearances. Maybe that was to be expected in such brutal conditions. Maybe something more than ghosts lived in those forests. It would be ideal cover.

I had to stop. This was ridiculous. Why did my mind instantly race towards whether or not there might be a killer lurking out there? I suppose that was one question I already knew the answer to.

Another groan lifted from the log walls as if something was trapped behind all that old wood, or perhaps inside it. A faint tapping began. I told myself it was the pipes but it didn't stop the image of those fingers drumming away, pattering on the other side of the wall. I could hear the soft crunch of the snow, as if footsteps were making their way towards our cabin.

Then, in the quiet, a familiar sound was near my window. A voice.

It stood out from all the other disturbances.

There were some muffled, undefinable words, but the tone was instantly recognisable. It was threatening.

I scurried over to the window, keeping low. It was garbled at first and I couldn't make out the words, but I managed to push the small window open a crack. The conversation drifted in.

'. . . Spear, oh yes, I know you. I recognised you.' It was the instantly identifiable East End lilt of Tapio. 'The only question is, how much is my silence going to cost? That pretty little bride must have a few quid.'

'Ursula!' It was Mother.

I crouched down further, my heart pedalling fast.

The conversation stopped abruptly.

In the thin moonlight, I could see Mother was sitting bolt upright in bed, but her eyes were closed. She paused, confusion drawing down her face, her eyelids flickering. Then she fell back into the pillow, into silence.

The voices outside had stopped. I waited, still crouched below the window, catching my breath, staring into nothing. Were they still there? Were they looking in? My bed was very clearly empty with the blankets pulled back, instantly making it obvious I'd got up. Perhaps even walked over to open this window.

I tried to calm my breathing and my eyes inched up to look at the very obviously open window. If I reached out now to close it and they were still there, they'd see me. But if I left it open . . .

I could hear the sound of their boots on the crisp snow. They were growing quieter, their voices becoming more distant. They were leaving.

My pulse was still racing, the sound of blood rushing in my head. I tried to stay completely still. I didn't dare move. The freezing air was creeping in through the open window, but it still felt too soon to reach up and close it.

I closed my eyes, trying to think. This was the man I was marrying and I was rigid with fear that he might see me. I was already hiding. Not only was he *unecstatic* but he still had secrets. Dangerous secrets that someone could blackmail him over. There was no time left. In a few short hours I would be bound to a man I really only knew the surface layer of.

I opened my eyes and looked to where Dad was watching. He leaned his head over to the side, sad sympathy scrolling over his face. He looked at Mother who was whispering half-garbled words in her sleep.

'It's never perfect, Ursula,' he said quietly.

Mother's face was suddenly disturbed.

'But it's enough.' He disappeared into the shadows again, leaving me with more questions. The biggest of them being, what is enough?

CHAPTER ELEVEN: URSULA'S WEDDING DAY

An urgency of voices, doors slamming, a turmoil of movement, all drowned out the silence of those stark hours I had sat in bed, thinking, turning over the same worries, the same questions, until each one was polished smooth. But, however clear the questions, and regardless of any answers, it was happening today. Time relentlessly pulled us to that one endpoint. Towards zero.

I knew it was going to be difficult when I saw Mother had already roused herself and brought me a cup of tea. That was the first red flag. Mother has never made me or anyone else a cup of tea. She'd used cold water but it was a gesture of some sort, I'm sure. I watched the lifeless teabag floating around in the cup like an empty lifejacket.

'Mother?'

'Hmm?' She was lining up all the make-up she wanted me to apply. Why I needed to paint my face entirely different to the usual way it looked was beyond me. Surely Spear would be expecting the same face he'd asked to marry him, not some clown-show parody, but I pick my battles with Mother. It had been enough that we were here and not at some stately home with me wearing a human-sized toilet roll cover.

'Did you ever . . .'

'I'm not playing that game again. I've still not recovered from Charlotte's revelations.'

Mother had started on the hair products now. One for gloss, one for full body, one for sheen, which apparently was very different to gloss. If Mother had her way with my hair, it was going to look like a giant conker.

'No. No, I mean . . . Did you have . . . I mean before you married Dad, did you have . . .'

She turned to look at me.

The word I was avoiding was obvious. Unspoken but clear.

At least I thought it was until Mother said, 'Sex?'

'God! No, Mother. I was going to say *doubts*.'

'Oh, that. Yes. I see.' She put down the strange hair tool that looked like a branding iron. 'Darling, we all have those, every single day. We'd never get anything done if we listened to them. Should I get married? Should I burden myself with a child?'

'Mother?'

'That's a much bigger decision because no matter how much you want to, there's no going back when it's still there every single day you wake up, whinging and moaning and needing food and nappies and—'

'Mother, I am here!'

'Better you know now.'

'But it's joyful in the end, yes? That's what you meant.'

Mother didn't answer that. She came over to the bed and sat on the edge. If this was going to be a touching maternal scene it could have been the final indignity in all of this. But I was safe on that score, at least.

'Ursula, get your lippy on and get out there. I haven't come all this way to spend a week with my sister and Bridget in the frozen wastelands without seeing this through. OK?'

It was all very far from OK but Mother's blunt appraisal of the situation did provide a spur of sorts. I put down the cold tea. It was time.

The next hour and a half was something I just endured. Make-up, hair, flowers, clothes. None of this had anything to do with what was spinning through my mind. In less than an hour, I would be inextricably tied to a man whose secrets endlessly unfolded, the layers peeling back as though he was being reinvented every day. But in spite of it all, whatever he was, I didn't want any of those days ahead of me to not have him in them. That was all I could cling to.

As we stepped out into the brittle, cold air, it seemed to clear my thoughts of any doubts. Even though my stomach stirred and my head burned, for the first time I felt absolute certainty. I held Mother's hand. She smiled and gave one definite nod as if to say, 'This is it. This is right.' It was all that I needed.

Aunt Charlotte was more demonstrative. Tears streamed down her face as she held me by both shoulders. She was wearing her full tweed ensemble, complete with tweed deerstalker. She looked resplendent, her soft smile pure love.

'Darling, darling Ursula. You are the most beautiful thing I have ever seen.' She could barely speak, her voice breaking with emotion.

I touched the brim of her hat. 'Very nice.'

She smiled. 'Nothing but the best for you. It is the greatest honour of my life to be your celibate. I've been training for weeks.'

Mother let out a laugh. 'More like a lifetime.'

Aunt Charlotte frowned.

I stifled my smile. 'I am enormously touched that you will be our *celebrant*.'

It was hard to believe that Aunt Charlotte, in her Sherlock hat, would very soon be marrying me and Spear. As strange as it might have looked, it somehow seemed very right.

'Oh, she's gorgeous, isn't she?' Bridget was fussing around, handing out small posies of dried flowers she'd worked on for weeks. There were no fresh flowers to be had out here at this time of year, so she'd set to work immediately gathering from Mother and Angela's gardens. Ours was pitiful, but Angela gardened so there was more to choose from. Although, anything would have been better than the single dead olive tree Mother had in a pot. Bridget managed to dry bunches of lavender and small sprigs of thyme, along with some more I suggested that had always been my favourites. Rosemary, lily of the valley, and even some heads of white hydrangea she'd dried in the airing cupboard were all carefully woven into my bouquet by Bridget. Even Spear acknowledged their beauty and requested that he too have a buttonhole to match. It had taken weeks, but the end result was perfect, their astringent, herb scent clinging to the frozen air.

'Thank you, Bridget.'

She glowed with pride. 'Bless you, girl. I wish you so much happiness.'

We stood for a brief moment, the four of us — me, Mother, Aunt Charlotte and Bridget — the air still and crisp around us. All our thoughts gathered, each of us knowing that we were picturing those who hadn't made it to this point. Mirabelle was there with us in those minutes, just as she'd always been. I saw the tears surfacing in Mother's eyes. I held her hand and she smiled.

We took a collective breath. This was it. This would change us for ever, all in different ways, but we were ready.

Matthias had arrived with the sleigh all decked in white ribbons, the reindeer's bell sounding clear on the cold air. I climbed in with Mother.

The sharp-faced man, Onni, was driving the sleigh behind for Aunt Charlotte and Bridget. Mother had arranged for Angela and Spear to be taken over ahead of us. She'd insisted some traditions at least had to be observed.

As we pulled away from the cabins, I saw Dad's shape, dark against the crystal snow. He held his arm aloft and smiled. Throughout it all, the image I'd held close was that of both of them, Mother and him, either side of me, walking down the small aisle towards Spear. All the worries, all the doubt melted away as I imagined Spear's face all radiant at the sight of us. Finally, it was beginning to feel like this was right.

When we drew closer to the main cabin, I could see Angela was waiting for us outside. I waved to her but as we slowed in next to the cabin, she had a grave look on her face.

'He's gone,' was all she said.

That was the moment my heart split.

CHAPTER TWELVE: AFTERMATH

The world was pushing in from all sides, crushing me until I couldn't breathe. I could feel Mother's arm around me, drawing me in. I could hear the initial disbelief. Aunt Charlotte issued a dismissive noise and a weak laugh before the realisation spread through them all.

There was deep shame in Angela's face, her voice thick with tears. 'I'm so sorry. I . . . I'm sorry. Oh, Ursula. I can't . . .'

'Where the hell is he?' Mother shifted from comforting to fury in one breath. I could feel her body stiffening next to me as though the blood was solidifying in her veins.

My thoughts had stalled. It was as if I was suspended there, floating in the cool, white air. I couldn't move. There were no thoughts other than Spear's face, that lingering look of sorrow on him, anguished and torn into an apology. I heard his voice in my head. *I'm sorry.* And then he turned away from me and he was gone. Gone from everywhere as if he'd never existed. An illusion. A *physical manifestation of* . . .

Dad's face was there instead now, so worried, his expression cut deep with concern.

I could see my hands shaking, but somehow, inside me I only felt complete and utter stillness. Even my heart didn't seem to be beating anymore. Every part of me was spent.

Mother was climbing out of the sleigh. 'Charlotte, stay with her.'

I could feel another arm around me, soft and warm. 'It'll be OK, love. Don't you worry.'

I wasn't worried. I wasn't anything.

'What the bloody hell is going on, Angela? Where the hell is he?'

Angela was breathing heavily, clouding the air in thick, white plumes. Panicked words stuttered out of her. 'I don't know. I don't know.'

'What do you mean, you don't know? There's nowhere to go!' Mother's wrath was building.

Angela tried to steady herself, slowing her voice down. 'We went to bed last night. He spoke to me a little about the . . . the . . . normal kind of things, you know.'

'No, Angela, I don't know.' That was true where Mother was concerned.

'Well, you know.' She glanced over towards me in the sleigh and grew quieter. 'He had a few . . . a few doubts, that's all. Just the usual kind of thing. Was he good enough? Would he mess things up again? He said how wrong his first marriage had been and the chaos it ended up in.' She paused and looked over again. 'But he kept saying how much he loved *you*, Ursula. How much he couldn't bear to cause you pain.' Tears coursed down her face.

Those words echoed in my head that he'd said so many times before, how he couldn't stand the thought of me being hurt. And now, he'd hurt me so conclusively that no one could ever hurt me again.

'He utterly worshipped you, Ursula. You have to believe that.'

I lifted my head slowly. 'Before he left me? Before he was gone?'

'Well, have you even looked for him?' Bridget was all angry confusion, her head switching around, searching us all for answers.

'Yes! I woke up this morning and took a cup of tea to his room. He wasn't there but I just thought he'd maybe gone outside or gone for a walk to clear his head.'

'Gone for a walk? It's bloody freezing! Where would he walk to?' Mother's eyes were furious.

'I don't know! I wasn't thinking straight. Then I saw the sledge thing, the *ahkio*, had gone and I started to grow concerned. I rang over here. Helmi was just on her way out to get us. She searched all around the cabin and there was no sign of him. She'd heard nothing. She's just gone inside to check at reception if he has left any messages about where he might be.'

I thought of Spear out there, skiing as fast as he could to get away from here. To get away from me.

Inside my head, the thoughts started to struggle out and writhe like newborn creatures all knotted and ill-formed. Screaming. Frenzied. Desperate.

But on the outside, I was perfectly still. I didn't blink. I didn't swallow. I couldn't feel the cold, or even the sleigh's bench beneath me. It was as if a great glass jar had descended over me, preserving me like those old displays of dried flowers. Sealing me off from the world. I was numb. I could feel nothing. See nothing. Hear nothing.

Until that visceral scream cut a hole right through the air.

It left a perfect silence behind it.

They all stopped, confusion rippling out from the noise. Then it came again, raw and loud. It was in Finnish but it was followed quickly by those unforgettable words that carried up into the grave sky. 'He is dead!'

CHAPTER THIRTEEN: 'TIL DEATH DO US PART

My heart restarted at a pace I couldn't control. The blood welled up in my throat until I felt I'd choke on it, the coppery taste harsh in my mouth. He could be gone, that much was real. Maybe someday I'd even grow around that scar. But he couldn't be dead. That couldn't happen.

'No!' Angela shouted. She looked around us in horrified disbelief. 'Not my son. No. No.'

All the anger, all the questions washed away in an instant.

'Please, no,' I whispered. Aunt Charlotte held me tight but didn't speak.

I could only watch as Matthias jumped down from the front of the sleigh and started running into the lodge.

The voice screamed out again. A woman. 'Help me, please! He's dead.'

Mother and Angela were next to run into the cabin, closely followed by Bridget. Aunt Charlotte's hold on me remained firm but I pulled back from her. She looked at me with confusion, the pain deep in her eyes.

'I want to see him,' was all I said before stepping out of the sleigh in a daze. I don't know how my legs were moving but I somehow got myself to the cabin door.

'Ursula, don't!' Aunt Charlotte was quick to follow me.

The only thought I had was to see him. Touch him. I wasn't going to let him go. Not now.

Inside, there was a small table to the right with glasses of champagne waiting for our joyous arrival. Dried flower garlands had been strung along the walls and down the banisters, just as Bridget had designed. I moved through the room in a silent dream, drifting through what could have been, seeing it all like another life that had been abandoned. On a stand, there was a large photograph of me and Spear, laughing. A small board to the side was littered with pictures of our past. Baby photos, childhood memories. Dad was there, and Mother. Spear was a little boy smiling with his mum. What if I could go back and look into those children's eyes? Would I tell them the truth of how this would all unfold, or would I keep it to simple, easier lies?

There were more flowers surrounding a door to the right. Dried petals and leaves littered the floor. I drifted through the arch with the strange weightless feeling of a dreamer. The intimate room was set with chairs facing forward and, at the front, a table draped in a plain white cloth was smeared with crude streaks of a muddy substance.

Mother and Angela were standing back from the woman hunched over on the ground, their faces caught in disbelief and shock. A strange, foul smell hung in the air. There was a frightening stillness to all this.

The woman's body was shaking with tears. It was Aino, her hair hanging down over her face, covering the body on the floor. A dark pool leaked out beside them, smeared in places across the stone floor. Aino leaned back and let out a wounded, distraught cry. 'Tapio!'

My thoughts unravelled. Spear was there again in my head, turning to me, a look of regret on his face. But this time it had so quickly morphed into something else. It was tainted with a bitter guilt.

'Tapio?' Aunt Charlotte was breathless.

The desperate woman on the floor turned her head mechanically. Her swollen eyes settled on me. 'This is you!

Your wretched man. He has killed my husband and fled like a dog.'

I stared at her, unable to comprehend what she was saying.

'Now wait a minute.' Angela was holding out her hands in a conciliatory gesture but the look on her face was firm. 'You can't know it was him. My son would never—'

'Your son—' the woman bit hard on the words, her accent sharpened with anger — 'has killed my husband and run. He's the one who's missing. He knew him! He knew what he did.'

My mind flashed back to a few hours ago and the conversation I'd heard outside my window. Tapio had threatened him. Tried to blackmail him. And now Tapio was dead, and Spear was gone.

I looked down at the pitiful woman crouched by the body. Her husband was on his back, his face blanched and set in a fearful expression of pain. The sickly sheen of his skin had taken on a tallow colour, a waxy, soft translucence that was grotesque. This had not been a quick death. His eyes were open, his mouth spread wide in a grimace with a line of dark fluid trailing down over his chin. His whole body was contorted, and his hand gripped his chest as if he had convulsed in pain in those final moments. Vomit and blood mingled and splattered all down his shirt. He was wearing no trousers, only a pair of baggy, grubby underpants. Even in the face of such a vile death, Aunt Charlotte wasn't going to let that go without comment.

'The murderer has stolen his trousers,' she mused.

'*Kalsarikännit*,' Matthias announced. He was standing solemnly at the door.

We left a pause for him to explain, the only sound Aino's sobbing.

'It is . . . how would you say? No-pants drinking.' He continued in a grave voice. 'You get drunk at home alone in your underwear with no intention of doing anything else.' He nodded, looking down at Tapio's pitiful state. 'It is a Finnish tradition.'

I stared at Matthias and then back at the half-naked body. Death had robbed him of a final moment of dignity.

Aunt Charlotte nodded solemnly. 'We call it goblin mode.'

Aino let out a strangled sound, her head falling back. She had the desperate look of a snared animal. 'How can you speak like this about my husband? He is murdered!' She gave me a narrow look. 'By your man.'

My heart clenched. I had no words to offer. How could I? The man who clearly knew Spear and his past, who I'd overheard trying to blackmail him, was lying dead in front of me and Spear had disappeared. He'd not just casually checked out either. Something had compelled him to run out into the freezing darkness in the middle of nowhere the night before his wedding. It was either the thought of marrying me, or the fact that he'd killed someone. Right then, in that moment, I didn't know which was worse.

'We don't even know how he died,' Bridget observed. 'This could have been a heart attack.'

'A heart attack?' Aino cried. 'He was as strong as an ox. He has been poisoned. Do you not have eyes?'

'That's a big conclusion to leap to. I've had experience of this before.' Bridget was right, we all had. And there was no escaping the fact that it looked just like this. Everything about the man on the floor said he had been poisoned by something very powerful.

Another scream broke out. Helmi was standing at the door, her mouth hanging slack, her eyes wide. Onni was behind her with a similar look of disbelief, although his was slightly tinged with a shrewd edge. His dubious eyes ran round us all. Suspicion sat very naturally on his face.

Matthias lowered his voice, adopting a portentous tone, as if he was delivering a grim omen. 'I told you darkness was near. The ghosts are coming. The beast has awoken and he won't stop until he takes us all.' He paused and widened his eyes. 'One. By. One.'

'Well, I don't believe in ghosts,' Mother said.

'I don't think they care whether you do or not.' He glared at her, then let his eyes travel around the room before finally coming to rest on me. 'You don't have to believe in ghosts to be haunted.' He continued to watch me closely.

'This is nonsense.' Mother doesn't do supernatural entities. Her view is that there are quite enough real horrors in this world without the need to invent new ones.

Matthias had started to edge out of the room.

'Dad?' Helmi searched each of our faces as if looking for the answer there. 'What have you done to him?' She was transfixed, staring at Aino.

Her mother held out her dirty, smeared hands in a humble, almost pious pose. The pitiful image made her seem like a woman looking for some form of forgiveness. A guilty woman.

'Helmi,' Aino whispered her daughter's name. She started to stand, still stretching out her arms, showing all the vivid smears down her clothes.

The girl stared in horror at her. 'What have you done, Mother?'

Aino shook her head, frowning. She opened her mouth to speak.

'You hated him. You did this!' Helmi shouted.

It was true that the woman had been the only person in the house with him in the last half an hour. Matthias and Onni had been collecting us, Helmi had gone to Angela's to search for Spear and found no sign of him at all. But then, who could say when this had happened. How long ago had he been poisoned? Perhaps I'd been the last one to hear the dead man as he issued his threats outside my window. The last one except for Spear.

'Helmi,' Aino's face collapsed. 'How can you say this about your own mother?'

The girl ran towards her but stopped, staring down at the slaughtered body. Her eyes were senseless. She turned and looked around us before finally focusing on the small table with the bloodstained cloth.

'I'll tell you how. This!' Helmi pointed to the table. As I looked at the blood and vomit more closely, it began to form into a pattern. The hand marks and smears from his obvious desperate fall now joined and circled one another until they met in something more recognisable.

Letters. A single word.

'*Kielo*,' Helmi hissed. She looked around us and then to her mother. '"Lily".'

The air was growing more rancid. My head pounded. I saw Dad's shadow drifting over by the far wall. He looked at me doubtfully, his face deeply troubled.

'You were always shouting at him,' Helmi was building into a frenzied pace that was barely controlled. 'Rowing with him about his supposed infidelities, his flings with the local young girls. With Lily. Well, now you've punished him, haven't you, and left this at his execution.' Helmi threw out the words like weapons before storming from the room. She pushed past Onni who made no effort to stop her.

'Helmi?' Her mother remained in a penitent's stance, her hands spread wide, covered in the guilty fluid. 'Where are you going?'

'Someone has to phone the police,' Helmi shouted back at her. Her meaning was very clear.

CHAPTER FOURTEEN: MOTIVES

When there were no more words, when it dissolved into disbelief and tears, we finally withdrew, slowly leaving the woman alone with her newborn grief. We gathered in the small dining room that was still set for the wedding feast. A dark wooden table was laid with white plates. Tall cream candles rose up from a central display of more dried flowers. Small place cards marked out the seating arrangement Mother had spent hours perfecting. Spear's name caught my eye immediately, his chair ominously empty as we all settled into our allotted places. None of us had been able to persuade Aino to leave her husband. Onni lingered by the door, a thin spectre who somehow seemed vaguely absent from all this, as if he was just a dispassionate observer.

Matthias appeared beside him, noticeably breathless. 'I've had a scout around the area and I went over on the snowmobile to his *mökki*. The *ahkio*'s gone.' He said it so matter-of-factly, as if a guest had just checked out and he was performing a basic inventory. 'But no skis or snowshoes have gone. Wherever he's going, it's on foot. He can't have got far yet, especially not pulling that sledge.'

Aunt Charlotte looked around us all in bewilderment. 'Why would he do this?'

'It is ill thought out to go off alone on foot.' Matthias shook his head. 'Did he not run expeditions?'

I nodded. 'A while ago.' My mouth was so dry. My thoughts a tangled mess. In the space of an hour, he'd gone from jilting me, to dead, to being a murder suspect.

'Ha,' Onni exclaimed. 'Ran expeditions.' He laughed. 'And the rest, I'll bet.'

Mother shifted in her chair. 'We need to act. The girl, Helmi, she was going to phone the police. Where's she gone?'

'I'm here.' Helmi was standing in the doorway, her face swollen and pulpy from crying, but she had a defiant look to her. She folded her arms. 'No joy. You'll be pleased to know your *boyfriend* cut all the phones and smashed the Wi-Fi box before he left us here.'

I shook my head in utter rejection but the feelings just beneath the surface were not quite so clear-cut.

'We can't start blaming him,' Angela pleaded.

'He has gone.' Helmi stamped each word on the room. 'My dad is dead. Spear clearly knew him and not in a good way.'

Nothing Helmi said was untrue. Spear's past was forever running on the tracks alongside him. But I wasn't about to tell this woman anything. Especially not that he'd once left me before because of it. Years ago, after our ill-fated boat expedition that sank, I'd let Spear into my life. Then he just left. He disappeared long enough for me to think he was never coming back. When he did, it was to warn me about the people he'd been involved with. He told me there'd been illegal stuff on the boat when it went down, mostly cannabis, and it didn't belong to him. The owners demanded payment in any form that felt appropriate. Spear had used that phrase then as well, that he couldn't stand the idea of me being hurt.

But when he came back, he'd sworn to me that it was all over, all sorted. He'd paid them off. It was gone and we'd lived a good life together for nearly two years since then. Yet the voice of his past misdemeanours had clearly come echoing back, even out here in the wilderness in the form of Tapio. He just couldn't escape it. Surely it hadn't been enough for Spear to kill him though, and then abandon me on our wedding day. If it was, then whatever he'd been involved in was more deadly than I'd ever imagined and it certainly wasn't consigned to the past, no matter what Spear had promised.

Onni, Tapio's weasel-faced wingman, had confirmed it as well. He'd recognised him too. He was watching us all intently now, a sardonic little smile on his face as if he knew more than he was saying. It felt like such an inappropriate expression of self-assurance, particularly given that his boss was dead in the next room.

'Only an hour ago, you were blaming your own mother, Helmi.' Bridget had taken out her notebook and placed it on the table in front of her along with her trademark fluffy-topped pen. She'd already written on the top of page one *MURDER SUSPECTS*. Spear's name was first on the list, followed by Aino and Helmi. After their names she'd written *in the house all night. Plenty of opportunity.*'

Helmi looked even more confrontational. 'It's no secret he was unfaithful. Mother left him. In October. She's only been back a few weeks.'

Bridget looked intrigued and wrote *MOTIVE — CRIME OF PASSION* next to Aino's name.

'Same time as me,' Helmi added.

Bridget gave her a puzzled look. 'You left too? But why did you leave if it was all about his infidelities?'

Helmi didn't answer but instead gave Matthias a quick look.

'We went for a holiday,' Matthias said bluntly.

'You don't look like the holidaying kind of man.' Mother eyed them closely. They both looked awkward. 'So you *are* together.' Mother sat back with an intrigued expression.

'No,' Matthias said.

'But you were.'

He paused before simply saying, 'Yes.'

'May I ask why you no longer are?'

'No.' He didn't elaborate.

Aunt Charlotte leaned back in her chair and pushed the monocle into her eye socket. 'Oh, I think you're going to have to do better than that now there's a dead body here.'

Helmi sighed. 'Father didn't approve. He thought Matthias was too old for me. Turns out he was probably right.' She glanced at Matthias. The skin around her eyes was puce and fresh tears were welling again now. 'Dad wouldn't give me any more money. Matthias was going to lose his job. We had no option but to come back and call it quits.'

Bridget immediately wrote the names *MATTHIAS AND HELMI* in bold letters and next to them *MONEY, REVENGE & BEDROOM MATTERS*. 'And after you'd searched for Spear, you came back here and entered the lodge, leaving you just enough time to poison your father.' Bridget hadn't framed it as a question.

Helmi froze. 'How dare you!'

Bridget repressed an irritating smile and set down her fluffy pen. 'Because, dear girl, this is a murder investigation and no one is immune from questioning, least of all the young woman who had *beef*, as I believe it's called, with her father. The same young woman who entered the lodge before the screaming started and seemed to take a little too long to respond to the cries of "he's dead".'

'I was in the back office,' she insisted, 'checking if anyone had left a note or any messages. I came as soon as I heard.'

Bridget turned her mouth down and shrugged. 'Perhaps.' She picked up the pen and wrote next to Helmi's name *PLENTY OF OPPORTUNITY*.

Her rather blatant, unsubtle approach did not go down well with either Helmi or Matthias, who both started speaking over each other in Finnish. They were rattled and it looked remarkably like they were arguing. Onni laughed cynically at whatever they were saying.

Mother glanced down at the little notebook and gave Bridget an exasperated look. 'This is getting us nowhere. We need someone to drive for help. Or you can get on your snowmobile again, lover boy.' She nodded at Matthias, who didn't look like he'd ever been called that before.

Angela was wiping her eyes with a handkerchief. She was quietly attempting to hold back tears, but they were starting to escape again. I put my hand over hers. She was shaking and I heard a deep sigh escape from her.

'I'm so sorry, Ursula. I shouldn't cry . . . but my boy is . . . my boy is out there and it's freezing and dark and . . . I don't understand why he would do this.'

I rolled my lips over my teeth and bit down.

'I'm so sorry, Ursula. I'm upsetting you. I just think we need to search again.' Angela appealed to the group. '*Please*. You can't leave him out . . . you can't believe . . .' Her voice failed and the tears fell unchecked.

Everyone was silent. No one wanted to say what I knew was running through their thoughts. Why would they go looking for a possible killer? Why not let him freeze to death out there? The idea turned my stomach. Spear was out there. Alone. The temperature was dropping. The wolves were circling and, if Matthias was to be believed, something else stalked these dead lands. I'd seen the shape of ghosts forming in the mist. Perhaps they were real after all and not just the product of a broken imagination, those *physical manifestations* rising up again. This place increasingly had a sense of unreality to it, as though we were in some halfway house where dreams and nightmares skimmed close to the real world.

No, I had to stop that kind of thinking. I had to hold on to reality if we were going to survive this. If *he* was going to survive this. I paused and my mind fell back to that moment when he'd proposed, his strangely worded reasoning. He'd said it was the only way he was going to survive. It seemed so odd at the time. It was hardly the most romantic reason for a proposal. But it had taken on a whole new meaning now.

I needed to hold it together. I needed to find him, no matter what the consequences of that were.

'OK,' I said.

There was a pause before the idea took hold.

Matthias was the first to fall in. 'We can split into two groups,' he offered. 'Someone can drive for help. Onni, you know the way.'

Onni nodded, still remarkably amused by all of this. In fact, he looked almost like he was enjoying himself. There was a malicious little grin on his lips.

'I can take the snowmobile out and do another round,' Matthias continued. 'I'll do a perimeter sweep and if there's no luck I can head out into the silent forest.'

Aunt Charlotte craned forward. 'Why is it called that?'

We all turned to look at her. And the monocle slowly fell from her eye.

CHAPTER FIFTEEN: CUT AND DRIED

'It's getting very cold. Shall I light the fire?' Angela looked hollowed out, half demolished by exhaustion and worry. A sort of weary dissolution had started to set in and was slowly wearing her down.

'That would be lovely, thank you,' I said.

Matthias and Onni had left to go and get ready for their journeys. Helmi said she was going back to see her father, or what was left of him. She refused to go with Onni. So did we. I made it clear I wasn't leaving without Spear. That set off a domino line of refusals to leave. Mother and Aunt Charlotte wouldn't go without me. Bridget was staying with us. So we all chose to remain here in the wilds with a killer close by. It seemed like a good idea at the time.

Maybe it was for the best. When there's a murder, the suspects can't all just go their separate ways. And I suppose that's what we all were. No one was above suspicion. We were all suspects.

But when I looked round the room, there was only us now, our little party. Somehow, we had actually let all the people we barely knew, the possible killers, leave and go in different directions.

'I need to keep busy,' Angela attempted a weak smile. 'There's wood and kindling. Has anyone got matches?'

No one had.

'I'll go and find some. There might be a box in reception. The guys are still out there getting ready, I think. I can ask them about the heating situation as well.' As she walked out, she looked so drained, so frail that I couldn't help thinking that we'd caused this with what we'd done. I was at least in part responsible for where we all found ourselves.

I clenched my hands together. They were yellow-white with cold. The temperature was dropping. My flimsy trouser suit, with all its elaborate embroidery, was doing nothing to keep me warm and only served to underline how foolish I looked. I was dressed as a bride without a wedding. Without a groom. Everything in the room was starting to mock me. The empty plates, the unfilled wine glasses, the wedding cake standing alone in the corner.

'I don't know about you, but I need a drink.' I pushed back my chair and followed Angela out into the hallway where I'd seen the welcome table loaded with champagne.

Mother, Aunt Charlotte and Bridget could do nothing but watch and exchange tense looks.

Matthias and Onni were outside the room pulling on coats.

'There should be matches behind the desk,' Matthias offered.

'Thank you.' Angela walked over to the reception.

'Otherwise, Helmi has gone for provisions, down in the kitchen.' Matthias looked across at me and explained, 'Onni has a long drive.'

'I need nothing. I have this.' Onni pulled a flattened piece of something dark brown and leathery from his pocket. He tore at it with the side of his mouth. 'Dried reindeer jerky.'

'Bambi doesn't stand a chance out here.' Bridget was in the doorway shaking her head profoundly.

Onni grinned and pulled up the collar on his coat. 'See you out the other side.' He gave another dramatic chew.

This man had such a startling streak of dishonesty running through him that part of me doubted we really would ever see him again. I could very easily imagine him driving away from here and abandoning us to our fates.

Onni nodded and cast his cunning eyes over us all before he strode out of the door. Would he come back with help? Could he be trusted to do that?

But my mind wandered further. What if he did? I thought of Spear out there alone in the snow. Would they mount a rescue operation for him, or would it more accurately be described as a manhunt? My head was such a mess of questions and conflicting fears that nothing would settle. The distant sound of an engine started up. We were about to find out the answer to some of those questions at least.

'There aren't any matches,' Angela called.

Matthias pulled on a glove. 'We'll ask Helmi when she comes back. She has a lighter.'

'For the *weed*?' Bridget enquired, provoking.

I grabbed a champagne flute from the golden array of glasses standing there poised for that moment of celebration that would now never come, those little lifting bubbles gently taunting me. I took a big mouthful and sank it down fast. The sour sharpness burned my throat. I took another.

'That won't do any good.' Bridget's voice was quiet with concern.

'Who said I was looking for good?' I took another bitter mouthful. A thin trickle of the liquid fell over my chin and on to the jacket.

'Careful with your . . .' Aunt Charlotte had appeared alongside Bridget. Mother joined them.

I bent my head in an ironic tilt. 'My what? My wedding outfit that might be ruined? I'm afraid I'm not cut out to be Miss Havisham.' I plucked at the lapel. 'I won't be needing this again.' I held out a glass. 'Mother? Waste not, want not, eh?'

She walked over and took it from me slowly.

I downed another glass. 'Expensive stuff, this. Might as well see it off.'

'You'll be no use to him . . . or us . . . drunk.' Bridget folded her arms.

'Again, who said I was here to be of any use? I'm just the decorative bit, aren't I, really?' I knew I sounded petulant, but I didn't care. Why should I care what people thought of me now, when the one person whose thoughts I actually cared about had gone? Perhaps he'd never really been that bothered. For a while, he'd made me think otherwise. I was fully prepared to be as self-indulgent as I wanted to right now. The cogs in my mind seemed to be detaching. Random thoughts were splaying out from that one uncontrollable truth. He'd gone. He'd left me.

Mother drank slowly, watching me over the rim of the glass.

'OK. I'm ready.' Matthias was doing a good job of ignoring all the drama. 'I'll take the snowmobile out round the grounds and do a sweep first.' He suddenly stopped and stared at us, his eyes a frightening zinc white and so intent. He lowered his voice to just above a whisper. 'Don't let anyone in. No one. The Devil himself is out there. I can smell him.'

'Eau de Lucifer,' Bridget murmured.

Mother took another drink. 'My God, man. Just go and get help. This is starting to resemble *The Wicker Man* on ice.'

Aunt Charlotte nodded in agreement. 'I used to love his travel programmes.' She paused, contemplating, before adding, 'No murders in those though, as far as I can remember.' She picked up a glass of champagne and drank with a thoughtful look.

'Just go and get help and stop talking about devils and ghosts!' Mother had reached that point.

Matthias shrugged and turned to leave. But just as he was heading out, Aino appeared beneath the doorway arched with dried flowers, some already crumbling and falling. It was beginning to look more like a wake than a wedding. She stumbled into the doorframe and more silent leaves dislodged from the arrangement and drifted to the floor. She unfurled her fingers and presented her palm as if she was revealing a precious treasure to us. Her face was rigid with disbelief, bloated with tears. She looked around us with glazed eyes.

'Dried lily of the valley. Our national flower.' Aino gave a dry, ironic laugh. 'He tried to tell us. He wrote it. *Kielo*. Lily of the valley. Not a girl at all.'

No one spoke. She searched for some hint of recognition among us but there was none.

'It was in his mouth,' she spoke violently, each word an attack. 'He was poisoned with it.'

I looked at the tiny, shrivelled buds in her palm. Such little husks that had taken a whole life. I frowned and stumbled a little, more champagne sloshing over the side of the glass.

Aino focused on me. 'The same flower as in your bouquet.'

All eyes centred on me. I rocked to the side, into the table.

'Did you help your fiancé out? Were you in this together?'

The room was a haze of people, suspicious faces. I took another glass of the champagne and drank it. I recognised the flowers in her hand. I did have them in my bouquet, she was right, the bouquet Bridget had carefully made for me. But Spear had also wanted a buttonhole made of the same flowers. I didn't add that bit.

'You are not Finnish. What possible reason would you have for drying these and bringing them here? Who would want such poisonous flowers in their bridal bouquet? Who, but someone who wanted to kill?' Aino was shaking now, the tiny petals falling from her hand.

'Oh, come on.' Bridget was trying to be conciliatory. It wasn't the time. 'Those flowers are in many bridal bouquets. Look in any wedding magazine. They're everywhere. You've even decorated with them. Look, all around you.'

But they weren't. The flowers arching around the door were all manner of leaves and foliage, but none matched the little dried buds in her hand. None except those in the bouquet and buttonhole Bridget had made. We had brought the murder weapon with us. As Aino moved towards me, her feet crunched the fallen leaves into the stone. She brought her other hand from behind her and reached out towards me. A large hunting knife gleamed in the dull light.

The room paused before descending into panic.

'Put it down!' Matthias commanded.

But Aino was in a world where she could hear nothing. See nothing. Except my face. She focused on me alone, her eyes searing.

The champagne washed through my head in a wave. I was unsteady, sweat pooling at the base of my spine. I couldn't form words. Spear's face drifted through my thoughts, set in fierce determination. He was holding the dried flowers out towards me. Then his image was gone. Covered over by a flurry of snow.

'You brought these into my home and you murdered my husband.'

'Now listen to me.' Mother stepped closer towards her.

Aino gave a swipe of the blade.

Mother spread her arms out. 'Put the knife down and we can talk. My daughter was with me all night. She couldn't possibly . . .'

'*He's* gone though, hasn't he? Spear. Run away. *She* brought the flowers.' Her words were becoming more incoherent as she slowly approached Mother with the blade extended. She bent around and looked towards me.

Mother spread her arms wider, filling the space between me and the blade. 'There will be no more deaths today.'

But, unfortunately, when Mother says that, she is often very wrong.

CHAPTER SIXTEEN: MORE DEATHS

My thoughts spun out into the blank world of ice. Spear was out there somewhere. I could still hear the engine of the car being warmed up outside. Mother stood firm between me and the mad-faced woman with the large serrated hunting blade. The woman who thought I was in some way to blame for her husband's death.

'She will pay,' was all Aino said as she drew closer to Mother.

Aunt Charlotte stepped in now too. 'It's time to stop this. Ursula had nothing to do with Sp — whoever killed your husband. The flowers are a coincidence. Whoever did this obviously knew they were poisonous. *You* know they are poisonous. I suspect Grizzly Adams here does as well.'

Matthias looked momentarily confused by the name.

Aino took another step towards Mother and Aunt Charlotte.

'I did the bouquet,' Bridget announced. 'If anyone's to blame, it's me.' She stood beside Aunt Charlotte, forming a sort of wall between me and the woman. 'Now put the knife down.'

I staggered into the table. The blood was flooding my head, overtaking me. The light started to pulse in strange, flashing shards and my mind went to the great display we'd seen in the sky over our heads. Spear was there, but as I imagined him now, his face was changing, finding a different expression. A cold one. I could feel my chest pulling in, my breath stuttered. I stumbled towards the wall and reached out, putting my hand out to steady myself.

And I felt the weapon in my hand before I even knew what I'd done. Everything was blurred and the large crossbow swayed in front of me. My fingers curled tight around the hilt. I held it up. It was so much heavier than I'd imagined. All I could see was the woman with a great shining knife approaching Mother, Aunt Charlotte and Bridget.

'Put it down!' Matthias's voice echoed in my head.

I drew it back, primed with the bolt in place. I couldn't think. The woman's eyes were locked with mine. I could hear Mother's voice. Aunt Charlotte.

Spear smiled out across the icy mist. He was disappearing into the far-off point where the ice melted into the sky. His image was fading. I had to find him. He couldn't have done this. I wasn't going to let myself believe that he'd poisoned that man. Spear was out there, alone. This woman was threatening my family. My head swam with the champagne.

I could hear my own voice as if it was a stranger in the room. 'Put the fucking knife down now or I'll shoot you.'

The silence hung over us all.

Mother turned to face me. 'Ursula, not this. Not like *this*.'

Dad's outline was forming in the air between us, his eyes shining out of his dark face. He shook his head slowly. 'Not like this,' he repeated.

Aino angled her head to the side in mock enquiry. 'So, you will be a killer then too?'

I could feel their eyes crawling over me in fresh judgement, my arm outstretched, gripping the crossbow. My eyes blurred. My legs were trembling as though they couldn't stand for much longer.

'Put the crossbow down, miss.' Matthias was taking big strides towards me.

The panic welled inside. I was dizzy. The light pulsing in my eyes.

'Miss?'

My eyes closed momentarily, and I saw Spear out there, running. Stumbling. A great dark shadow was approaching him. Matthias had said the Devil was here. Perhaps he was right.

'I have to find him,' I said desperately. And that was it. I ran.

I was at the door. I could feel the crossbow, heavy at my side. As I stepped out into the frozen air, I felt the breath stall in my throat. I could only see the white air, hear the noise of the engine running. The car was still there. I ran towards it, through the freezing mist, over the ice and snow, my feet slipping with every step, the crossbow swinging at my side.

I couldn't think. I ran round to the driver's side, furthest away from the lodge, and stood in front of the open car door. I held up the crossbow, ready to tell the man to get out.

Then all I could see was blood.

Their voices carried towards me on the misty air.

'Ursula!'

'Ursula, come back.'

Dad was by my side. 'Ursula, no.'

And then it was all happening too fast, out of my control. I saw the bolt wedged into Onni's neck, pinning him hard into the headrest, a frozen look of horror set in his face.

All I felt was the hand run through my hair on the back of my head, the fingers meshed in close to my scalp. His familiar smell was there.

'Spear?'

I tried to turn and look but my head was slammed against the edge of the open door. Pain broke through the side of my skull.

I fell to the ground, the ice instantly driving through into my knees. The world was growing dark. The light flickering out. I could see nothing, hear nothing except for the soft movement of the feet beside me. There were boots next to my head. Someone reached down next to me and took the bolt from my crossbow.

'Shh,' was all they said. As my eyes closed over, the last face I saw was his.

CHAPTER SEVENTEEN: BONNIE AND CLYDE

There was a rising madness of voices as I began to resurface into the cold world. My name was being called on the air all around me, frozen in waves that travelled through the mist. Faces eddied in and out of focus.

'I saw him.' My voice was raw and the iron-rich taste of blood filled up my mouth. I pictured him again beside me. Clear as light. I looked up at Mother now, her face growing out of that flint-grey sky. 'He was here. He was here beside me. Dad was here.'

'She's delirious.' Mother was firm but I could sense the alarm.

'She's a murderer!' Aino's voice was manic.

I looked for the blade in her hand and gripped harder on the crossbow. I turned my head slightly, remembering the bolt being removed. As I shifted my neck round, I felt the sudden shock of pain travel from my temple down the left side of my face. My eyes instinctively closed as it rippled down the whole left flank of me.

'Don't move.' Mother's voice was right beside me. She was crouching now, her face close enough for her warm breath to touch me.

'Dad was here,' I breathed. My voice was no more than a trail in the air. 'I saw his face just as I . . .'

'I know,' was all she whispered. 'We're going to get you out of this.'

My face gathered in confusion and then I remembered the sudden wash of scarlet against the bleached-out scene. In the car. The blood. Onni.

I let my eyes travel up slowly until I found him. The bolt from the crossbow had shot deep into his neck, impaling him on the leather seat of the car. The dark blood spread out into the cheap beige leather like offal. A thick stream ran down his neck, stark against the pallid skin. The smell of it was rancid, clinging to the cold air. His eyes were fastened open, wide with his last view of this white world reflected across them.

I looked again at my own hand gripping the empty crossbow. I'd just told them all that the ghost of my dead dad had been here. But in my dazed thoughts I was certain there'd been someone else here too. I could still smell them on the flat air. I could smell the coppery blood mingling with the familiar odour of waking in Spear's bed, my face nestled into his T-shirt, the daylight warm and safe.

The ice lifted up through my veins now, my head fixed still, looking up at the man that either me or Spear had killed. It came down to a choice.

I said nothing. I'd already told them Dad was here. That's all they'd need. I'd been mad enough to grab the loaded crossbow, to run out here into the wilderness dressed as nothing more than a jilted bride, with the small guilty flowers embroidered all over my jacket. I looked down at the beautifully stitched lily of the valley and slowly let my hand unfurl from the crossbow. In my life, I'd seen so much death, almost been killed so many times. Now, the time had come for me to finally be labelled 'murderer'. Somehow, it seemed an appropriate last bow. I let the bitter smile form on my lips of its own accord, knowing too well how they would all interpret that.

There would be a pleasing inevitability in all those readers' eyes as they lapped up every detail of the Queen of Death's descent into the madness that was always waiting.

What better occasion for Ursula Smart to finally lose her mind completely and embark on a killing spree than on her own wedding day — jilted by the man she'd once thought could be a killer? And, in fact, probably was. But the world didn't need to know that last part. It was time for my last act as a Smart Woman.

I turned to face Mother. 'I'm sorry, Mother.' My voice was flat. 'I must have lost my mind.'

I heard her heavy sigh. She leaned close to my ear. 'You and me both. But you're no killer, Ursula Smart. Do exactly what I say.'

Mother stood up and addressed the shell-shocked group. 'She's not well. I'm going to take her back to our cabin. Matthias, do you have another vehicle? We can't move this man. The police will need everything just as we found it.'

'What the hell?' Aino's voice was filled with anger and fire. 'You're not taking her anywhere! She's just killed my husband and then fired a crossbow bolt into Onni. Both of them obviously knew Spear and he's disappeared pretty fast too. He's probably waiting in the trees right now, ready to race off with her. No, no, no. Bonnie and Clyde aren't getting away with this.'

'Who?' Aunt Charlotte was crouching down next to me now, holding my hand where only moments ago I'd gripped the brutal weapon so tightly. 'We'll sort this out, dear. We always do, don't you worry.' She said it as easily as if I'd just got a little mark on this farcical white suit. But this was going to take a lot more than tea and sympathy to wash away. It was a new stain on my soul, soaking through everything. A new ghost ready to haunt me.

'Onni?' Matthias was at the car door.

'Ursula?' Angela was confused. 'Is she . . .' Then her eyes found the dead man. She looked at me in disbelief.

'Touch nothing!' Bridget was there, busily photographing the body with her mobile phone.

'What are you doing? This is sacrilege,' Matthias said in stunned horror.

'Not for him. He'll know nothing about it. Stand aside, please. I need every angle.'

'You people are insane.' He strode away but paused as he saw Helmi walking towards him.

'Matthias?' she called. 'Why is everyone out here?'

He didn't speak immediately and looked towards Aino as if looking for permission.

Aino spoke first. 'The mad bride has murdered another.'

'The mad bride,' Bridget repeated, and took out her notebook.

Aino swung around and pointed firmly at me. 'She has killed again. Onni is dead now. How many more?'

'Onni? Dead?' Helmi was still walking towards us. As she drew closer and saw inside the vehicle, she put her hand over her mouth. The act had a strange, almost contrived nature about it. She glanced over at her mother and then towards Matthias. 'How has this happened?'

'I should think that was fairly obvious, young lady.' Bridget continued to take notes. Then said slowly as she wrote, 'Shot through neck by crossbow bolt. Ursula Smart on floor unconscious next to body, holding crossbow. No longer has bolt.' She looked up. 'Some people might call it an open-and-shut case but we are not *some people*. Ladies and gentlemen, it's time for the Smart Women to do what we do best.'

'Be around dead people?' Aunt Charlotte asked.

Bridget flinched. 'Solve the murder.'

CHAPTER EIGHTEEN:
PUBLIC ENEMY NUMBER ONE

Being the only suspect, or perhaps technically the only suspect present, was actually quite liberating in some ways. No one asked my opinion. I wasn't called upon to do any mental gymnastics around some impossible crime. I didn't even feel under threat. After all, they needed me to survive more than anyone, since if I was killed then the murderer had to be one of them. All they had to do was keep me, the guilty party, safe and sound until one of them could bring help.

We'd gathered in the dining room again, strangely occupying the same seats, with the place cards still displaying the names as if we might each be a player in a game, one where steadily the seat beside each name card became empty. I'm sure that's been done before though. Spear's was perhaps the first. His name was starting to sound so different in my head every time I said it now.

My thoughts rattled like marbles in a bag, angry, annoying, too loud for anything to make any sense. But under all the chaos and turmoil of ideas ran one smooth thought. He would not have hurt me. Ever. No matter what he'd done in the past. No matter who he'd been. Who he knew. No

.

matter what it took to rid himself of those anchors dragging him down, he would not have hurt me. I knew that in my core.

I held my hand to my head. It throbbed under my hair, hidden from view, the telltale sign that someone else had been there. But if it wasn't me, and it wasn't anyone who'd been inside, that left only one person. I banished the thought again.

I circled back to the same few words. Spear would not have hurt me. If I was going to prove his innocence, I'd have to work out who the murderer was, or take the blame myself. They were my only choices. I looked down the lineup of Aino, Matthias and Helmi, sitting at the end of the room, away from the wedding table. I certainly wasn't going to be taking the blame for any of them.

One thing was for sure though, I'd been wrong about my role as chief suspect. It in no way seemed to excuse me from the usual mental gymnastics. In fact, they were getting worse and this time they were clouded by my own doubts. In some small part, I even doubted myself. Why had I run out there with a loaded crossbow? My brain was so scalded with all the pain and confusion of Spear leaving, and the idea that he could have killed a man, that I would have had no defence to anyone who said I was momentarily out of my mind. Perhaps I had been. Perhaps I still was. Thoughts bubbled up to the surface and burst, spilling out, spreading like some disease. Was I a killer? Was Spear a killer? Was someone in this room a killer? Perhaps there was more than one. Perhaps it was some lone hunter out there picking us off one by one. Or even, as Matthias had suggested, the Devil himself.

My brain blistered with pain. I closed my eyes and put both palms to my head. I felt Mother's hand on my leg.

She didn't speak, but when I opened my eyes, she was staring straight ahead with a steadfast look of determination about her.

Aunt Charlotte and Angela were opposite, both watching me with concern and worry. One thing seemed certain, wherever this was going, it would cause pain and heartache to those I loved. My role now was to minimise that damage as much as possible.

Bridget, however, had other ideas about her place in all this.

'OK, so what have we got?' The notebook was out on the table again and she was ready for business. 'Tapio was poisoned with dried lily of the valley flowers which you, Aino, found in his mouth.'

Aino held a handkerchief up to her face and made a desperate sound.

The three members of staff didn't have an allotted place at the wedding table so had taken seats on the opposite side of the room, as if drawing the battle lines.

'Can I just ask—' Bridget continued tapping the fluffy pen on the pad — 'what exactly you were doing looking in his mouth?'

It wasn't the question anyone had been expecting.

Aino paused with the handkerchief still in place and frowned. 'That's none of your business.'

Bridget laughed. 'It's everyone's business when there's a killer in the room.'

So Bridget, at least, wasn't suspecting Spear.

'If you must know—'

'I must.'

Aino fixed her eyes on Bridget. 'I was kissing him goodbye.'

Bridget raised her eyebrows. 'How would that necessitate having access to the contents of his mouth?'

'With tongues,' Aunt Charlotte said flatly.

'With . . .' Bridget looked confused first and then appalled. 'He's dead.'

'Cadavers. It's a thing.' Aunt Charlotte took a swig of champagne. 'Quite pop—'

'Enough!' Mother held up her hand. 'The dead man had the poisonous flowers in his mouth. The end.'

Bridget leaned back in her chair and folded her arms. 'I'm afraid we're very far from the end, Pandora.'

'Do we need something else to drink other than alcohol?' Angela asked. She looked weary, her eyes falling back further into their dark depressions.

'No.' All three of our voices were very definite.

'Nope.' Aunt Charlotte took another mouthful. 'It's freezing in here though.' She got up and walked over to the large, empty fireplace.

'There weren't any matches,' Angela said apologetically. 'Perhaps some food might be an idea, you know, to soak up the drink a bit?' she suggested before a thought clearly passed over her eyes. 'Wait, wasn't someone going for provisions? For the journey? Food for them.'

'Onni had his Bambi jerky,' Bridget confirmed.

Angela shook her head. 'I know. But . . . but . . . Helmi, you went for provisions. You went to get food for Onni for the long journey. You were gone for quite a while.'

Helmi's eyes widened, and she looked around us all. She gripped her hands together as if in prayer before appealing to Matthias. 'I went to the kitchens! I must have forgotten to bring the food when I heard all the shouting. I just ran up. Matthias, you were here.' She swung her head round to Aino. 'And you, Mother. You were both with this group of crazy women. One of them has killed *Pappa*.'

Bridget let out a laugh. 'Oh, so it's *Pappa* now, is it? Only a few hours ago he was a wicked philanderer who'd ended your love affair, wasn't he?'

Helmi was out of her chair. 'He was still my father! I wasn't going to kill him. And if I was, I wouldn't wait until we'd got a house full of guests to witness it. We're on our own most of the time, miles away from civilisation. It's very easy to kill someone out here and leave them in the snow!'

My mind paused, treading through the same thoughts. I looked at her. The words circled my head, each one coming to the front again. *Kill. Someone . . . And. Leave. Them. In. The. Snow.*

'Oh my God,' I whispered. 'We need to find Spear. Now.'

I stood up quickly and the chair fell back. I started grasping for the words. 'He's out there! One of you bastards has tried to kill him. Yes! You know him, all right. Some of you, at least.' My eyes ran along the line of them. Aino, Helmi, Matthias. 'I don't know how you do but—'

'I think I do,' Aunt Charlotte said slowly. She turned to face the room, holding a small, charred piece of paper in her hand. She read from it. '"Breffni".' She looked up. 'It's dated at the top: fifteenth of October.'

'That's a page from the reservations book.' Aino's hand was on Helmi's arm, pulling her back into her chair, her expression one of warning.

Aunt Charlotte looked at me and held out the paper. 'Spear stayed here before.'

In one moment, every part of the machine just rearranged again. All the cogs started to slot into new places. Whether they were the right ones or not wasn't clear.

'You must have seen him, then?' Angela looked at Aino doubtfully, her eyes red with tears. 'You must have seen him!' There was a seam of desperation rising in her voice now.

Aino shook her head slowly. 'I was not here in October.' She clearly wasn't about to offer more without provocation.

'You weren't here? Why not?'

Aino tightened her mouth as if she was refusing to be fed anymore.

'Please,' Angela implored, 'this is my son's life!'

The tired Finnish woman studied Angela for a moment. For a newly widowed woman, Aino seemed more exhausted than distraught now, as if she was already resolved to her new life. It had seemed like a very quick shift in her whole demeanour. 'I'd left him.'

'I already told them.' Helmi said.

'And that was in October?' Bridget asked, pen poised.

Aino nodded. 'I've only been back a few weeks.' She let out a heavy, burdened sigh. 'It was too much. There were too many things to forgive. Too many women. Too many indiscretions. It chips pieces off you until you're a whole different shape. I didn't even recognise myself anymore. I had to get out.' She sniffed. 'I don't know if I wanted it to be permanent then, but I knew I had to go. I went to stay with friends in Oulu. They were kind. Tapio was distraught.'

She paused. There was a subtle shift in her voice. 'Or so he said, anyway. He phoned every day. Begging me to come home. He'd change.'

I thought of all the promises Spear had made, all the assurances that his past was buried.

'It would be better, Tapio told me. He ground me down. He always did. So I came back and it was all the same. All the young girls, waitresses, receptionists, cleaners. They all left eventually.' She paused, a look of regret on her face. 'It was just us marooned out here in the end with Matthias, Helmi and Onni. We don't get many guests. We haven't had any since October. Until you.' Nothing in the way she spoke would have indicated to anyone that her husband now lay murdered in the next room.

Bridget wrote in clear capitals, *WIFE A MAJOR SUSPECT. COLD FISH.*

Aunt Charlotte glanced down. 'What the hell have fish got to do with it?'

Bridget tutted and continued her intense scrutiny of the three staff at the end of the room.

Angela's look of disbelief was slowly falling into suspicion. 'And you two?' She settled on Matthias and Helmi. 'You said you were off on your *holiday* then too, at the same time as Aino wasn't here. Very convenient.'

Matthias held out placating hands. 'Wait! Wait.'

Tears were forming in Angela's face. 'Someone must have seen him!' She was sounding increasingly alarmed. 'Someone must have seen my son!'

'Yes, Onni and Tapio. And they're both dead now.' Bridget wasn't helping.

'None of *us* did.' Helmi was as cold as her mother.

Bridget held out her fluffy pen towards the piece of paper Aunt Charlotte was holding. 'Someone removed the page from the reservations book that proved he was here and tried to get rid of the evidence. Disgraceful!' It was unclear what Bridget was more appalled by, the fact that Spear had stayed here before and they'd hidden that, or that they'd attempted to destroy her precious evidence. She quickly wrote in the book, *EVIDENCE TAMPERED WITH.* At least there was an answer to that question.

'You can think what you like. Mother had gone,' Helmi sneered. 'Me and Matthias had gone. We left. Together. My father didn't approve of our relationship. Said Matthias was too old for me. I was too young to know my own mind, *apparently.* We went to Helsinki for a while. That was in October. When Spear stayed, none of us were here then.'

'And yet here you are now.' Bridget leaned over the table. She was in full cross-examination mode. 'There seems to be a missing piece, does there not?'

Both Matthias and Helmi looked away — from us but, more noticeably, from each other. They studiously avoided one another. There was an awkward pause where they both shifted uncomfortably in their chairs, aware of all the eyes on them.

Finally, it was Matthias who broke the deadlock. 'It didn't work out.' He sniffed, drawing the air in hard through his nose, and sat back as if closing the matter.

'I see.' Bridget left a difficult pause, tempting one of them to speak. She has, admittedly, honed her questioning technique over our years of confronting killers and liars.

It worked.

'We had no money,' Helmi continued. 'I couldn't get a job. We couldn't afford to keep renting even our tiny room. I got in touch with Dad but he wouldn't send us anything. Refused to accept our relationship and told me to get myself home.' She glanced at Matthias but it wasn't a loving look or even a regretful one. There was spite in her eyes, resentment even. 'I didn't know he'd already made a *deal* with Matthias.'

Matthias's face crumpled. 'It was hardly a deal.' He looked around each of us with an imploring face. 'There was no other option. He agreed not to fire me if I brought his daughter home. I had no choice. It was heading into winter. I was just doing bits of temp work that would dry up. My savings had gone. I couldn't cover the rent. I . . .' His head fell. 'I'm sorry.'

Helmi had a bitter look. 'So he brought me back for his lousy job as a lackey for my father. That's how much I was worth to him.'

Matthias's mouth fell open. 'That's not true! I had to make sure you were safe. I couldn't take care of you properly. I . . . I wanted it to work but it was just a dream.'

I watched his pleading eyes as he looked at the remnants of the dream. Helmi was all sour rejection now. She had no space for dreaming anymore.

Matthias shook his head slowly. 'The bastard got you back here, made sure you'd never trust me, and then, last week, Tapio told me he was firing me after Christmas. After this wedding party. I've lost everything anyway.'

Bridget took up her pen again and wrote while saying the words out loud. 'Matthias — powerful motive. Had been fired by victim and relationship ruined. Says he lost everything because of Tapio.'

Matthias was growing increasingly agitated, fidgeting in his seat. 'And why would I kill Onni? I had no problem with him.'

Aunt Charlotte waved the paper again. 'Perhaps he knew too much. Perhaps he'd seen something. He had to be got rid of. Just like Spear.'

The words fell like stones in my aching head. But the look of instant realisation on Aunt Charlotte's face couldn't take them back now. She knew she couldn't unsay them.

'Oh.' She looked at me, then Angela. 'I'm . . .'

'Charlotte,' Mother sighed. Her disappointment is always close to the surface.

Angela took a breath and then the tears fell. Her head dropped forward in defeat. 'My boy,' she heaved. 'He can't . . . I can't . . .' She gasped, her chest rising and falling faster. 'I can't lose him. He can't be dead. I can't . . .' She covered her face and wept as if no one else was there.

My stomach clamped and all the thoughts of Spear tumbled over one another. The panic raced through me again.

Disbelief and dread are such easy partners. I tried to hold back all the thoughts that were waiting impatiently at the door. His body out there, one dark shape in all that white expanse of nothing. The cold biting his bones. His eyes blank, misted over with death. I tried to wish away the demon thoughts but they kept coming. One then another. My eyes were instantly drawn to the back corner of the room. I saw the clear figure of my father lingering there. Being that *physical manifestation of trauma* again.

I'd never really loved many people in my life. Not since Dad died. Death does that. It whittles away your desire to invest in anything. Anyone. But I had let myself believe in Spear, started to slowly detach myself from the dark shadow of grief. I'd clung to this new soul. Spear. Had he gone? I widened my eyes questioningly at the spirit of my father. He watched me closely before shaking his head.

If I'm honest, which I'm not sure I ever am entirely, I'd known all along Spear wasn't dead. I could still feel him with every breath. But then, Death can be very cunning. Devious little beliefs are easy to hold on to when you're desperate for hope. That's the point at which you're most open to betrayal.

But right then, every fibre of me wanted to be convinced by what I saw, what I felt.

I walked round the table and put my arms over Angela's shoulders. I could feel her shaking uncontrollably. She turned and buried her head into my stomach.

'Oh, Ursula.' She gripped my hand and looked up pleadingly into my face, as if I had the answer.

I thought I did. 'Shh,' I said. 'He's alive, I know he is. I can still *feel* he's alive.'

I looked over at Mother, who was watching that same corner of the room where Dad stood waiting. Her eyes refocused on me. She studied me for a moment. They all waited, in uncertainty.

But Mother doesn't do uncertainty for very long. She placed her hands on the table in front of her, her face undeniable. 'Well, what are you waiting for? Let's go find him then.'

CHAPTER NINETEEN: SABOTAGE

That's how we ended up outside, staring into an abandoned world that had suddenly become more hostile than any of us could have envisaged. Someone had turned the car engine off and I thought of the warnings we were issued with at the airport. I imagined the liquid freezing into all the pipes inside the engine with the same undeniable force as the blood solidifying in Onni's impaled body. He was nothing more than another object to freeze for this world. All that liquid just sitting perfectly still in his veins, cooling with every passing moment until he was petrified, his face set in that last moment of horrified disbelief. His skin would be glassing over with ice, sealing him into that tomb. Mother was right, we couldn't attempt to move him before the police came — if we could ever make contact with them. We couldn't drive the car with him in the driver's seat though.

'There's always our car,' Mother said. 'The people carrier. Where is it?'

'I put it around the back. I'll get the keys from reception.' Matthias walked back inside.

'Ursula, you need to put this on.' Mother had the large parka I'd worn over my wedding outfit to travel over.

It had been less than twenty-four hours since we'd travelled here and yet I could remember so little of anything that had happened since we arrived. But what I did recall very strongly now was the ominous feeling that had dominated everything from the very first moment. Spear had been anxious, disturbed as soon as we got here. Possibly it had been Tapio and Onni recognising him from when he'd stayed here before. Had he said he'd been before? I didn't think so, although it had been his idea to come here, to revisit this place. He couldn't have been that concerned about them, or perhaps he'd planned it all along. Perhaps he had to be here.

But as I cast my mind over those initial moments of our trip, that trepidation had started before we ever set down here. Back home in London, he'd been distracted, unable to engage in anything wholeheartedly. It had started almost as soon as we got engaged. If that was the effect marrying me had fostered in him, then why had he suggested it? Unless it was something else, something out here.

The crunch of thick boots on snow approached round the side of the building. Matthias had a heavy-hearted look. 'It's no use. It won't start.'

'Can we defrost it somehow?' Bridget was hopping from foot to foot on the spot to keep warm.

'It's not that. I've lifted the bonnet and someone has sawed through the fuel line. I think, with this.' He held up a mini hacksaw.

I felt the sick turn of fear.

'Snowmobile has been done too.'

'Someone wants to keep us here. Why?' Aunt Charlotte searched our faces for an answer.

It was Helmi who was quick with one possibility. 'To kill us all!' She was starting to sound manic.

'No, no.' Matthias shook his head. 'If they'd wanted to do that, they'd have done it by now.'

'Unless they're enjoying picking us off one by one,' I added. It didn't seem to help the atmosphere. But things were just happening around me now. Things just being said. None of it had any meaning at all. There was one over-whelming thought. Whatever happened, I had to find Spear.

'Right.' I pulled on the parka and lifted the hood over my head. 'I'm going to walk.'

'Where to?' Aunt Charlotte looked increasingly con-cerned with every passing minute. 'Look at this place! You'll freeze to death out there.'

'That's if the bears don't get you first.' There was a slight accusing tone in Mother's voice, as if I was somehow to blame for the presence of the dangerous animals.

Matthias looked horrified. 'You must never speak their name. It is sacred!' His words came as a sharp rebuke.

'Oh, for God's sake.' Helmi turned away from him dis-missively, emotions playing across her face. Any previous affection I'd thought I'd seen between these two had paled with the deaths. Fear can easily devour any other weaker emo-tions. '*Karhu*—'

'Helmi!'

'Forget it, Matthias. All your superstitious nonsense isn't going to amount to a hill of shit now. It's not going to protect us or save us. We need to get out of here.'

'I'm not leaving without Spear.' I was unshakeable.

Helmi turned on me. 'Well, it looks like nobody is leav-ing any time soon.'

Matthias started to walk away.

'Where do you think you're going?' Aino shouted.

He turned and paused. When he spoke, his voice was low and steady. 'You *must* have faith. I believe in the ways of our ancestors. Mead-paw is the sacred embodiment of our forefathers. These are our guardians. They will see us through. It is the time when the doors to the spirit world are opening. We are at the very edge of the living and the dead.' He was solemn, as if we stood on hallowed ground and these words were sacred. He leaned closer, his eyes sparkling in the gloom. 'I can feel it. This is the thin place and tonight the ghosts are coming out of the dark to collect their dead.'

Bridget stamped her feet again. She was starting to look like a petulant child now. 'There's no point trying to frighten *us*. I cannot see how this helps. Are these spirits going to magic another car? Transport us to safety?'

A smile touched the edges of Matthias's mouth. 'No. But we can harness this natural land to travel out to the other cabins where the phones might still be working.'

'What, man? Speak human, for Christ's sake!' Mother isn't at her best when people have been murdered around her.

'You will see, witch woman.'

Mother balked but no one questioned the description.

The first whisper of cold wind circled us. The mood was shifting with the light. Until then, the air had been dead, but now something stirred in the high trees, shivering the snow on the tops of the pines. A dark line was settling between ice and sky. Night was coming in fast but there'd been no day to speak of.

A distant wolf cry lifted from the woods.

'How can it be getting even darker?'

'Because light is a precious gift.' Matthias had settled into this new strange, spectral voice he'd adopted. There was an eerie sound to him now, his eyes searching the horizon as if he knew something was out there. 'You must start to see the world in a different way if you're going to find this man. This is a frozen country. The light will come from the ice, from the spirits inside it. Let them guide you. Let the land and her creatures help.' He stalked away, a new energy to him.

'He's going mad.' Aunt Charlotte had a look of conspiracy. 'It happens to men out here in the wild and snow. I've read about it. Wilderness sickness. Their minds start to unspool. Think they see things out there, out on the ice. It begins with strange lights. Movements. But it can spiral out of control very quickly and become full-scale hallucinations.' Her eyes travelled around us all with a sinister look. 'He's entering an altered state. He could be very dangerous.'

The first we heard was the harsh barking, then the eyes appeared through the mist, brilliant, piercing blue eyes reflecting the lights from the lodge. Mother held my arm and instinctively drew me back.

Eight grey-white dogs pulled round the side of the building, dragging a small kick sledge. Matthias stood behind the seat holding the reins, a fixed look of purpose on his face. 'I have two seats. You, sad lady—' he stared at me — 'if anyone can sense this man, it is you. Get in.'

Mother stood in front of me before I could move. 'Not a chance, Sasquatch! You're not dragging my daughter out there into the wilderness alone. How do I know you're not the killer?'

A thick grin spread under his beard. 'Because if I was, I'd have come for you first.' He laughed and pulled back on the reins. The dogs barked and jostled, eager to run. Impatient. 'We must go quickly. There is enough room for one more. The old mother can come too if she must.'

Mother looked suitably offended before marching forward. 'Very well. Come along, Ursula.'

'Wait.' Angela sounded shaky. 'I . . .'

Mother paused. 'We will do our very best.' She could see it wasn't enough. Mother's shoulders fell. 'OK. Maybe you go with Ursula. But watch her closely. She has a tendency—'

'A tendency to what, Mother?'

'A tendency—' Mother drew out the word— 'to fly close to disaster.'

There wasn't really any arguing with that.

'We can follow in the reindeer sleighs.' Mother looked to Matthias for verification and he nodded.

'Or go for help in them?' Bridget asked.

Matthias shook his head. 'It would take too long. It is too far. Too dark. Too *cold*.'

'We need to find Spear,' I added.

'We stay together,' Mother said firmly. 'We will follow Ursula.'

'Helmi,' Matthias called. 'See to the reindeer. I will meet you at the *mökkis*.'

This time Helmi didn't offer any resistance.

'Stay together,' Matthias repeated. He'd let a small note of concern enter his voice.

There was a surreal look to our party now, gathered in the freezing gloom, waiting to be dragged out into the darkness by eight dogs and a mythical-looking man, in search of the person I was supposed to marry. Weddings are often unpredictable, but this was very far from what I'd imagined all those weeks ago with Spear. He'd been so keen when he'd first proposed it. I don't know if it was the relentless preparation and organising that diluted his enthusiasm, but as the weeks rolled on, his anxiety every time our trip was mentioned was palpable. Now I knew why. He'd been here before. There was something waiting out here in all this darkness for him. We could have gone anywhere in the world. Increasingly, it was becoming obvious he must have had a reason for coming out here and it wasn't anything to do with marrying me. Whatever that was, I had to find him. I stepped into the sledge.

'Matthias!' Helmi faltered. 'Take care.'

He nodded. 'Get the sleighs out. Aino can take one. We will see you there.'

As I settled into the precarious small seat close to the ground, I could feel the eager power of the dogs barely being restrained by Matthias. We slipped sideways a little as he struggled to contain them. I was grateful to be wedged in next to Angela. It brought comfort. She pulled up the reindeer skin over both of us and gave a weak smile but I could see the fear drawing out across her face.

Aunt Charlotte ran forward. 'Ursula, Angela, is this a good idea?'

'It may not be good, but it's definitely an idea.' I held her hand and looked into her concerned face. 'I have to find him, Aunt Charlotte. He's out there. I know it.'

'Stand back, crone,' Matthias called.

Aunt Charlotte glowered but reluctantly let my hand fall. 'This is madness, Ursula!'

I gave a single unhappy laugh. 'What else did you expect?'

Matthias shouted to the dogs and we shimmied forward a little at first before surging into the mist. It instantly took my breath and I held the sides of the flimsy sledge. The sudden rush of power dragged us out over the ice at a speed I'd never expected. I concentrated on the fast gush of air in my chest, releasing it slowly, calming my heart.

I turned to see the shocked looks on Aunt Charlotte and Bridget's faces. Mother was attempting to remain stoic but the cracks were appearing.

My back was shoved into the seat. I could feel Matthias standing behind me, half leaning over, the reins held high above my head. Out in front, the huskies raced with a vicious speed across the snow. Our sledge skated behind them as if it weighed nothing. The dogs were focused on some far point and nothing would stop them now. I felt the freezing air rake through my hair. I pulled up the thick coat, grateful for its hood but struggling to hold it in place around my head against the fast wind. The sledge jolted and fishtailed, slamming me into the seat as if we were on storm-wrenched seas. I held on to Angela's arm. She attempted to lift a smile but there was fear nestled deep in her eyes, whether for this precarious journey or what we might find at the end of it, I didn't know and I wasn't about to ask.

I looked out into the deepening sky, to that point we were racing towards. He was out there. Or at least something was that these creatures were resolutely hunting. They were insatiable, bounding their way through the frozen air, racing towards the gloaming. And there, out beyond the trees, over the planes of ice, those flickering shocks of light began again. Green glowing fluorescence burned then faded across the leaden grey, coruscating over the sky. It was living light, turning and breaking like some unimaginable sea creature in the farthest depths of the ocean. The strange phosphorus murmurings reflected off the frozen lake, mirrored in its black, still surface. Matthias's warnings may have seemed farfetched but out here beneath this sky rippling with what looked like burning gas vapours, it was hard not to see these strange, spectral lights as some sort of omen cautioning against our course. A warning.

The sound of the kick sledge below me was a constant whisper sluicing through the snow. The dogs yelping and barking incessantly. The bullying wind relentless in my face. I could barely open my eyes. All I could see was Spear's face and it was slowly drifting away from me like a ghost.

CHAPTER TWENTY: THE WATER SPIRIT

When we arrived at the cabins, the Northern Lights were illuminating the lake in a great sea of livid green. Matthias had said the snow would soon start to cover the surface as they headed deeper into winter, so now was a perfect moment, with the ice a clear mirror of the luminescence above. He pulled the dogs into an uneasy stop, their breath frantic, panting and clouding the air.

Matthias, still dragging on the reins, called stern but calming noises to them. We'd drawn in next to the frozen jetty that led out onto the lake. None of us had ventured this far from the cabins before.

'We don't stop too near the cabins. I don't take them in too close. The dogs will smell the food, or whatever else is in there.' He didn't elaborate on that last comment but it was enough on its own to pass a shiver over my skin. Was this where Spear was hiding? Or had someone else taken up refuge here? One thing was certain, no one could stay out in this cold too long without some form of shelter, and our cabins had been left empty all day. Anyone could have been using them.

Neither me nor Angela wanted to ask any more.

'OK?' she said quietly to me.

I nodded. 'I'm scared though, Angela. But I don't know what of.'

She gripped my arm tight and stared at me. 'I know,' she breathed. 'I am too.' She looked so fragile that I wondered if I'd done the right thing agreeing to her coming out here with me now. There was a spent frailty to her. Her face so sallow, the skin paper thin, a weary grey round her eyes that were sunk deep and bloodshot with tears.

I looked back for the others. Surely they wouldn't be far behind.

The climb out was unstable with the dogs jumping at one another and shifting the sledge. I helped Angela out while Matthias tended the over-excited animals, trying to calm them.

'Let's find the phone and get some help out here to this place.' Matthias started to walk towards the cabin, then paused and looked at Angela who was wandering closer to the jetty, staring out across the lake. 'Don't go near the water. *Nakki* could be there.'

'*Nakki?*' I repeated.

'You really know nothing about my land. Nothing. They are water spirits that lurk beneath the surface, waiting for more victims. They will lure you in and grab you. Now, I'm going to telephone for help. Stay there.' He seamlessly shifted between talking about the real world and that of some surreal spirit land as if they were one and the same, living beside one another out here in the snow and ice. He made it seem almost believable.

I looked towards Angela. She'd paused at the end of the small jetty, looking out over the surface of the lake. I knew who occupied her thoughts and it wasn't water spirits or devils. I walked slowly down towards her.

The lake was exactly as Matthias had said, a perfect glass for the spectral display. The acid green slipped over the frozen waters, flickering with darker blues before failing. And out there, drifting, I thought I caught the black outline of Dad, rising over the waters as if he was sailing through the lights.

'How are you holding up?' Angela peered up into my face, searching.

I didn't directly answer. I had no idea how to. I just said, 'You?'

She closed her eyes and let out a laboured breath. 'We'll get through this. I know we will.'

I had to keep it together. I was falling, my thoughts splintering again. Dad's shape was there all the time now, hovering near me. I remembered all those therapists queuing up to repeat the same thing. *It was a manifestation of extreme trauma.* They said it with such assurance, as if that would in some way fix me or make the so-called hallucinations stop. But only I could do that, they informed Mother. That was convenient, of course. They'd told me what was necessary, and all that needed to happen was for me to do it. It was like repeatedly telling a child to stop sucking its thumb and just about as effective.

I reasoned to myself that I'd stop seeing Dad when the time was right. But it never seemed to be the right time. And this definitely wasn't the moment to think about letting him go. I needed him more than ever. I let my foot hang over the edge of the jetty and touch the solid lake below.

'Hey, just be careful,' Angela cautioned. 'Remember, the *nakki* might catch you.' She attempted a smile but there was no life to it, wilting before it had even begun.

I looked down into the frozen black surface. It was hard to understand how a grown man could believe in all those superstitious notions of creatures lurking beneath, ready to drag unsuspecting travellers to their watery death. There were no water spirits under there.

But something else was.

As I looked down from that small wooden pier jutting out into the solid black waters, something caught my eye as the peculiar green light rolled over the ice again. But it was gone as the colours burned out.

'Everything all right, Ursula?' Angela was looking at me and then at the ice. She was growing increasingly anxious and the lowering light level wasn't helping. The temperature was sinking fast too. I could hear the dogs barking. I turned to see one rearing up. They were so restless. Spooked perhaps. We should go back. Matthias had warned us against being out too far. He'd warned us against the water.

But as another chain of light fed out, I saw it again, under the ice.

I bent lower towards the surface, crouching right down over the end of the jetty, glancing back up towards Angela again.

'What? What is it, Ursula?' There was a rising, hectic edge of fear to her voice now. 'Ursula?'

The others would hopefully be here soon in the sledges, and if they caught me being this reckless near the ice, that would definitely elicit some form of reaction as well. The ice had been forming for weeks now and we'd been told it was pretty thick at this time of year. Later in the season, this would be solid enough to bear much greater amounts of weight, but if I fell onto it now, I had no idea whether there was any guarantee it would hold me. The dangers of falling through the ice occupied many online travel blogs, particularly the ones Mother had showed me when she was attempting to dissuade everyone from coming out here. But, by this point in the year, the ice would go deep.

Another pulse of light travelled through the sky and spread its feathery tendrils out across the ice. It lit a meandering path towards me like a great crack opening up, a long fissure breaking through the ice, with the light pouring up from the dark waters below as if there was another world down there.

It wasn't a world down there at all. But, as I peered closer into that depthless pond, I could see that I was right. There was *something* down there.

A face staring back up at me.

My heart hit the front of my chest in one sudden surge before the pulse started running fast behind my ribs.

I fell back, gripping the edge of the ice-hard jetty. My eyes strained wide in horror. Was this my mind? Was I conjuring new ghosts from my *trauma*? Matthias had said there *were* spirits down there.

'Ursula? Ursula, what's wrong?' Angela was down next to me, panic deep in her face now. 'Ursula?'

The vibrant shocks cut across the sky again, casting that same filigreed web over the lake, opening out in great wings of light. The ice glowed. I scuttled to the edge again, my chest tight with fear.

'What is it?' Angela repeated.

I hung my head over the end of the jetty and, in a moment of light, I was staring into that suspended face again, trapped beneath the thick ice. I couldn't breathe. I wanted to scream but the noise caught in my throat. I was so close, staring into the face I knew so well.

Spear.

The air stopped around me.

What new illusion was this? I squeezed my eyes tight shut, willing it away.

'Ursula, are you OK?' I could hear Angela's voice but the words had no meaning anymore. 'Maybe we should go back now, Ursula. It's not so safe out here.'

The still waters below were solid black like rock. The flickering lights played across what I could see of his face, a strange mosaic of colours drifting in and out. As the light began to disappear again, the dead grey stone of his eye stared out blindly. He was on his side, his neck curved, bent round, foetal style. He'd half turned as though trying to look up at something before the life had all gone, and that was how nature had kept him, setting him into the ice like nothing more than an animal.

I reached out to the ice in slow disbelief, my gloved finger touching the surface as if it could push down into the water. My hand lingered above his face but hit the hard surface much further above him than I had imagined. The ice was thick. The lights above faded, and he was blurred by the darkness as though drifting down away from me into the depths.

In a haze, I slipped from the jetty, my face pressing into the cold, solid water. My mouth hung slack in bewilderment. I could taste the ice on my lips. And I stared into his face, half hidden by darkness, distorted by the vast thick pane of ice. I pulled off the gloves and held my hands flat to the surface to feel his heartbeat under there. He didn't move. He was held fast in that distorted position.

Only one side of him was visible, trapped in black layers like coal poured around his face. It was squeezing him so tight. I banged on the window into his world but he couldn't hear me.

'Spear?' I called into the ice. I smacked my hand down again and he didn't even move.

'Ursula?' I could hear Angela in the back of my thoughts.

'Get up, Spear!' I slammed my hand into the ice again and drilled my forehead into it hard enough to split the skin. 'What the hell are you doing down there? We've got a wedding to be at! Our wedding!' I frowned at the sudden feeling of light headedness. 'My God, man, you haven't even got changed. You can't wear that parka to get married. Where's your suit?' A small, warm trickle of blood traced down my forehead, and when I pulled my face back from the ice, a little berry of blood landed on the surface. For a moment, it looked as though he felt it. Had he moved?

'Wake up, damn it! Come on!' I screamed into his unmoving face. 'Spear! Don't ignore me! Move. I need you up here, this side of the ice. I need you. I need you to be with me!'

'Ursula! Ursula! What . . . what are you doing?' Angela was so near but I could see nothing beyond his face under the ice.

The lights had paused and I could barely make him out. Then the celestial energy came back afresh across the sky and ice, and he reappeared, so close but trapped.

The breath shuddered through me. 'I need you! I can't survive without you.' I slammed my head against the ice, determined to break through to him. But he didn't even blink. How could he not hear me? I put both hands on the ice and pulled back my head, giving him a firm look.

'Stop! For God's sake . . .' Angela's voice was frantic somewhere in the darkness.

My hands lay splayed out across the ice. Another wave of fluorescent light gathered and pooled around us, lighting him again. It touched the surface of the ring he'd given me. The black opal. And the colours wove through in a river of luminous greens.

I stared down at Spear. He still didn't respond.

'Spear! Now, listen,' I was panting, my heart hammering through my chest into the ice as if it could chip him out of that tomb.

Angela was screaming somewhere in the background. 'No!' was all I could decipher.

A trail of spit fell from my mouth and mingled with the tears and blood. I scrubbed my hand across the ice, feeling the bite of cold. 'Oh, look, it's dirty now. Come on, enough. Let's get going!'

I could see him through that grubby veil of ice with the light flaring above us. It was a dark hole he'd managed to get wedged in, with black on all sides and beneath him as if it fell all the way to the bottom of the Earth. No, no, he couldn't go down there. That wouldn't be very nice at all.

I looked into the one eye I could see through the murk, so separated from me. I could see that familiar colour I knew so well, shining out as if to say, 'I see you, Ursula. I know you're there. Wait a minute, I'm on my way.'

But he was not on his way to me. He was on his way into that dark labyrinth below him, disappearing as the lights above flickered and drifted out as if they were giving up and leaving with him.

'No! No! No!' I leaned back my head and screamed at the light as it ran away. I breathed out in great shocks of white, frozen air. 'Please!' I lay out across the ice, curling round to match the shape of him. Angela was screaming, shouting unintelligible words. Weeping uncontrollably. Grabbing at my shoulder.

I don't know how long we were stranded in that moment but it had grown even darker when I heard fresh voices. All the light had escaped from the world.

Matthias was first to call out, his deep voice carrying over to us.

'Lempo!' he shouted. 'I saw from the window. Evil spirit. Will-o'-the-wisp. It was a ball of light, forming over the lake to lure her in.'

Then more familiar ones. 'Ridiculous man.' It was Mother. Always Mother. 'Ursula?'

More running footsteps were coming along the jetty. Always someone is bothering me when I am busy.

'Angela? What's happening?' Aunt Charlotte was breathing heavily and shouting.

But Angela couldn't speak.

'Ursula!'

Now all the feet were running in time with one another, like wind-up toys, pounding on the frozen wood of the jetty, shouting my name as if they owned it. Always shouting.

'I've found him!' I called back nonchalantly. 'We'll be out in a minute.'

I looked down at the dark outline of his body, no more than a ghost beneath that unlit ice. He was twisted and gnarled by the incredible pressure of its grip all around him, the force of it all compressing him, distorting him and puckering his skin into thick lines as though he'd stayed too long in the water, leaching the life out of him.

Too long in the water.

How long must he have been in there to freeze under it?

That was my last thought as I felt the thick ice floor hard against my head and my hands sting with the cold. The world went black and would stay like that for too long.

CHAPTER TWENTY-ONE: SPEAR IS DEAD

Some people might have seen my actions that night and supposed I was losing a grip on my sanity. A man frozen into a thick layer of ice is, of course, dead. You might think from the number of deaths I have encountered that I, more than anyone, would know this. But when you are looking into the eyes of Death, you know nothing. Feel nothing. See only what you want to. Only what Death wants you to.

I could still see him now in my feverish semi-consciousness. He was smiling up at me from his cold grave. Flashing that breezy smile that always had enough weight to sink through to my soul. Turning me inside out with a madness only one thing can inspire.

Death.

Most people say love. But it is simply the other side of the same coin. Death has always inspired me to live this life. I have never run from it. I have clung to my ghost, the lingering images of a dad who left so long ago. I have held that close, even when all of them said I must abandon this nonsense. Let go of that *physical manifestation of trauma*. I don't remember a life without being haunted. But now I had a new ghost.

'She's delirious.' I heard the voice. Another side of me. Mother.

'No, I'm not. Spear is dead.' I didn't need to add any emotion. I didn't even need to open my eyes to know all the expressions arrayed in front of me. 'Have you dug him out yet?'

'Shh.' Someone was placing something cold on my head. 'You're hurt. You must rest.' The comfortable smell of Aunt Charlotte flooded my face.

My eyes blinked open a little. 'You'll need a pickaxe or something. The ice is pretty thick. Then sit him by the fire. We'll have to do the wedding tomorrow.' My voice was savagely raw from all the screaming. 'When he's thawed out.'

I heard a muffled cry and someone left the room.

I lifted my eyebrows in casual enquiry.

Aunt Charlotte breathed a heavy sigh. 'Angela. She's not good.'

I could see their outlines. Mother, all angular and bent. Bridget, overly keen and jittery. Some people I didn't know. Ghosts perhaps, seeping through the walls from the ice beyond. So much I'd read had talked about how this was an ancient land of spirits. This was a world for the dead to walk freely. Good. I would wait for him.

'Go and fetch him up,' I murmured.

'We can't, dear,' Aunt Charlotte said quietly.

'And why not?'

'It's too dark to see anything down there. We can't see him, my dear.' I heard the faint glimmer of doubt in her voice, and when I looked around the room, I saw it on every face. Even Dad's.

I let my eyes close over and my mind fill up with that freezing ice water just as his had done, drowning out every thought, numbing every emotion. I didn't want to feel anything again. But I would, and the cruelty would begin all too soon.

They came and they went with tea, laboured feet and hushed voices, as if I was the dead one lying in state and this was my wake. My fitful consciousness was haunted by Spear, trapped in his underworld of ice, begging me to free him. He was so perfectly formed beneath there. His shadowy face

135

and glimmering eye shining out at me, unable to blink but seeing me in the land of the living above him, on the other side of the glass.

My tenuous link to this world was breaking. What was there to keep me here now? And then I heard Mother, by my side. She stroked my hair and whispered words beneath the drum of my thoughts.

I pictured him out there, imagined him there through time, held in stasis. Time just passing away as he slowly thawed and decomposed. Time would be meaningless to him. He would be there for so long.

'So long,' I murmured through the blur.

'Shh.' I felt Mother's hand touch my forehead. 'You're hurt.'

'Concussion,' Bridget said decidedly. 'From beating her head against—'

'Yes, thank you, Bridget.'

'Long time.' I imagined the days falling like snow as the season changed and covered him entirely. It would be a long time until spring, until the ice began to melt, freeing his bent limbs. A long time.

'Ursula, you need to rest.' Aunt Charlotte was on the other side of me.

I flicked open my eyelids and fixed my eyes on her. 'I will not rest until his killer is dead.'

Her face blurred and faded away. The dark was here and it was all-consuming.

CHAPTER TWENTY-TWO:
THE MONSTERS ARE REAL

My soul was numb. All around me, a void. I knew nothing. I tried to think of something simple, how the bed must feel beneath me. But it was as though I was inside someone else's body, and they were just describing what they could feel. I heard voices that I knew I should grasp, should recognise. But their sense slipped over the surface of my mind like cool water. I was senseless. The world had been drained of meaning.

I had tried but now it was easier to just let myself drift under that ailing darkness again. I knew my head was pounding but the pain was another irrelevance. I was still. Very still. Not just my body but my whole self. Everything about me had stalled, ground to a halt. And I welcomed it. I had no more need for thoughts. I'd thought enough. My mind had a loose feeling of being untethered now. Cast adrift into nothing.

I don't know how long I was there. The occasional murmur of words passed by like stations outside the train window, but they'd gone before I could place the speakers' names.

The blood's stopping.

Silence.

Keep her warm.

Silence.

She's in shock.

Silence.

She'll survive.

My hot brain lingered on that last word before letting it go. *That* word. Spear had said he couldn't survive without me. In fact, the truth had ended up being entirely the opposite.

Behind all this, a tiny thread was forming, spinning a fragile web. A pattern of days was mapping itself out from this very point. I had no will, no inclination to stop it or even protest. I had no stomach for the fight anymore. I was ready to abandon myself. Falling was easier than I'd thought.

Memory seeped in underneath it all, slow and steady like water under a door struggling to hold back a flood. I knew this place. I knew it well.

I was standing at a fixed point. As I turned to look around, I saw there was not just one but many doors surrounding me. No walls. No ceiling. Just doors. All of them closed. There were no handles.

They opened in turn as if there was a preordained rhythm to the moment of revelation. Behind each stood an unmoving man.

Spear.

I studied each version in turn. All so similar. None alike. But in all of the models, he was haggard, his skin stretched thin as if he was being worn away. Scoured of everything I knew of him. Slowly draining of colour. Diluted by the waters. Fading away from me.

It is the dream all dreamers have, to grow together with those we love, the roots of our lives so inextricably entwined to another soul over the years. Spear and I had just started to grow together. But all those years of ours that lay ahead were cut away. I was left to wander the loneliness. I reached out towards one of the silent figures but my hands fell flat just in front of his face. There was a pane of glass between us. Spear's eyes flicked open, such dead grey pearls. I called his name but he was deaf to me. Sealed away.

The light began to fade, his face withdrawing, melting back into the darkness. I called again.

'He's gone, love.' I couldn't see Aunt Charlotte.

All those threads I had been so busily weaving snapped one by one. When I looked at him now through the dark water of dreams, far below, in that ice-locked tomb, all those years had gone in an instant. Without me.

The wall of ice thickened beneath my hand. His face blurred.

'No!'

'Shh.' I heard those distant voices purr.

'Don't go,' I cried, my hands still flat on the ice, the ring he'd given me glinting in response. 'Please, don't go.' I lay my hot forehead against that cold sheet between us.

The past falling away. The future so unobtainable now.

Warm blood spilled down my temples. A surprise of pain struck me.

'He's gone now.' Mother's voice peeked through the fog.

The slow, steady stream of ice water grew to a rush and the flood came in a blistering wave. Her words felled me in an instant.

Everything froze into that moment. Clarifying it. Clearing the rest of the world away.

If I was entirely honest, which no one ever is, it had always been there, this moment. In the back cupboard of my soul, I'd always known this was how it would turn out.

I let go of the dream — the last fine string slipping through my fingers before sailing off, a tiny kite buffeted on the wind.

He was gone and, in his place, rose a much darker creature — the features shadowy, the outline indistinct. It lifted from the ground, a phantom with long hands and a malicious look. Its cold eyes slid towards me and a dead smile cracked the face as if to say, 'It's time to do this dance again, Ursula Smart.' The spectre filled the door, rippling thin fingers in keen anticipation. My skin sank from the crawling sensation.

I knew this monster. I knew it so well. Grief is as familiar to me as life. There would be many phases to come.

Matthias had spoken of the superstitions and demons that roamed out there. I don't believe in many things, but I know there are monsters and ghosts in this world. They will never stop haunting me. And out here, alone in this frozen darkness, fear lived everywhere. The monsters were real and they were coming for us all.

In a disintegrating, broken voice, I whispered, 'The monster is coming.' My eyes flashed open and I looked at each of them in turn with total candour. Mother, Aunt Charlotte, Bridget — their fearful confusion was so tangible.

'The beast is out there in the night and it's coming for you, for each of you in turn. We are all going to die.'

The shadow dragged me back into the intimacy of the darkness, under the water where my thoughts froze on that last view I had of him.

My last image of the room was the window opposite, and the shape framed within it. It was here. Watching us. Waiting.

CHAPTER TWENTY-THREE:
A LOCKED LAKE MYSTERY

It was wrong. It was all wrong.

The words jangled in my head like chains that didn't link.

'It's wrong.'

'I know, dear,' Aunt Charlotte soothed, 'but sometimes it just is.' Her sigh was heavy on my cheek.

My eyelids lifted cautiously and the room bled in. Faces round me, locked in sadness. My voice was weak, but I wheezed out the words again. 'It's wrong.'

Mother was nodding.

I pushed myself up in the bed and felt the pain rip through my temple. I let my fingers gently explore the mess on my forehead.

I looked at Mother, whose eyes were fixed on the open wounds. Her expression was as if I'd inflicted every one of those on her, not me. 'I'm sorry,' I rasped.

She gripped my hand even tighter.

'Mother.' I leaned a little closer to her. 'It's very wrong.'

She frowned.

I looked to Aunt Charlotte and then over to Bridget, who hovered at the end of the bed, still unsure of her position.

'Listen to me, please.' A shiver of pain passed through my head. I widened my eyes and stared intensely. 'You have to get him out,' I whispered.

Bridget audibly sighed. 'We've been round and round this. He's dead. He's beneath too much ice. We need to leave him where he is for the police. I'm not making a note of any of this and I think you'll thank me later for that decision.'

'Why must you always speak like you're giving dictation?' Aunt Charlotte made no effort to disguise her exasperation. 'Where is your pity?'

Mother gave her a crisp look before turning to me and attempting to soften it, but I could see she was struggling. 'I'm not going to say she's right. But Ursula, darling, you saw him under the ice. I'm afraid not even he can survive that.'

'Don't you see? How can he be? We only saw him last night. He can't have gone under the ice that far. The water can't have frozen over him that thick in a few hours. The lake has been solid with ice since we got here.'

Aunt Charlotte nodded. 'We'd considered this, obviously.' She tried to look judicious, steepling her fingers in front of her. 'I have come to the conclusion that there is some form of entry point elsewhere in the ice. A fishing hole perhaps, or an ice water plunge pool. I'm told they're very good for the more intimate areas.'

'Yes, thank you, Charlotte! May I just say—' Mother stared intently — 'that sounds like absolute horseshit.'

Aunt Charlotte looked vexed and fell into the chair.

'There are no holes in the ice out here.' It was Matthias at the door, his face muted. 'We do not cut it yet for the fishing. Whatever is under there must have been there some time.' He paused. 'Or else the spirits have something to do with it.'

Bridget gave me a very deliberate look. 'I'm sure the spirits have!'

'I know what I saw, Bridget.'

'I'm just saying, you'd drunk a lot, you were in a high state of emotional distress.'

Mother interrupted. 'That's not a new phenomenon. We can discount that.'

'Thank you, Mother.'

'I'm just saying, it wouldn't cause you to start seeing spirits and ghosts.'

I glanced over at Dad, lingering in the corner of the room. He'd been out there, hovering over the lake. I'd seen him. He'd lured me there. He'd wanted me to see that body under the ice. But why? Why break my heart even more? That wasn't like Dad. Perhaps Matthias was right, perhaps there were other phantoms lurking out there, playing tricks on my mind. But I'd seen Spear. I knew I had. Angela had seen him.

'Where's his mother?' I asked.

'She's in a bit of a state, Ursula.' Aunt Charlotte shook her head. 'Helmi and Aino are with her. She's in shock.'

Bridget stepped closer. 'She needs a doctor. We need to get help out here.'

'How can we do that when someone's cut all the phones?'

I looked at Mother. 'Here as well?'

She nodded. 'The ice wind is rising too. We'll have to wait for it to pass. Matthias says it's bringing heavy snow.'

'Can you give Angela anything to help?' I asked Mother, knowing full well she always travelled fully pharma'ed up.

'It's gone. My zolpidem. The lot. I didn't get hardly a wink last night.'

That made sense. She'd tossed and turned all night. 'There was me thinking you were nervous about my wedding.'

'I was prepared for it to be challenging.'

'Challenging?' Bridget laughed. 'Heavens, the groom dead under an impossibly thick layer of ice? I'd say that's challenging, yes.'

Everyone glared at her.

'What?' She pulled out the tedious notebook and pen in the fashion of a malign schoolgirl recording our every move in a diary. Bridget could very well have been doing that over the years and at some point there'd be a warts-and-all exposé that would put Mother's blog to shame with its indiscrete revelations.

Bridget started writing in the notebook, the balding, yellow-feather-topped pen twitching like a canary in a mine. 'Impossible crime. A locked lake mystery.' She looked round at us all, the pen hovering over the top of the page. 'Right, what do we know?'

I suppose I had to admire her blatant disregard for compassion. It was the only way we were going to get anywhere near the truth. I thought of what I'd seen out there. A body under the ice. Just as he was the last time I saw him. His jacket. His unseeing eye staring up at me. I turned the ring on my finger and looked into its shifting colours. 'I looked into his eye,' I murmured, staring at the ring. 'I saw it.'

'Eye.' Bridget wrote again. 'Colour?' she glanced at me as if she was just asking what flavour of ice cream I'd like.

'His eyes are blue-green, like the ring,' My voice was barely a whisper.

I saw him again, lying on his side in the dark ice, staring out. The room fell into an uncomfortable silence.

I could hear the windows being tested by the wind. Noises surfaced from the wooden walls and conjured thoughts of some hidden form of life buried within them. The logs cracked like ancient bones moving around us. It was as though something was breaking in, or perhaps breaking out from the wood. There was an overwhelming sense of this world closing in on us.

Bridget moved towards me, which is always disconcerting. She looked down at the ring. 'There's no green in that.'

Her blunt manner in the face of such an ordeal was starting to grate. 'It's a black opal,' I said sharply. 'It changes depending on the light. It was his great-grandmother's. He told me she had the same eyes as him.'

'I see.' Bridget's bedside manner was positively reptilian at this point.

Mother couldn't contain her frustration. 'This is getting us nowhere. He's under the ice. How he got there will no

144

doubt become clear as soon as the authorities arrive. For the moment, we have to sit tight and keep everyone on an even keel. Raking over the bones isn't going to help.'

'There'll be no bones for a while.' Matthias was a still grave sentry stationed at the door. 'There's a track out there. It's being blown over by the wind and snow though. The *ahkio*'s definitely gone as well.' He looked around us all. 'Track leads out into the forest. Pair of skis gone too.'

'We need to follow it.' I pulled myself up straight, my eyes appealing to each of them in turn. 'Quickly, before we lose it.'

'What? Are you mad?' It wasn't the best question Mother could have asked in the circumstances.

'Could be Tuoni gathering more souls,' Matthias offered in a low, warning voice. He'd adopted a strange, prophetic look. He saw our blank expressions. 'God of the underworld.'

Bridget frowned. 'You mean the Devil?'

He cocked his head, his eyes clear and decisive.

Mother stood up and folded her arms defiantly. 'I don't think the Devil needs skis.'

Matthias turned down the sides of his mouth and shrugged as though this was perhaps a debatable matter.

'How can we go out there following anything, dear?' Aunt Charlotte looked pityingly at me and then pointed towards the window. 'It's dark and freezing. Whatever it is that's out there, it won't bring Spear back. It's a dangerous killer. We shouldn't put any more lives at risk.' She placed a hand on my arm and shook her head. 'He wouldn't want that.'

'Stop saying *whatever*.' Mother was still impatient, even with the added thought that the Devil himself might be stalking her. She seemed familiar with the idea. 'It's a *whoever*. There is no such thing as *whatever*.'

Bridget assessed me for a moment. 'What do you hope to find if we do go out there and follow the tracks, Ursula?'

'The answer,' I said simply.

'Out there?' Bridget was turning over the options.

'It's started snowing.' Aunt Charlotte stared intently at the window as if she was half expecting to see someone standing out there looking back.

'And there's probably a killer in the woods,' Mother added, which seemed a bit unnecessary.

'One capable of *magically* getting the body under a thick layer of ice.' Bridget sounded ponderous, which is always irritating.

'It's absolute madness to go out there.' Aunt Charlotte shook her head.

'Then that's what we should do.' I started to get out of bed.

But then I paused, doubt catching me. The five of us looked at one another, waiting for someone to confirm that this was really what we should do.

It was Matthias who nodded once and spoke simply. 'I'll get the reindeers ready for you to follow on behind with Helmi. And the dogs. They are fast.' He paused and looked at each of us in turn. 'But just remember when you are out there, the ghosts are close. The air is at its thinnest between us now. We must travel with care.'

I didn't tell him they were already here in this room with us.

'So, we are agreed? We definitely need to go out there and follow those tracks into the forest, right?' Aunt Charlotte wasn't really looking for a response. We all knew the answer. I wasn't going to let his killer get away and forever be left wondering if we could have caught them.

We gathered together in what had quickly become some sort of base camp in the living room.

For the next ten minutes, we dressed soberly in outer layers, standing in front of the fire to savour those last moments of warmth. No one spoke. A nervous apprehension had settled over us, each of us casting one another quick glances, trying desperately to focus on nothing more than fastening ourselves into the various pieces of extreme clothing as if it was armour. There was a definite eve-of-battle feel amongst us now. But that had no meaning for me. Whatever or whoever was out there had killed the rest of my days. I had no problem with taking theirs.

Aino and Helmi watched us in disapproval, resolutely offering no help.

'You're all going to die.' Helmi had reverted to her charmless self. She leaned against the wall by the fireplace, nonchalantly looking us up and down. She had that expectant look of someone who enjoyed provoking a reaction.

'We've been told *that* before.' Aunt Charlotte put another reindeer hide round her shoulders. She increasingly had a budget *Game of Thrones* look about her.

'Helmi.' Matthias looked at her. 'I . . . We need your help. I cannot take them all with the dogs alone.'

She glared at him but didn't speak.

'Helmi?'

She drew a breath, her eyes fixed on Matthias, then nodded once.

I dressed silently. As I pulled the hat down I didn't even wince from the hot pain that ran across my forehead. I traced my finger underneath the fur trim, along the line of the cut from where I'd struck my head into the ice. It was still raw, the traces of blood staining my fingers.

Mother was giving me avid glances. She didn't speak. She didn't need to.

Our quiet, solemn gathering felt almost religious. Ritualistic. Matthias waited by the door. He was to be our guide. It struck me that he'd been oddly accepting of a plan that was clearly dangerous. One that could lead us straight to the savage murderer of three people. But all I could picture was that moment and how I would end everything right then.

'Please take care of Angela,' I said to Aino.

'Likewise, my daughter.' Her face was grave.

My mind went to those cruel moments out on the ice. I'd screamed his name. I'd given Angela no consideration. What would Spear be thinking now? If I'd been under the ice and he'd found me, would he have shown so little regard for

147

my mother and let her discover I was dead in such a brutal way? I already knew the answer to that.

I was ashamed. I needed to prove to him, or his ghost, that I could be better than this. Even if I couldn't bring him back to life, I could find his killer and punish them.

'OK.' Aunt Charlotte clapped her mittened hands together. 'Let's go hunt the Devil.'

CHAPTER TWENTY-FOUR: THE SILENT FOREST

'I've tracked many things,' Matthias spoke almost to himself, 'but never a man.' He pushed the knife down hard into the sheath hanging from his belt. There was a decisiveness to him. He seemed almost keen.

Outside, the darkness was clear and crisp, the sky sharp with stars. The ice infected my skin immediately, and ran to my bones, snaking down my back. But it made no real impression on me. It was as if I was just recounting the effects to a stranger. I was cold, I knew that, but I didn't really feel anything.

My eyes were instantly drawn down to the jetty. The urge to run over and peer into those frozen waters was almost overwhelming, to lose myself for ever in the icy reflection of the stars.

Mother reached over and grabbed my elbow. 'You won't see anything now.' She stared at me, if not with understanding, then definitely with knowledge of where my thoughts had travelled.

Bridget leaned in. 'The best thing you can do is find his killer. Come on, you won't solve this by standing around looking all gothic. Let's move out. They're getting away. We can't waste a minute. The snow will cover the track.'

She climbed into the reindeer sleigh and waited, her eyes set on the frozen forest ahead. Helmi was holding the reins, murmuring quietly to herself in Finnish. It had a sharp little edge to it, a malevolent sound, as if she might be hexing us or delivering some sort of deathly curse. I tried to banish such a foolish idea, but the truth was, I was seeing treachery in everything now. I couldn't trust anyone, least of all myself.

There was another blink of green out over on the other side of the lake beyond the pine trees. It seemed to twist with the movement of life somewhere inside it. I wondered if he was up there, in those coloured wisps. Watching. Willing me on to find his killer.

Aunt Charlotte climbed into the sleigh with Bridget.

I got in next to Mother and sat with a grim determination. The dogs yelped and panted into the night air.

As we drew out in front, I looked towards the eerie darkness of the high trees. I leaned my head right back and let the snowflakes fall like feathers on my face. I stared into the depths of the sky.

'Lintukoto,' I whispered.

'Ursula?' Mother asked.

I remembered what Matthias had said to us, to me and Spear, about it being an imaginary, happy place, *warm and peaceful like paradise*. When he'd told us, I'd almost thought I'd found it.

I pictured myself that night with Spear. I'd come so close to the dream.

But now was not the time for peace. Reflection and grief could wait. There would be plenty of time for that later. Now was the time to catch a killer and they were still close. I could smell them.

'We follow the *ahkio* tracks. But beware the forest spirits,' Matthias called out from where he stood behind us. 'Do not look at them. They are cruel creatures that will draw you in.'

Mother sighed dismissively.

'And also the trolls.'

Matthias leaned over and called out to the dogs as he flashed the reins. He didn't wait for us to settle in before we were away. There was an unwavering resolve in his face, focused out there in the darkness. But his firm resolution didn't bring any feelings of assurance. Quite the opposite. It was unnerving.

There was no time for any more discussion. We were off, scything through the snow behind the insatiable dogs. They were eager for the hunt. So was I. I felt the adrenalin rush through me. It might have been reckless, dangerous or anything else that people were going to accuse us of after all this had played out. But right there, in that moment, as we faced the prospect of Spear's murderer getting away, disappearing for ever and leaving us without any answers, it seemed like the only sane option we had. We had to chase them down. If it ended in disaster, at least we wouldn't face all those long years stretching out from this point without ever knowing the truth.

As we ploughed on into the silent forest, a disorientating calm descended. The only sound was the panting of the dogs and the swathe of our tracks through the snow. We followed the single *ahkio* trail out into the darkness. The trees lining our path disappeared into the sky, an occasional ribbon of colour passing over the stars between the branches. It was so eerily still. We were the only things moving. Perhaps the only things living. But it didn't feel like that. I caught the occasional reflective button of light at the edge of my vision. Eyes? Round the trees, small clouds of white air ballooned out like breath. It was a lonely, silent space and we had no place being there.

Matthias drove the dogs with the fierce intensity of a man focused on the hunt, his shoulders tensed, head jutting forward. I didn't understand his resolve, but there was so much here beyond my reasoning. Tapio and Onni had both been slaughtered. Perhaps it had had more of an effect on Matthias than he'd shown. He'd hidden most of his emotions, even when faced with bitter scenes of blood and death.

His hardened stoicism had been there from the beginning, never faltering once. Nothing seemed to disturb him. It was almost as if he had never really been quite present. When he'd spoken about leaving with Helmi back in October and the humiliation and upset of having to come back, he'd shown very little emotion at all. Nor when he'd relayed the fact that Tapio had then decided to sack him. Matthias had lost a lot. He had reasons to kill, and if anyone was capable it was the large woodsman with a big hunter's knife, racing a pack of dogs into the forest. There were many reasons to think this wasn't a good idea but the extremes of grief do have one benefit. They unhook you from the world, numb you, disconnect you until you are immune to fear. If Spear's killer was out there, I was going to find them and have my revenge. Even if it killed me.

CHAPTER TWENTY-FIVE:
WHERE THE DEVIL LIVES

I couldn't say how long we followed that trail. The slow, almost motionless fall of snow through the silent darkness created an unreal, altered state. We'd lost sight of Bridget and Aunt Charlotte in their slower reindeer sleigh behind us. We were the only life now, Matthias standing behind us driving on the huskies that raced on up ahead as if the Devil was indeed at their heels.

In among those cathedral-high trees, tiny movements filtered through. Lights glimmered then disappeared. Just beyond our sledge, as we skirted past the base of the trunks, shapes formed from thin tendrils of mist and ice, then disappeared into the snow. Silvery faces traced through the air like spirits circling the trees. There was a solitude to this place but there was no calm. It was a frozen, dead zone.

I held Mother's hand under the rug like I was a child again. She gripped tight, her face taut, body rigid. She knew the devastation a dead husband brings, like a fireball through life, burning down all in its path, everything it touches, laying waste to it. She knew all too well the charred path I would have to walk from this moment. It would consume everything. This hunt to salvage something from the blaze was only granting us a temporary reprieve, an interlude before we had to let all that grief roam free. For the moment, we had something to focus the rage on, a purpose for all that loss and disbelief. To let his killer just go out into the night was unthinkable.

The first we saw of the hut was a thin line of smoke snaking up through the trees, a single thread to lead us through the woods towards an end, whatever that might be. We had found where the Devil lived. Now all we had to do was kill him.

Matthias pulled the dogs into a stop behind the trees at the edges of the small clearing. He whistled at them to quieten down. Through the haze of snow and ice as it came in waves, I could occasionally see the details of the small, rustic-looking cabin in the centre of the glade. It was the perfect image of a fairy tale, one where the unsuspecting children could so easily be lured in.

Mother had a rare look of fear on her face.

'It is a *riihi*.' Matthias climbed down from behind us, hauling in the reins tight. 'Where the *haltija* come to dry their grain.'

'*Haltija*?' I asked.

'Elves,' was not the response I'd expected.

'Elves?' Mother frowned.

'Surely even you people have heard of elves,' he sighed.

'Of course we've heard of elves, in the same way we've heard of fairies and ghosts, neither of which actually exist.'

I glanced off into the trees and caught sight of Dad's shape floating at a distance. He was there all the time now. Like they told me, a *physical manifestation of trauma*. Perhaps they were right. But out here, it felt like anything could be real.

Matthias dragged on the lead again. 'They are the mill elves. Every building has an elf. You treat them well, they bring good luck.'

'I presume you guys must have been horrendous to them then, given the run of luck we've had in the last few hours.' Mother started to climb out of the sledge, gently unthreading her fingers from between mine.

'The tragedy only started when you people arrived. We were fine until then.'

I couldn't even begin to think of the number of times someone has said that to us.

But Matthias wasn't looking for approval or agreement. 'You must have done something bad to anger Hiisi this much.'

He looked at our blank faces.

'The bad spirit? A monstrous creature who attacks travellers?' He bent his head towards us and lowered his voice. 'He lives out here, in this forest.'

Our eyes travelled towards the hut.

'Well, I can only thank you for bringing us out here to visit him.' Mother raised a sharp eyebrow.

A stream of cold traced down my neck as I watched the tiny shack in the snow-covered glade. The tracks led right to it, and there, propped against the wall outside, was the *ahkio* that had made it, along with a pair of skis.

'Look,' Matthias whispered. 'More tracks.'

The set of ski tracks also led to the house. They were fresh in the new snow.

'It's the track from the cabins.' He followed its line through the trees.

'They've gone back there?' Mother looked puzzled.

'Or they came from there.' Matthias remained stony-faced. 'Since the skis that made them are here, I'd say that was more likely.'

The idea that it was a random outsider seemed increasingly unlikely.

Matthias finished tying all the reins to a tree. 'We walk from here. Less noise. Keep your eyes open.'

'For what, more monsters and ghouls?' Mother sighed. 'Elves, pixies . . .'

'No, wolverines. There are many out here.'

A creature shot from the cover of the trees straight across our path. Mother grabbed my arm.

'It's a squirrel,' I reassured her. 'Just a squirrel.'

The scrawny-looking animal paused and fixed its eyes on us before it bounded out of view.

'I thought they were red, not mangy grey little rats like ours.'

Matthias started walking, his boots crunching on the snow. 'They are red. They only change to grey in winter.' He walked away, shaking his head.

It somehow didn't even seem surreal that we were discussing squirrels as we hunted my almost-husband's killer. But we'd slipped anchor from reality and anything seemed possible now.

Something was nagging at the edges of my thoughts. But nothing was clear anymore. It was distorted, as if we'd fallen into some parallel world where spirits and the elements crossed over the boundary and conspired against us. Everything was constantly changing, even the colours.

As we drew closer, Matthias turned to us. He held his finger to his lips and widened his eyes. We instantly looked towards the cabin. A light had come on in the window.

A door slammed at the side of the cabin and someone walked out to where the skis were. They had a helmet on. Whoever it was quickly stamped into the skis and, without pausing, set off into the woods proficiently.

The sound of the skis slicing through snow trailed away into the forest as the figure disappeared.

'Now what?' Mother whispered.

Matthias turned to her. 'We go see the ghosts.' He nodded towards the window. In the flimsy light, I could just make out a dull, floating shape. It was no more than a dark stain, formless and unrecognisable as anything at first.

We warily moved towards the hut, listening, our senses keen, heightened by the hard silence. There was an unbearable tension in my head, as if a string was being pulled to breaking point. Any sound seemed magnified, our boots crushing down on the brittle honeycomb snow, our breath freezing in stuttered clouds. And those thin skeins of misted light threaded through the edges of the trees, forming shapes, following us just at the edges of my vision.

My head pounded hard as if beating out a message. I looked at Mother and Matthias, forging on with dour, remorseless expressions of grim determination chiselled into their faces. Could they hear it, the thrum of my blood, the veins straining to contain my thick pulse? Dad was there, as clear as reality now, unable to help, just watching, rubber-stamping that word — *trauma*. The word seemed so maddeningly inadequate, something you might use for a single event that would heal, that could be treated. Not something that realigned everything. Destroyed everything. An unhealable future.

I watched all those other ghosts now, flit through the dark among the snowy branches like smoke. I'd thought this place would be special. We'd chosen it together, hadn't we? My memory was weak. In a way it was unique, a place of spirits and darkness, of unreal moments. Had it been real, any of it? Perhaps I'd imagined his folded-up face down there, squeezed by the crushing force of the ice, twisted in the heavy darkness. That unfocused eye looking out into nothing. I'd seen that, hadn't I? I see a lot though, and not all of it is true.

The strange shape at the window still hung there. It had been quite blurred through the mist and snow at first, but as we moved a little closer, the edges grew clearer.

My mind was framing it into a figure. Cast in silhouette, the arms and shoulders were obvious now but the strange thing about it was its feet. They were halfway up the window as if it was levitating from the ground.

No head was visible as it was above the level of the top of the window. The figure must have been unfeasibly high up, as if suspended and dangling down.

Matthias turned to us. 'There is some evil here.'

'Excuse me if I don't applaud, Sherlock.' Mother had stopped, a look of disbelief on her face. She pointed to where the floating shadow still hung in the window. 'That does indicate something might be rotten here in Deathland, don't you think?'

He looked affronted at the slur but, faced with three gruesome deaths and a possible fourth, he didn't have much to offer in the way of a response.

'You can see it too?' I asked. 'The gho—'

'Of course I can!' Mother gave me a purposeful look. She'd cut me off before I said more. 'There's a bloody body swinging there. A hanged man!'

'Or woman,' Matthias added.

Mother didn't acknowledge that. 'Well, why the hell are we standing around, Thor? Let's go!' She strode out like it was Black Friday.

I followed.

'You are going in there . . . with that?' Matthias had a stranded look about him.

'Why not? I have nothing left to lose. Let's go see the hanged man.'

'You are unarmed.'

I didn't answer that.

'This person may come back. They have brutally murdered people.'

I shrugged and carried on.

My mind was so detached from my body that I could barely feel the snow beneath my boots. A loud crack filled the air, echoing round the clearing. We paused, caught in the open like prey.

'Don't worry. That one was the trees,' Matthias said. 'When it gets cold, their wood cracks.'

'That's no tree. It was loud, like a gunshot.' Mother was scouring the area with keen, avid eyes. 'Why aren't Charlotte and Bridget here yet?'

'The reindeer are much slower. They will be here soon enough. Helmi will be sure to take care of them.'

'It doesn't help when you make it sound like she's going to dispose of them.'

He sighed and continued trudging away, murmuring in English about how little we knew and how foolish we were to walk into such danger. I didn't say anything, but the truth was I had no wish to know anything anymore. I felt nothing, least of all fear. I just wanted to kill whoever it was who'd taken Spear from me and I was happy to do that, whatever it took or whoever it was. At that moment, it seemed entirely rational and I was almost pleased at my own honesty. It was the only truth that I had left.

I reached inside my pocket and felt the serrated edge of the blade. A hunting knife I'd taken from the wall of our cabin. If they were going to use weapons as decoration, the guests might as well make use of them. I smiled to myself. Matthias had said I was going in unarmed. I certainly wasn't, no matter what they might think. At least Mother's blog followers would have something really salacious to get their teeth into. If they wanted blood, I was going to give it to them. In rivers.

CHAPTER TWENTY-SIX: THE HANGED MAN

As we neared the *riihi*, thin trails of icy mist wandered between us, forming and reforming, pausing to watch our approach as if the drifts were curious spirits. Closer in, I could make out a rough, tangled mess of fur and blood nailed to the doorframe. It was a large, burly-looking hare, its coat white for winter just as I'd read. Everything here was bleached out for the arrival of the snow, to make it disappear. Nature's conjuring trick. But it hadn't saved this poor creature. Its fur was filthy with blood. The animal had been slit along its length and the insides just left to tumble out in a grisly display. The ribcage was visible like long bone fingers unfurling from the hare's insides. The anguished look of defeat in the beads of its eyes was pitiful. Death had been ruthless. Pointless. And from the looks of the gutting, this hadn't been cleaned and prepped for food. This was sport. A statement. A warning. Or perhaps it had been slaughtered just for sheer enjoyment. Had that been the only reason for Spear's death? For all the other deaths? Someone's momentary pleasure? An indulgence?

There was an anxious silence among us now. Our eyes and thoughts all concentrated on whatever lived in that small hut. Whatever was capable of such a cruel, barbarous act could very easily have been responsible for the other slayings that were equally ruthless and, as far as we could work out, meaningless.

The door to the *riihi* had no lock. An abandoned grain store in the middle of a bleak wilderness had no need for security. It swung open to reveal a shadowy entrance hall, with a faint dim light coming through from another door. The small entrance instantly forced all three of us to bend low and remain like that as we clustered in the cramped hallway. Matthias looked so constrained by the thin passage and its low roof.

The smell of damp wood was cloying, hanging on the frigid air. It had an unused, decaying taint as if the timbers were slowly rotting.

Like all the other buildings, it was built almost entirely of logs, but these had a more ancient look about them than the other lodges, the bark almost black with age and heavily encrusted with some thick, grimy residue. Matthias had said it was for grain drying and the large hearth ahead of us seemed to agree. But then he'd also said the work was undertaken by elves. It was difficult to know how much credence could be given to anything the man said.

A fire was smouldering in the grate, casting long shadows over the dark walls. It didn't give off much light or, indeed, heat. There was a dank cold that settled easily into the bones, unlike the sharp, frozen air outside. It was a mildewed air that had a sickly staleness to it, an illness lifting from the old wood.

But I had no need for fear now. If there was a dead man in there, it was just another for the tally. That would make four. I'd once googled how many people you have to kill to be a serial killer. Not that I'd thought of killing anyone. Not then. It was more that I was curious to find out if there might be an opposite. A serial victim.

Three or more murders is the baseline for a serial killer. But I only needed to kill one.

I could hear a strange whispering sound coming through the walls. The freezing air moved a little as though something had disrupted it. As we walked further along the small corridor, I could hear our footsteps on the wooden floor. We paused at the door. Was there one more step after we had stopped? I turned round, but there was no one there.

'OK?' Mother mouthed.

I nodded.

As we entered the small, murky room, I heard the rope creak as it shifted. It was hung from the thick beam that crossed the ceiling and below it swung the body of a man.

Mother's hand went to her mouth.

Matthias took out his hunting blade.

My mind tried to make sense of what I was seeing, piecing together a rough image out of the scraps that the mean light was providing. The man's arms were up in the air. He was tied by the wrists, not hanged by the neck as I had first assumed. What looked like an old grain sack was pulled down over his head that lolled on to his chest, his spine bent over unnaturally like a melted candle in the gloom. He was wearing a long funeral-black coat that looked old and threadbare. He wasn't moving.

Matthias approached with his knife held out. He grabbed a small, rickety chair from the side of the room and placed it next to the man. Cautiously, he reached out and put his fingers to the man's neck. He waited. Then said nothing before climbing onto the chair and sawing through the rope efficiently.

The man dropped to the floor in a heap and let out a single groan. Whoever it was, they were alive. The crumpled shape didn't move. Matthias looked over at us before crouching down next to him and slowly turning the man on to his back. Another sigh fell out of the body.

Carefully, Matthias replaced his hunting knife in its holster at his side and then reached out to the hood. He gently lifted the man's head and pulled the sack over from the back and off.

The man's face was slowly revealed.

It was Spear.

CHAPTER TWENTY-SEVEN: YOU ONLY DIE ONCE

Books and films may have fanciful ideas about living more than one life. Perhaps there's some truth in that. But you can only ever die once. And Spear had already been given his death.

I stared, unable to move, unable to process the face I knew so well, lying there on the floor as if he'd just fallen asleep. But my mind wouldn't let me say the words *he's alive*. It was as though a protective membrane had formed over my brain. To think that, to believe it, would send me into a chaos, a madness I might never shake off.

As if to tempt me further into believing what my eyes were conjuring, he made a weak, wounded sound. I pushed away all those thoughts so desperate to be set free, like voices in another room that I could only vaguely hear but made no sense.

It was Aunt Charlotte's voice that finally cut through them all. 'Bugger me, he's alive!'

She was standing at the door, transfixed.

Spear groaned again in agreement and tried to move.

'Stay still, dead man.' Matthias continued to hold Spear's head in one hand and the grain sack in the other.

Everyone's eyes slid towards me.

'Ursula?' Mother was hesitant. 'Why did you say . . .' Her voice faded out.

I started to walk towards him in slow, dream steps. He was still there with every beat. He wasn't disappearing, melting away like all the rest of the ghosts. He was real. He was there. He was alive.

I fell to the floor beside him and grabbed his arm. It was a solid limb, not a spirit sent to taunt me, not a fragment of my imagination. Not a *physical manifestation of trauma*. Spear was alive and there right next to me.

I threw my head on to his chest and listened. A strangled sound fell out of him.

'Be careful with him,' Matthias warned. 'He is not well.'

I pulled back, my eyes burning and blurred. 'Spear?'

He coughed but didn't open his eyes. 'Ursula,' was all he said.

'Oh God, he's alive!' I turned to the others. 'He's alive! He's here.'

I pushed my cheek into his before turning and kissing his cold skin. I heard him whisper my name again into my ear, his warm breath touching my face.

'You're alive,' I breathed.

He mumbled in agreement and attempted to lift his head.

'Don't try to move too much,' Matthias said.

I put my hands around his face. 'You're alive.' It was me I was trying to convince. I pulled his head in close to mine and stared into his face. He forced his eyes open into two small, dark slits and looked at me. A frail smile attempted to form on his face, but his eyes drifted shut and the smile died. He was losing consciousness.

I frowned at Matthias, my desperation quick to resurface. Spear's whole existence at that moment seemed so tenuous, so unreal that it could very easily slip away.

'Spear?' I said tentatively. Then with more force. 'Spear.' I grabbed his face harder and Matthias placed his hand on my arm.

'Has someone dug him out of the ice?' Aunt Charlotte looked confused.

Mother scowled. 'Why must you always say the most unobvious thing?'

'Because someone has to.' Aunt Charlotte lifted her chin. 'And sometimes it's the answer.'

Mother sighed and glanced at Matthias for confirmation.

'He has been drugged.' Matthias pointed to the floor where a packet had been left and most of the pills popped from their blisters and used.

Mother walked over and picked it up. 'My zolpidem. The cheeky . . .'

I looked at Spear, barely clinging to consciousness. 'How many have gone?'

Mother thumbed through the pack. 'It's not too many. He'll be out of it for a good while, but it won't kill him.'

Aunt Charlotte moved in beside me. 'He'll live.' Her voice was soft.

A single cry fell out of me. I let my head fall on to his familiar chest and breathed him in. 'Thank you,' I whispered. 'Thank you.'

I could hear the distant note of his pulse. Feel the rise and fall of his breathing. It was real. He was alive. The urge to never let go was overwhelming. I gripped his arms, screwing my fingers down into his coat. I sobbed until I thought my chest would crack open. I was breathing too fast, the air rushing in and out of me as if I was drowning. I never wanted to come up for air.

'OK, OK, shh.' Aunt Charlotte held me round my shoulders. 'It's all going to be OK.'

Mother was on the other side of me. 'Come on. Let the man breathe. He's going to be all right. It's all going to be all right.' I heard her voice break. Did her thoughts reach for Dad in that moment? The image of him lying on the ground in front of us. Dead. The comparison was inescapable. But his untimely death could not be undone. He had not been granted such a reprieve. Nor had Mother. Dad had stayed dead. I lifted myself and looked at Mother through my hazy view.

Tears pooled in her eyes. 'Oh, my Ursula.' The look of poignant delight was etched deep into her face. I had been spared the same fate as her.

I could see Dad's shadow lingering behind her. He reached out a hand to touch Mother's back then disappeared into the air. She would never hold him again, never feel his touch, see his smile. All these things had been snatched away in one moment. And I knew the hysterical pain of that and how it burned a hole right through a person.

To be given all of that life back was an unthinkable dream. One I would cling to. One I wished I could give to her. I put my arms around her and held her as hard as a child.

'Mother,' I whispered into the side of her head.

I felt the sharp breath she took and felt her arms around me. 'Thank God,' was all she said. 'Thank God.'

Aunt Charlotte leaned in and put her arms around both of us as if sealing us together. It felt unbreakable.

We pulled back and looked at one another, our tears running unchecked.

Mother took a moment and wiped her hand quickly across her face. 'And Bridget?'

'Outside, being sick.' Aunt Charlotte cleared her throat. 'Too much *salmiakki*. Salty liquorice filth. Then there was the sleigh ride and the dead hare outside and, well . . . it's all been just a little too much.'

The ease with which we fell back to reality was so quick. And it was real. This was no physical manifestation of anything, nor a lie conjured up by my scarred mind. He wasn't a ghost. He wasn't dead. This wasn't a dream. All of it was real.

Unfortunately, so were the next twenty minutes.

CHAPTER TWENTY-EIGHT:
THE NIGHT OF TOO MANY KNIVES

'Oh, I see what's happened here.' Helmi was standing at the door with her hands on her hips and a look of fury set firmly on her face.

Mother and Aunt Charlotte stood up but I remained with Spear, unable to break from him.

'What a perfect scene of family bliss,' Helmi sneered. 'You have killed my father and hidden this man here so now you can sail away into all that happiness.' She shook her head slowly. 'Well, you're in my world now.'

'That's not it at all. You've got it all wrong.' Aunt Charlotte was astounded. 'Why on Earth would we do that?'

Helmi stiffened. 'My father obviously *knew* him.' She cast a derisive look at Spear and I instinctively moved myself in front of him.

'My mother was right,' Helmi continued, 'with her Bonnie and Clyde theory. You worked together to kill people who were a threat. This was carefully staged by both of you to disappear. I can see exactly how you wanted this to play out. His problems would never stop chasing him unless he was dead. So you told everyone he'd been killed and was in a place deep under the ice that we couldn't get him out

167

of for a long time. Long enough for you to disappear. He's killed my father, then you've hidden him out here until the time was right to get away. I'm going to see you all in jail for the rest of your lives.'

'Helmi.' Matthias approached her carefully. 'Helmi, listen to me. We found him. Strung from the roof!'

'I'm sure he was. This scheme's all been very carefully set up, hasn't it, Ursula Smart? Nothing has been left to chance.'

I looked to Mother and saw the doubt forging on her face.

'Oh, yes. I did my research on you before you came,' Helmi continued. 'Sad, crazy lady who wanted to get married out here in the middle of nowhere. How strange!' She gave a little hollow laugh.

'You don't know anything about me,' I said. 'You've no idea what it's like to have every move I make dissected, everything scrutinised over and over again. Marrying Spear was going to put me so far under the spotlight, I'd burn up. If I was ever going to be free, just once, if I was ever going to get away from the circus of it all, it had to be done out here, far away from everyone.'

'Ursula?' Aunt Charlotte's voice wavered.

Helmi pulled a long hunting knife from a holster at her side. 'I wasn't about to go hunting a killer without this. And now I've found him.' There was a look of barely contained hysteria in her eyes. The kind I'd known until only moments ago. I'd been ready and willing to plunge a knife into anyone who stood against Spear. Was Helmi prepared to do the same to the man she thought had murdered her father? I couldn't take that chance. I slipped my hand into my pocket and carefully pulled out the knife. It was time to end this.

'Oh, so it *is* Bonnie and Clyde then, eh?' Helmi's smile was vindictive.

'Them again, what is this . . .'

'Quiet, Charlotte.' Mother looked down at my hand. 'Ursula, you're going to need to give that to me now.' She used her undeniable voice.

But I was ready to do whatever was necessary to keep Spear safe. I wasn't going to let him die again.

'No, Mother,' are not words my mouth is used to, but they came out loud and clear. 'Not this time. He can't survive without me, that's what he said. So I have to make sure he does.'

'All right, we all need to calm down and put the knives away.' Matthias drew out the thick blade from his side.

'Matthias.' Helmi looked wounded. 'She *lied*. He's not dead. Look at him! He's not under the ice. Like she told us he was.'

'I saw him.' I said it in an unmoved voice. I had to keep my emotions under control now.

'Miss Smart, you could not have.' Matthias motioned to Spear. 'He is here. Alive. We saw him yesterday. That ice formed weeks ago. He could not have got under it then got out of it and be here. That is impossible.'

'I saw him.' I kept my eyes steady on all three of the blades in the room.

Mother spoke in a low voice. 'My daughter sees many things that others don't.'

I frowned.

'What the hell is that supposed to mean?' Helmi was losing patience. 'Are you telling me it was a ghost? Some *supernatural* event?'

'It has been known.' Matthias was grave. 'Inside the ice are many spirits.'

'Oh, for God's sake, wake up, Matthias.' Helmi shook her head. 'All that nonsense and rubbish. This is something these people have cooked up to get rid of my father. The man has even been here before! We know that.'

'And Onni?' Matthias said.

'He was the only other person here when Spear came before. These people have come out here to kill. Ask yourself, why would anyone want to come here to get married? And now they're trying to slip away. What better way than to pretend he was dead? But I'm not going to let that happen.'

She held out the blade firmly and I responded in kind.

Matthias stepped forward with his knife extended too.

'Wait.' Mother held out her arms. 'We need to put down the knives and be rational. Just lower the knives and we can talk.'

'Talk?' Helmi snorted. 'What good has that ever done?'

'Quite a bit actually.' Aunt Charlotte sounded almost as if she was speaking to herself. 'It's always worked that way before.'

Helmi looked confused for a moment. 'I know who all of you are. I've done my research. You're the Smart Women. You go around seeking out murders.'

'Well—' Aunt Charlotte looked doubtful — 'that's not strictly true. Murder just seems to be attracted to us. But it turns out we're quite good at solving it. Probably the practice, you know. I mean, they do say practice makes—'

'Oh my God, be quiet!' Helmi echoed everyone's sentiment. 'I don't care for your *sleuthing*. This man killed my father and he's going to pay for it. This woman lied to protect him. Now, move aside.'

I rose to my feet and held out the knife. 'You'll have to come through me.'

Helmi turned down the corners of her mouth. 'If that's what I have to do.'

'Stop!' Matthias shouted. 'This is not the way.'

'Well, what is?' Helmi's anger shifted easily from person to person. 'Spirits and ghosts?'

'No,' Mother said firmly. 'It can't be that. We must think rationally. Ursula says she saw something she thought was Spear under the ice. If she says that, then it must be true.' She looked directly at me. 'Clearly, it wasn't him. Ursula had been drinking, she had just been jilted and seen the corpses of two men brutally killed. We were all in a state of high emotion. You saw how she was. She was almost delirious. It was dark. He was deep below the ice. Whatever she saw, it wasn't Spear but she was convinced it was. How?'

'It's twins!' Aunt Charlotte announced.

Mother sighed. 'It's never twins, foolish woman.'

'I'm under pressure! There are a lot of knives.'

Mother pinched the skin between her eyebrows. 'Think!'

'A hallucination?'

'Possibly.'

'A reflection?' Aunt Charlotte offered.

'Of what?' Mother shook her head. 'A ghost?' She looked at me and raised an eyebrow.

Matthias nodded. 'The water spirits.'

'No, no, no. It was real,' I insisted. 'I saw him. He looked at me with his eye.'

'I thought you said he was dead?' Helmi sneered. 'Very odd thing to say that he *looked at you*. If he was dead, he wouldn't have been able to see anything.'

Aunt Charlotte reached out to me. 'It can't have been, dear. Look. He's *here*.' She paused, considering. 'It was his idea to come out here, wasn't it?'

I couldn't tell if that was a question or a statement.

Helmi took another step towards us with the knife held out.

I thrust my hand forward, the dim light catching on the blade. My hand was shaking wildly now, my thoughts flailing. I looked back behind me just to make sure that Spear was really here and not still wedged in that icy tomb. I saw that face again, so pathetic and weak, twisted beneath the ice. It had been so dark. But then it never seemed to be light here.

Helmi fixed her eyes on me. 'Maybe it's not the Bonnie and Clyde scenario. Maybe it's just Clyde.' She waited for me to understand and then the smile spread across her face. 'Maybe he wanted *you* to think he is dead, no?'

I saw both Mother and Aunt Charlotte look round at where Spear was lying.

'And he drugged himself and hung himself up there?' I raised an eyebrow.

Helmi had a cruel playfulness about her. 'Who said he did it in that order?'

'Oooh, I like it!' Aunt Charlotte's eyes sparkled.

'Aunt Charlotte! Whose side are you on?'

'At this moment in time, dear, I'm so confused I wouldn't even be able to make out where the sides were, let alone choose one.'

Mother sighed. 'I think this would work a lot better if everyone lowered their knives. It's not very conducive to thinking to find yourself in the middle of *The Good, the Bad and the Ugly*.'

'Which one am I?' Aunt Charlotte asked.

'There's no Stupid, so none of them.'

Matthias started to lower his blade. 'The old woman is right.'

Mother made an astonished noise.

'This will not be solved by any more bloodshed. Come, Helmi. Put down the knife.' Matthias looked at Helmi in a way I hadn't seen him look at her before. The story of their elopement started to seem more possible. 'Please, Helmi.'

She paused, considering each of us.

'Ursula?' Aunt Charlotte focused on the knife.

I looked at Mother and then back at Spear. He was so vulnerable, lying there on the floor with nothing to protect him but me. I'd had so many doubts about all of this, but one constant from the beginning had been that I wanted to spend as many of those fifteen thousand six hundred and eighty-five days with him. The thought of sacrificing any of those was unbearable.

When I looked at Helmi, she had started to lower her knife. I was the only one with a weapon held up.

'Ursula . . .' Mother was waiting.

I lowered the knife slowly but I was still ready to use it.

'We need to *think* if we're going to get out of this alive. We must circle back to the beginning, before all this ice and blood. Before any of this,' Mother continued. 'We need to take it apart piece by piece.'

CHAPTER TWENTY-NINE: ANGEL DESTROYER

'This is going to take a while.' Aunt Charlotte pulled out a small bottle from her sporran. 'Bit of the old *pontikka* always helps.' She winked at Helmi and then Matthias before swigging a mouthful. She passed it to me. 'Hooch.'

I took it and drank, then hesitantly held it out to Helmi. She looked at me distrustfully before slowly taking it. Just as she was about to drink, I said, 'It's not poisoned, don't worry.'

Her face darkened. She drank without taking her eyes off me.

Matthias was deep in thought. 'Is there anybody you can think of who might want to harm you. Perhaps even kill you?'

I looked around us. 'Where do you want to start?'

He frowned. 'It is possible though, is it not, from what I understand of you people, that a stranger also might know of you and have . . .' He paused, almost afraid to let the words out. 'Followed you out here?'

I nodded slowly.

'Maybe you should start at the beginning. Go back to when this all began for you.'

Mother went first. 'Spear proposed to Ursula.'

I remembered that dream. It seemed so long ago.

'Then we started the planning.'

'You did!' Aunt Charlotte took back the bottle from Helmi. 'God, bits of fabric, visiting venues, phoning churches, announcements, dress shops, flowers, cake tasting, wine tasting.' She paused. 'Actually, that last one wasn't too bad.'

My thoughts ran through all those weeks spent in preparation, most of which didn't seem to involve or require me in any way. I became fairly irrelevant to the process. It was public property from the very first moment we told everyone. They all came out of the woodwork, professing to know one of us, wanting an invite, telling us how our 'work' had changed their lives. That had been the moment when it all started to change.

Yes. I paused. That had been the moment it started to change. 'Mother—' I began, my thoughts turning — 'when did you put the announcement in *The Times*?'

'As soon as you told me. I always like to strike while the iron's hot. Can't miss an opportunity like that.'

'You made an announcement?' Matthias was perplexed. 'You . . . people?'

Mother shrugged but I could see the doubt forming.

'Well,' he prompted. 'Did anything odd happen after that? Anything at all. Anything out of the ordinary?'

Aunt Charlotte sighed. 'There's always something odd happening.' She took another drink.

I thought back. I'd seen a few weird tweets round that time, not much out of the ordinary though. As the so-called Queen of Death, you can expect to receive a few odd messages and see some strange articles. But there was one in particular that had caught my attention at the time. I'd not given it much thought afterwards. There'd been plenty of other things to think about, not least of all heading off mother-of-the-bride-zilla before she embarked on her scheme to approach Westminster Abbey.

No, this had been a direct message to Mother's account. I'd long since turned off the ability for anyone to message me, but Mother loves the attention. She said it boosted traffic to her podcast and blog, *Death Smarts*, and afforded her the opportunity to engage directly with her fans. She doesn't mind the intrusive, the macabre, the ghoulish or the insane so long as she gets traction. But this message she'd left up on her screen was disturbing enough for me to sit down and pay attention to it. It came from the account with the handle @ Angel_destroyer.

We'd known a few Angels over the years and none of them had enjoyed pretty deaths. They'd all been poisoned, some even with mushrooms that bore the name Destroying Angel. Seeing that account name sent a chill through me, as if a dead voice was calling in from the past.

I thought of Tapio, poisoned with the dried flowers that had been in my wedding bouquet. Perhaps I was just gathering everything and grasping at coincidence.

But then Spear had also led the expedition where another man named Angel had been poisoned. Was that just chance?

Whether it was accident or design, when that account name came up, @Angel_destroyer, and I read the message they had left for Mother, I was in a cold shock. *You take my life. Now there will be death.*

It was more of a threat than most of the tweets and DMs, and I told Mother so.

She'd brushed it aside like she always did. 'If you think *that's* a threat, you should see some of the others.' That's the problem with being a *controversial figure*, as Mother describes herself — you never know which of the threats will prove to be the important one.

That account had sent a few messages before, but this one had a bizarrely personal tone, as though it was referring to something very specific. I always knew our past would come back, and now I was increasingly convinced it was here with a vengeance. If only Mother could have kept the wedding private and quiet as Spear and I had both wanted.

'Mother, do you remember that message?'

She looked at me in confusion. 'I get a lot of messages.'

175

'The threatening one.'

'Again, I get a lot of threatening messages.'

Helmi gave an empty laugh. 'Why doesn't that surprise me?'

'I write about death and true crime. It's an occupational hazard. Some people don't like it. Some people were affected by it.'

'What do you mean, Mother?'

She knitted her eyebrows together. 'Just what I said. We've been involved in a lot of murder cases. It affects a lot of lives. Tears some people apart. I'm still in touch with lots of the people we've met, and their relatives.'

'What?' I stared, seeing yet another new light on her. 'Are you insane?'

She drew her head back and made an incredulous face. 'This from the girl who is infamous for her crazy times? You're very popular with the more *fringe element* of our fans.'

I shook my head. 'Why have you never told me about any of this?'

'You know I run the blog. It's very popular. Who did you think it was popular with? Nuns?' She paused. 'Actually, we have got a couple of those following us.'

'*Us*? This is you! You've announced our private, secret wedding to a bunch of people who like reading about death and murder. It could be any one of these lunatics.' I looked around the group.

'So . . .' Aunt Charlotte trailed out the word. 'The unknown, mad killer theory moves into the lead. It could very easily be someone out there, watching us right now, picking us off one by one. That's what we're saying. Right?'

A lull descended. The vague wind tested the windows. I looked over and saw the night staring in at us. Faces formed in the mist. If I closed my eyes, the slow, steady patter of snow could easily have been tiny fingers tapping on the glass.

'Wait.' Matthias was the first to speak. 'You put an announcement in a *national newspaper* and details on your blog? So it is very possible it is someone who knew you and does not like you? Someone from your past perhaps. An ex-friend, or lover, or relative? Is there anyone—'

Aunt Charlotte clicked her fingers. 'Spear was married before. Remember?'

'It hadn't slipped my mind, Aunt Charlotte.' I sighed.

'She was murdered.'

'Yes, but they also tried to kill Spear, if you recall.'

Helmi and Matthias were looking utterly dumbfounded by the continual revelations. It must have seemed to them that everyone we ever came into contact with died a horrible death.

'Perhaps it's someone trying to *frame* Spear. Revenge, you know. And Ursula too.' Aunt Charlotte thought for a moment. 'Or perhaps it is just someone who likes murdering people.'

Matthias shook his head. 'Mr Spear was brought out here on the *ahkio* from the cabins. The ski tracks come from the cabins. A pair of skis is missing now. They've been using lodge skis. They've not skied here. They *were* here.'

My mind was a random mess of ski tracks. Aunt Charlotte looked utterly confused.

Mother tried to straighten out the tracks. 'So far we have scenario number one, let's call it the Unknown Killer theory.'

'Comforting,' Aunt Charlotte nodded.

'Someone, perhaps spurred on by our past, perhaps linked in some way to that, has decided to come out here to our wedding—'

'My wedding,' I corrected.

'And kill some people — perhaps framing Spear and Ursula, but that seems unlikely. As Matthias says, the missing skis and tracks clearly point to it being somebody already at the lodge.

'Scenario number two is the Bonnie and Clyde theory, namely that Ursula and Spear cooked all this up to rid themselves of someone who knew about Spear's past and people who saw him here before when he visited.'

I looked at Mother open-mouthed. 'Do you need to make it sound so plausible, Mother?'

'I'm just going through the options, darling, as an impartial observer.'

I was aghast. 'How the hell are you impartial if I'm a killer? I am your daughter.'

She considered this for a moment. 'Then there's the more attractive Clyde scenario, where Bonnie—'

'That's you, Ursula,' Aunt Charlotte interjected.

I widened my eyes. 'Yes, I was following. Thank you.'

Mother cleared her throat aggressively. 'If I may continue! The Clyde scenario, as I was saying, involves Bonnie being duped into thinking he is dead so he can do a runner.'

I watched Mother intently, hoping for some additional comment along the lines of, 'But that would never happen, of course.' She remained silent.

'*Mother*!' I glared. 'I don't think he would really need to go to such elaborate lengths. He could just have said, "I don't want to do this, I don't want to get married," rather than resorting to killing two people and faking his own death. He could even perhaps have not proposed in the first place.'

I stepped towards Spear and crouched down. His eyelids were flickering as if something was playing out behind them. But what? What had he seen? Had he known his attacker or was he drugged and brought here? But why would someone do that? If it was a revenge attack, surely they would have killed him. They were obviously not afraid to take lives, and in a brutal fashion. I held his hand. Was it my imagination that he gripped a little tighter? He was in there somewhere, hidden behind a wall of drugs, fighting to get out.

I turned to the others. 'We need to get away from here. Whoever that was we saw leaving is going to come back, and they take no prisoners.'

'Well, they do actually, Ursula.' Aunt Charlotte's voice was tentative. 'They clearly do. They've drugged him and strung him up like the hare outside.'

My thoughts went to that pathetic creature with its guts hanging out. Was that what they'd had planned for Spear? A long, vile death out here in the middle of nowhere. I bent to kiss him and felt him breathe out. He smelled different. Strangely toxic.

I remembered those words he'd used the previous night, the eve of our wedding day. The last time I saw him. He'd said *everything just tastes foul tonight*. He'd been so overwhelmingly tired. I'd seen it as part of this change in his behaviour, but it was obvious now. He'd been drugged already by that point. How long had he been out here alone in this hut? He could have frozen to death. But then I looked at the hearth, stoked with some wood. Not a lot, but enough to keep it warm in here. They were keeping him alive. Drugged but alive. This was becoming more unsettling by the second. Whoever it was had gone out, but they were certainly coming back. And probably very soon.

'I think we should go.' I was working hard to stay calm.

Mother watched me closely. 'OK.'

'Wait a minute,' Helmi interrupted. 'I'm not going anywhere with a bunch of killers.'

'But you're happy to sit in an abandoned hut with us.' Aunt Charlotte was right.

The cabin walls groaned again. The weather was closing in. I checked out of the windows. The woods were watching and whatever they were harbouring was coming back, particularly if they'd gone to the lodge and found we'd all gone. The tracks out here had come from the cabins originally. How long would it take to circle back? Not long. Twenty minutes maximum. We didn't have much time left.

Time had run out for someone. The next sound we heard was screaming from outside. The darkness was lit with a desperate cry for help. The door slammed back. A sudden thud followed. I could half see a body of some sort, gasping and spent, falling to the floor.

A wave of freezing air circled the room.

Helmi was nearest the door. With eyes wide and the knife held up again, she turned and began to move towards the little entrance area.

Whatever had come through that door wasn't moving anymore.

CHAPTER THIRTY: ANOTHER DEATH

Matthias strode through the room, the timbers vibrating beneath his feet. I stayed where I was, gripping Spear's hand tight, feeling him breathe softly into my side.

Aunt Charlotte and Mother started to move.

'Wait! You don't know what it is.' I felt every muscle tighten, holding me in.

Mother locked eyes with me. '*What* it is? Don't be ridiculous, Ursula, there are no *ghosts* out here. *It* is human.'

Aunt Charlotte looked between us. 'But even if it is, we don't know whether it's a good one or not.'

'Oh my God!' Helmi shouted back to us. 'Come quickly. I need help.'

Mother and Aunt Charlotte ran for the door. I looked down at Spear. There was no way I was moving from his side.

Their voices came in broken snapshots. Hurried. Panicked.

'Get the skis off.'

'. . . alive?'

'Barely.'

'She's freezing.'

'Bleeding heavily.'

The door was slammed shut, muffling out the sound of the wind. There was a dragging noise, and I could see their bodies moving through the light.

Aunt Charlotte was first to back into the room, her frame obscuring any view of what was happening. 'Gently!' she cautioned. She was carrying something. As they edged into the room after her, I could see they were carrying a person. A real person, if they were in fact still alive. They all shuffled awkwardly into the room in a broken line, too many people making it more difficult to manoeuvre the limp body. Mother edged round the side and Matthias came in last, taking the majority of the weight, his arms under the shoulders of the body. The head was resting into him, lolling to the side. I could only see who it was as they swung round into the room. The battered, bleeding face didn't move.

It was Angela. Or what was left of her. Thick blood ran down the side of her head. A deep cut was visible on her cheek. One eye was almost closed over with a livid, swollen bruise.

'Angela,' I breathed. I let go of Spear and ran over. 'Angela!' I looked at Mother and then Aunt Charlotte as she lowered the woman's feet to the ground. 'Is she alive?'

Mother gave a single unconvincing nod. There was definitely a doubt over how long that would remain the case. 'Looks like they've come for the mother as well.'

I hadn't even thought about that. But now she'd said it out loud, it seemed obvious. If they could come for the son, they could definitely come for the mother. That was a distinct possibility.

'We shouldn't have left her alone!' I cried.

'We didn't,' Mother said.

I glanced at Helmi. We'd left Angela with Aino, Helmi's mother. The grief-stricken widow who'd been so quick to shower us all with blame.

Matthias set Angela's head down gently before quickly taking off his own scarf and rolling it into a makeshift pillow. He lifted her head slightly and wedged it underneath. Angela made a thick, rasping noise as if her throat was filled with blood. One eye struggled open. The injured one remained sealed over.

'Ursula,' she wheezed. 'Is that you?'

'Angela, I'm here!' I fell to the floor beside her and put my hand to her face. It was covered in blood. 'What happened?'

'It came . . .' She coughed violently, gasping for breath. 'It came while I was asleep. I thought . . . I thought I was dreaming. I couldn't see it properly. So dark . . . It struck me. Again and again. Cut me. It was enormous. Frightening.' Her voice had dissolved into nothing more than a whisper. 'It was a great . . . a huge *monster*.' She faded and her eye sagged. Her head fell to the side. A tear traced a single line through the blood. 'It killed her. It savaged her. Like a beast.' Her eye struggled open again and found Helmi. 'I'm so sorry. I'm so . . . She is dead. Aino is dead.'

There was an instant unplugged look to Helmi. She drew in a great chestful of air as if she was drowning in our silence and angled her face to the ceiling. The noise that followed was raw, stripping her throat until her voice cracked and failed. Her mouth stretched in anguish until her lips were nothing more than white lines, a thread of spit joining them. She scrunched her eyes tight as if she wanted them to disappear into her head. The knife fell to the floor and she clenched her hands into small fists, balling them into her scalp, crushing her head.

She hurled out words we couldn't understand. Matthias dropped his knife and grabbed her. He pulled her towards him, burying her screams into his chest. He held her so tight, as though he was trying to absorb all her pain.

Helmi pulled free from him and paused, her face torn. She was shaking her head in defiant denial.

'No. This is not true. Not both of them. No.' She ran from the room, through the small entrance way and slammed the door open. The night air entered again in a swift, icy strike. She paused for a moment and looked into the darkness. Then ran. Out past the reindeers and sleigh, into the trees beyond. Matthias followed her quickly, calling her name repeatedly.

Angela groaned and gripped her hand to her chest. She tried to open her one good eye but it remained partially closed, only a slim line of white visible. It flickered shut and she let out a long breath.

I looked at Mother quickly. She held her fingers to Angela's neck and paused.

'She's alive,' Mother whispered. 'Just. We need to get her medical attention, and quick.'

'Angela, please hang on.' I gripped her hand. 'Spear's alive! He's alive. Please hang on.'

She didn't respond. There was nothing. Not even a vague movement. She was so frail. So beaten.

'Dear God.' Aunt Charlotte was bewildered. She looked at me and Mother. 'We've got to get away from here. It's coming.'

Mother was letting the anger take over. 'What do you mean *it*? Get a grip. It's a man. A human. Maybe more than one. There are no monsters. She's delirious. They came out of the darkness and attacked her. She was asleep. We have to keep our heads.'

'She used the word "monster", Pandora. I heard her.' Aunt Charlotte was genuinely afraid. 'It could be some . . . some . . . animal. Something that . . .'

'What? Armed itself with a knife? Had some reason to attack two women in a lodge? Don't be so ridiculous, Charlotte. It's definitely not a berserk animal.'

The distant screams of Helmi resounded through the darkness, trailing further away. I looked out of the window. A blanket of icy mist had descended so fast that it had swallowed the world entirely. This was a place where, right then, in that moment, even monsters seemed possible.

'I'm scared,' I breathed.

Aunt Charlotte tried to steady herself. 'We all are. But that won't help us now. We can talk about that afterwards. For now, we need to get Angela and Spear in those sleighs and ride out of here like Bad Santas.'

I nodded.

'And where the hell is Bridget?' Mother held up her arms in frustration. 'She can't still be sick. Go and check on her, Charlotte.'

'What? Why me?'

'Why not? Just do it. You were her sleigh partner. You let her eat all that filth.'

'Sleigh partner? That's not a thing. I'm not her keeper.'

Mother folded her arms. 'Sitting in a reindeer sleigh with someone brings some responsibility. Now, you need to go and see if she's dead too.' Mother had a way of making the horrific seem commonplace.

Aunt Charlotte paused, before abandoning any further argument and stomping out of the room. The door was still open and she left it that way.

CHAPTER THIRTY-ONE:
BRIDGET, MISSING IN ACTION

'Ursula.' Mother stared at me intently. 'We've got to try and move them.'

I looked at Angela, bloodied and broken. I turned to Spear, still unconscious. What had I brought them to? How had it ever been a good idea for us to come to this wilderness? Spear had wanted to come and may well have had his reasons — though what those were was still unclear. But I could have said no. I'd embraced it with open arms. I'd run so quickly to the idea of isolation and escape, but all it had brought was the inevitable danger and catastrophe. I brought it with me. I'd put these people I loved in harm's way. I had to fix this. By running away? It seemed like the best idea, but wouldn't it, whatever *it* was, just keep hunting us until we were all dead? It would never stop. But then what was the alternative? Were we really going to trek out there in the freezing cold, leaving all of us utterly exposed? At least here we could defend ourselves. We would be warm and have some form of base to be holed up in. Out there in the bleak, dead lands, among the snow and darkness, we stood little chance of survival from attack. I had to keep them safe. And right then I decided there was only one way of doing that. Find the killer.

'We need to stay here.' I kept my voice flat, unemotional.

The remark bounced off Mother as if I hadn't even spoken. She was bending down, checking on Angela, slipping her hands under her arms and testing her weight.

'We can drag them out to the sleighs,' she murmured, as if she was planning this out to herself.

'I said we need to stay here.'

Mother's face just closed. 'I heard you. Lack of response is not an invitation to repeat your idiocy. Sometimes when you say insane things I just have to ignore them.' She carried on shifting Angela's weight around in her hands.

'We can't go out there into the freezing night with no protection and two people who are barely alive. We'll be sitting ducks for whatever is hunting us.'

Mother dropped Angela to the ground. 'Stop saying that. It's not a *whatever*. I've told you, there are no ghosts, ghouls, monsters or trolls out there. There is a person. A murderer. Someone who left your intended here dangling from a beam and drugged him so they could perform whatever last rites they'd got planned for him. Do you seriously want to stay here and wait for them to come back and finish the job? We have to get out of here.'

'No, Mother.' That was twice in one evening I'd managed to say that. It was becoming a little easier every time.

'Don't be so ridiculous, Ursula.'

'She's got a point.' Aunt Charlotte had reappeared at the door. A freezing ribbon of night air ran through the room. She was alone. 'We can't leave without Bridget.'

Mother was growing exasperated. 'What do you mean? Where the hell has she gone now?'

'I can't find her.'

'What do you mean, you can't find her? She's always there, wherever you turn. She never just disappears, however much I've wished for it.' Mother threw up her hands as if we'd just lost a set of keys.

A sudden image came to me of Bridget standing in our kitchen, dangling the keys to our house that she'd had cut without asking anyone.

Aunt Charlotte stamped the snow off her feet. 'Well, she's disappeared this time and we can't go anywhere without her.'

Mother left too long a silence there for it to be acceptable. I knew a little idea of us sleighing away with Bridget's empty face watching us was creeping into Mother's head.

'No, we can't,' I added, just for Mother's benefit.

Mother's face fell and she shrugged. 'Something like this was bound to happen when we keep getting into these *situations*.'

'Pandora!' Aunt Charlotte scolded.

'I'm just saying, you can't expect the Smart Women to go on for ever without some collateral damage.'

Aunt Charlotte's eyes glazed over. 'You may have a point. Remember poor Mirabelle.'

As soon as the name was out, she knew it shouldn't have been. Mother was rigid. She had suffered the loss most of all. The thought of losing another one of us was too devastating to contemplate, but increasingly a possibility.

Mother's eyes refocused. She sniffed. 'Bridget's not a Smart.'

Aunt Charlotte frowned. 'Really, Pandora. I . . .'

'OK. OK. Right,' Mother said in frustration. 'We'll bloody well stay to die! But we'd better batten down the hatches before Bigfoot arrives then, hadn't we?'

Aunt Charlotte looked blank.

'I mean, shut the bloody door, Charlotte. For Christ's sake, we'll freeze to death before any *monster* arrives.'

Aunt Charlotte searched the night again, before slowly closing the door over with a defeated look. 'We have to find Bridget. She could be in danger.'

'And she could be dead.' Mother isn't one for shying away from the obvious. 'Right now, we have to think about the living and the barely living. We have to keep them safe. That has to be our priority.'

There were some old wooden chairs by the side of the room, human sized, so presumably the elves hadn't been in habitation for a while. We gathered them together and settled like a small council, just separate from where Spear and Angela were lying. We spoke in conspiratorial, hushed voices.

'It still makes no sense,' Aunt Charlotte began.

'None of it makes any sense!' Mother remained indignant. 'Why we're staying here, waiting for the inevitable slaughter to begin, *makes no sense*.'

Aunt Charlotte looked troubled, as if too many thoughts were causing her genuine pain. 'I just keep coming back to the same question. How can a man go under the ice, ice that was formed weeks ago, that is a metre thick, and then miraculously get out?'

I looked over at Spear just to reassure myself he really was there and not some spirit of my imagination.

'What does that matter now?' Mother's voice was sharp. 'The killer is still out there!'

CHAPTER THIRTY-TWO: THE ILLUSIONIST

'No, Pandora.' Aunt Charlotte was ponderous but the words still startled Mother. We were all getting far too used to using them now. 'I think it *does* matter how the trick was performed. I think that will lead us to our performer, as it were.'

'What the hell are you talking about, Charlotte? This is not some staged event. This is life and death.'

Mother had hit on something, I was sure of it. 'Staged event,' I repeated.

'Oh, you're just as ridiculous as your aunt. I don't know why I've let myself get caught up in all this nonsense again.'

'It'll definitely be popular on your blog.' I knew how to push Mother's buttons. 'They'll lap up all these murders.'

'And with a locked lake mystery at the icy heart of it,' Aunt Charlotte added. 'Just think, if we could solve that, we'd be universally applauded.' Aunt Charlotte wasn't bad at the button-pushing, either. 'Everyone will be hooked on *Death Smarts* if we can crack the ice on this one!'

A new, shrewd look took up residence on Mother's face. 'I suppose it could be good, if it's written in the correct way, of course.'

'Oh, of course, Mother. That goes without saying. In your capable hands . . .'

'Love, sex, blood, betrayal . . .'

'What the—'

'It sells! No one's interested in all that figuring-it-out nonsense. They just want a sea of blood with you and Spear right at the centre in a passionate embrace.'

'Jesus, Mother.'

'I just can't understand *why*,' Aunt Charlotte mused. 'Why put him under the ice and then take him out?'

Aunt Charlotte's forensic analysis was bringing back all those images, playing in a nightmarish reel, again and again.

'Why resurrect a dead man?' she continued.

The phrase ran cold through my veins.

I pictured myself again, sprawled across the ice above him. Calling his name.

I said it again now. 'Spear.'

In a drug-addled voice, he murmured my name in response.

But I was far away, out there now, drifting onto the lake, its glassy surface glinting with the phosphorous lights from above. I stared down into that darkness again. The ghost-grey face looked up at me with the illusion of life, frozen deep beneath the water, the skin contracted into deep ridges from the pressure of the ice, his bones sinking back into the flesh. Crystals had colonised his face as if a disease was spreading over his skin. His body was rolled in tight against the cold. My hands beat on the unforgiving surface. It seemed as if he was disappearing beneath the layers of ice, drifting down into the grime. I could barely see him. I called his name again, and the heavens lit with another intense charge of lurid green. Colours stained the white landscape, the snow-covered trees momentarily tinged in vibrant shades of spring, the lake's surface glowing with the reflected light. His face was illuminated again, casting him in a pool of that vague, eerie stage light. He looked up at me from the other side of the glass. I heard my own voice, the hysteria rising, my hands flat on the ice as if they could sink through to him, the skin tinted a sickly green by the lights.

I glanced over at Spear, lying on the floor of the hut. His skin now ash grey, that vague malaise Mother often had after too many zolpidem. But he was alive. He was real. I had to keep repeating that. I clasped my hands together as if in silent prayer and felt the ring dig into my fingers. I looked down at my hands. The opal was night blue in the barely lit room, the amber tinge of the firelight did little to colour its darkness.

I saw myself again, out there on the lake, the unearthly lights had sent fractures of green light through the dark. Another acid seam lit the sky as my hand struck the ice. I looked down again into that face in the frozen tomb, partially illuminated in the darkness below the ice, lit by the Northern Lights.

'The light,' I said, my voice strangely absent. 'The light changes things here.'

'What now, Ursula?' Mother had an impatient edge to her voice.

'Let her speak, Pandora.' Aunt Charlotte leaned forward and put her hand on my leg. 'Go on, Ursula. The light.'

I refocused on her face. Then looked at Mother, keeping my voice steady. 'The light here, the Northern Lights, they change everything. Nothing looks how it should. It's a new lens.'

'Good God, now is not the time for your poetic musings. We are being hunted. Save the angst for back home, *if* we survive.' Mother leaned back.

'He wasn't there at all. It was the lights.'

'What the hell do you mean, he wasn't there? Are you saying the lights created some ghostly image of him under the ice, because that, Ursula Smart, will finally get you sectioned this time.'

'Thank you, Mother.' I paused to think. Had he really been there? What had I seen? 'It was the lights that made him—'

'Now I've heard everything!' Helmi had reappeared at the door with her head tilted and a look of hatred on her face. 'So the Northern Lights killed my father, did they? Reached out and poisoned him. Shot the crossbow from your hand into Onni's neck? Then they beat my poor mother to death.' Her voice failed. She held her hands to her face.

Matthias was behind her and pulled her round into him. 'There are spirits in the lights. They are very powerful.'

'No,' I gasped. 'Please, you don't understand. It was an illusion.'

Helmi spun round viciously. 'It's no illusion that they are dead!' She pushed her whole face forward, her mouth an angry gash.

'Please, I—'

'The lights create things in the mind,' Matthias continued. 'They are powerful magic. It could very easily have all been an illusion, as you say. She may not be lying, Helmi.'

Helmi shook free from him, her eyes frantically searching the room for something.

'No, I saw him,' I insisted.

Mother made a frustrated sound.

'So now you *did* see the man dead under a metre of ice,' Helmi shouted. 'The man who is very much alive and in this room.' Matthias was now actively restraining her.

'No.' My voice was bland. Distracted.

I saw Mother clench her jaw so hard I thought it might shatter.

'She is a liar!' Helmi tried to wrench her arm free from Matthias. 'And a killer.'

'How could she have killed Aino?' Aunt Charlotte cut in. 'She was here, with us, with *you* when she was murdered. See sense, girl.' It wasn't exactly the most compassionate statement to make to a grieving daughter but it did momentarily silence Helmi.

'I saw him in that green light,' I continued, my voice calm. 'He was in the water, under the ice. Surrounded by darkness. I could see him as the lights passed over.'

Both Mother and Aunt Charlotte were looking very sceptical now. Helmi made a dismissive noise.

But it was Matthias who was nodding along enthusiastically. 'The lights change the colour of everything. The snow, the ice, the trees. Everything. But—' he paused and frowned — 'I can't see why that is important. They do not *create* men under the ice.'

My head was a frenzy of sudden thoughts, snapshots of what I'd seen shifting in those whips of light travelling across the surface of the lake. I remembered every moment of the nightmare, him trapped beneath the ice, the dead grey stone of his eye staring out at me.

The dead grey stone of his eye.

'Grey?' I stared at them. I held out the ring. 'It changes colour in the light.' I looked around them all. 'He said . . . he told me, it was the colour of his eyes. I saw his eye under the ice. Only it wasn't his eye.'

'This makes no sense!' Helmi was barely being contained by Matthias now. 'First you saw him, then you didn't. You're just a liar. Or a fantasist, seeing dead men who aren't dead. Making ghosts who do not exist!'

I was beginning to doubt myself. 'Please,' I begged, 'just listen to me.' I looked at them all imploringly, desperately trying to make sense of it myself. 'The eye under the water was grey. His eyes aren't grey. But it kept appearing blue-green, just like his. It . . . it was the light reflecting on his eye, just as it was on the surface of the ring. *That* made it blue-green. It *wasn't* his eye.'

They looked at me as if I had lost my mind.

'So, he was under there but he had someone else's eye?' Aunt Charlotte had a tortured look on her face. 'But he's here! Alive and with his own eyes.' She paused. 'I assume he couldn't switch his eyes in and out.'

'He could not have got out either, miss,' Matthias added. 'The ice is almost a metre thick. There was no way in or out.'

'So . . .' I continued, 'if he can't get out and it isn't his eye, then . . .'

'Then?' Mother said.

'Then it wasn't him.' I looked around them all for a glimmer of understanding.

'But *you* told us it was,' Helmi insisted.

They fell into a disturbing silence. I started to see how I must look to them. I'd thought I'd seen the man I was about to marry dead, but I'd mistaken someone else for him. How could I have done that?

Aunt Charlotte's next comment didn't help much either. 'Was it a doll of him then, or something? I know some people do have such things made of their partners. Or celebrities. Richard Madeley—'

'Charlotte!' Mother shouted. 'Now is not the time.'

Matthias looked at her in confusion.

'No, Aunt Charlotte,' I said, 'it was a man, not anything made to look like him, I'm sure of that.'

'But you were sure it was your husband-to-be.' Helmi's aggression wasn't abating. 'How can we trust anything you say?'

I couldn't argue with that. I'd asked myself the same question. How could I have mistaken him for someone else? But I knew what I'd seen. There was a man under the ice and I'd been so certain it was Spear. His eye colour changing in the light had been part of the illusion, but it couldn't have been the only thing that fooled me.

I held out my hands to placate Helmi. It had no effect. 'Look, whoever was there had to have gone in the water before the ice formed. Do we all agree on that?'

'October,' Matthias confirmed. 'The ice starts to form in October.'

My thoughts started to rearrange.

'Which is when he came here before, according to the remains of the reservations book Charlotte found burned in the grate,' Mother clarified.

I went back in my mind to his face under the ice, all puckered and compressed, wedged in the dark hollow that had grown around his body over the weeks. His skin furrowed, as if the ice had drained him.

'That man came here in October,' Helmi fired. 'His name was in the reservations book, and someone tried to destroy it to hide the fact that he did.'

The ideas fell in a wave through my head. 'Yes, he did come here in October. His name was in the book.' I thought back to when we told Mother we were getting married. She'd needed to know his name. An unusual name for many reasons. 'It's an old Irish name,' I said in a flat voice. 'Breffni Spear did come here in October, and it wasn't the ice that aged him. It was time. That man, the man I was going to marry—' I pointed to Spear — 'was named Breffni Spear after his father.'

They were silent.

I thought of the photograph I'd seen so many times. The man who looked just like Spear. The man who would still have looked just like Spear, only aged, like the creased face I'd seen in those depths. It wasn't the water or the conditions that had made his face look so haggard and wrinkled. It was age. I tried to place the picture I remembered next to the dead face I'd seen.

Mother looked at me quizzically. 'But his father is dead.'

As I lined up the two images in my mind, the photograph I'd seen of Spear's father as a young man against Spear himself, there was one thing that didn't look the same. 'His father didn't have the same eyes as Spear.' I was sure of it. Spear said, when he gave me the ring, that it was his great-grandmother whose eyes were the same unusual colour as his, the same as the ring. No one else. I looked at Mother. 'That man who came here in October, who was called Breffni Spear, *is* under the ice. He looked just like Spear, but older.' I thought of that photograph again. 'He didn't have blue-green eyes. He had *grey* eyes.' I saw the grey stone of the dead man's eye. 'The man under the ice is Spear's father. I'm sure of it.'

CHAPTER THIRTY-THREE: THE DEATH OF
ANOTHER DEAD MAN

'No, that can't be right.' Aunt Charlotte frowned. 'Spear's father died before he was born.'

'Wait.' Matthias looked doubtful. 'So you are telling us the man was already dead when he went under the ice?'

I pictured that photograph so clearly. It was the man I'd seen under the ice. 'It's him. I'm certain.'

Helmi scoffed. 'Just like you were certain it was your boyfriend.'

'He looked just like him!' I appealed to them all. 'He was in the dark water, with a face just like Spear's and he even looked like he had his eye colour. What else would I have thought? That his dead dad had been dug up and shoved under the ice weeks ago? Of course I thought it was Spear. He was missing.'

We paused, the wind singing discordantly round the outside of the small hut. The thin wolf cry carried out from the trees again. It seemed nearer.

'It can't be him. His dad is nothing more than dust by now,' Mother said without a trace of emotion. 'He's long dead.'

Aunt Charlotte spoke as if she was afraid of the words. 'Well, he will be now, of course, if he's under all that ice.'

I tried to rearrange what we knew. 'In the beginning, when we realised Spear was missing, the idea was raised that he had disappeared, that he'd run away from all this, run away from his past, the people who knew him, his wedding . . . *me*, to start a new, unburdened life somewhere else. We now know he hadn't, of course, but it seemed like a possibility. But what if his father did do that all those years ago? What if he actually survived but no one knew and he went to live elsewhere, far away from all the responsibility. Start afresh? In a remote place? Like this.'

'Really?' Aunt Charlotte frowned.

'Why not? We thought it was a possibility for Spear when he went missing.' I tried not to linger on that thought too long. I took a moment to think. 'Mother, we thought your ill-judged announcement might bring out all the crazies.'

She tutted. 'There was nothing *ill-judged* about it. Everyone makes a wedding announcement in the newspapers.'

'But we're not everyone.' Aunt Charlotte sounded almost proud.

I stared, unwilling to let the idea settle. 'We thought it would bring out murderers and *crazies*. What it brought out was something even scarier. Something everyone fears at a wedding. Bridget even warned us that weddings bring these people out just as reliably as funerals.' I paused and looked around us all. 'Relatives.'

Mother drew her head back. 'Long-lost relatives, per-haps. But not *dead* ones.'

'Hmm.' Aunt Charlotte was pondering. 'I've been to some weddings where that might have been a possibility. Remember old Aunty J . . .'

'Quiet, Charlotte! How can anyone think?' Mother was definitely out of patience.

Helmi made a frustrated sound. 'I don't understand you people. You are saying someone has come back from the dead for this wedding but they came here in October instead? Why would they come here when there was no wedding then?'

My mind was so tangled, the broken pieces of ideas all mingling with one another until they made no sense. 'We need to look at it the other way around,' I said. One thought was leaking through from the back of my mind, a thought I was trying to push away it was so unthinkable, but it kept resurfacing. 'From the beginning, this has all felt too preordained, as if someone knew what to expect. As if they'd been here before. Think back. Why are we here?'

'Well, Spear liked the look of it and I said it was shit but you wouldn't listen.' Mother looked pleased with herself. 'No change there.'

'That's right,' I said. 'And when we arrived, Tapio greeted us. He was a little unseemly, too flirty, or so we *thought*. He also said he recognised *the name* Breffni Spear. He didn't say he recognised Spear. It was the name he knew. Tapio had been here in October, unlike his wife and daughter. Onni was here and he too started to voice his recognition. He said, "Well, hello again." Bridget instantly laughed at this, saying we'd come to the middle of nowhere and "you seem to know everyone". But that was the wrong thing to say.'

Mother sighed. 'Trust Bridget.' Somehow these words didn't sit well together.

I continued, thinking it through out loud. 'But Spear said nothing in response. He didn't make any acknowledgement that *he* knew Tapio.'

Helmi gave a mirthless little laugh. 'Probably thinking how best to get fistfuls of lily of the valley into my father's mouth! He even brought his own murder weapon with you in your wedding flowers.'

Something snagged in my head. A little thought began to unfurl, petal by petal. It was a dark idea but it made more sense than anything else so far. And I wasn't the only one having it.

'The flowers.' Aunt Charlotte, Mother and me stared at one another.

'She insisted on doing them.' Aunt Charlotte looked like she couldn't believe the words were coming out of her.

'Where exactly did you say Bridget has gone?' Mother sounded dubious.

We waited for the thought to percolate.

'I think we really do need to find Bridget now,' Aunt Charlotte added slowly.

'No. Wait!' I held up my hand. 'That's not what I'm saying at all. How can you be so quick to blame our friend?'

Mother looked incredulous. 'We're not. She's not our friend.'

I rolled my eyes. 'Of course she is. We've known her for years.'

'I've known the postman longer and he's a shit.'

'Mother!'

'What? He's always *losing* my fan mail.'

I'd been present for some of these conversations and the poor man had no idea what Mother was talking about.

Helmi and Matthias were still at the door. He was whispering soothing words into her ear and she was gently sobbing now, with intermittent outbursts. Angela and Spear were still unmoving on the floor, laid out with no ceremony or comfort. I couldn't see anything I could use to help either of them in the modest little hut. This had been abandoned for some time and was clearly only intended to be used temporarily. There were no more logs near the stove and the fire was dwindling. There was no evidence of any food or water. Perhaps that's what the killer had gone back to fetch from the lodge. They would, as Mother had pointed out, no doubt be back, but to go out trekking in the dark seemed like suicide. Was that our choice, suicide or murder?

I looked out of the grimy window. Snow spiralled in the air. The patter of flakes on the glass was constant and picking up pace. Bridget was out there somewhere. Alone. But the doubt was rising as to whether she was in danger or, in fact, she might well be something else entirely.

She'd been so keen to do the flowers and had started work immediately, cutting them and drying each little spray. Choice had been thin on the ground in Mother's garden, given that its sole use was for Bridget's various pets. Mother is not a natural horticulturalist, her primary objection being there is too much reliance on animal excrement, which is ironic given that it's now full of that courtesy of Bridget's menagerie. Bridget had done such a good job on the flowers though. They were genuinely beautiful and so heartfelt. I couldn't imagine that she'd carried them out here as a handy disguise for a murder weapon.

Mother and Aunt Charlotte started rising from their seats, ready to go out there and search again for Bridget, this time more warily. I hovered, half out of my seat, the floor creaking below me. The sound of another animal drifted from the woods. Helmi's gentle sobs were running under everything.

'The flowers.' I focused on the window and the snow sifting through the air.

Mother and Aunt Charlotte scrutinised me.

I didn't dare move. I couldn't even shift my eyes to look. In that moment, every cog turned and fit with pinpoint accuracy. I knew.

'Ursula?' Aunt Charlotte's forehead gathered in confusion.

'Someone *had* been here before. They knew too many things about the place. I was *supposed* to think the man I was about to marry was dead. But who would want me to think he was dead? Someone who didn't want me to ever go looking for him again.' I paused, unable to believe what was so very clear to me now.

I took a deep breath before I let out the words and opened the door to chaos.

Confusion spread over their faces as mine slowly gathered into realisation. 'They'd been here before. Tapio and Onni recognised Spear, all right. I even heard Tapio trying to blackmail Spear outside my window.'

'What?' Helmi shot. 'You're lying!'

'Oh yes, Tapio even used their name. He called this person that he recognised Spear. The other Spear who came here.'

'His supposedly dead father in October?' Aunt Charlotte frowned. 'But he wasn't here with us. He was under the ice by then if it was him.'

'No,' I said, disbelieving myself. 'The *other* Spear.' I paused. 'The third Spear.' I stared. 'Angela Spear.'

Slowly, we all turned to face her.

But we were too late.

CHAPTER THIRTY-FOUR: NO RED HERRINGS

Angela was standing over Spear, her swollen face contorted into a smile.

'Took you a while,' she rasped, her mouth a bloody slash where the wounds had opened slightly.

She was holding out a gun.

'And there was me thinking the Smart Women might never live up to their name.' She laughed, but it quickly fell away into a grimace from the obvious pain. With her free hand she wiped the blood from her eye. 'Put up a fight, your mother.' She nodded over at Helmi, who stood tear-streaked and open-mouthed.

'You . . .'

Matthias grabbed both Helmi's arms and said something in Finnish.

'No—' Angela laughed — 'I have the knives.' She'd understood whatever he'd said.

I looked around us and realised we'd all put down our weapons at some point and not thought to pick them up. Not thought that the danger wasn't out there in the darkness, but in here with us.

'Ursula . . .' Spear groaned, desperately trying to lift his eyelids.

The smile evaporated from Angela's face. 'You'll soon forget that name.'

I went to move forward but she waved the gun a little at me. 'You just stay there, lady. Thank goodness that sewer rat Onni was armed. I was fed up having to get creative with the murders. A good old gun is always best.'

I paused. 'I was right, wasn't I? You had been here before.'

She smiled.

I stared at her. 'You knew too much about the place. About everything.'

She laughed. 'I'm afraid I can't say the same about you.'

'There was something that wouldn't stop nagging me about that very first moment when we arrived here. I couldn't stop thinking about it. Something was out of joint. But it was the smallest thing. When Tapio handed out the keys, he already knew who *Mrs Spear* was.'

Angela nodded. 'Yes, that did become a bit more problematic than I'd imagined.'

'Then when he was asking after a *Mr* Spear, it wasn't because he was interested in whether you were attached. He was looking for the man you came here with before. He knew, didn't he? He recognised *you*.'

She shrugged. 'I was prepared for that but I didn't think they would make it quite so obvious to everyone else.'

'You made it obvious yourself,' I said.

She attempted to raise her eyebrows under the thick mess of congealed blood.

'Just in the little things. You knew which cabin your key was to. You walked off towards it before any of us knew which cabin was which.'

'Ahh, so you are slightly smarter than the others then.'

'What is going on here, Angela?' Mother looked bemused.

A thin laugh gurgled out of Angela's mouth. She was clearly in a lot of pain. She coughed, the blood making a ruckling sound in her throat.

'When Onni said "hello again", he wasn't talking to Spear. We all assumed he was because you'd manoeuvred us

203

to think that. But Spear was helping you with your bag. He was standing right next to *you*. Onni was saying "hello again" to you, Angela, not Spear.'

Spear groaned and tried to surface again but the drugs held him down. Angela gave him a little nudge with her foot.

I instinctively moved towards him, but she waved the gun at me. 'You can stay right there, little Miss Smart, otherwise it's you next. I think I've adequately illustrated to you that I am willing to kill anyone who gets in the way.'

'And it was *you* outside the window, wasn't it?' I was treading carefully, torn between flattering her and confirming to myself what I'd suspected. 'You are the devil who has always been there stalking us from the beginning.'

Angela nodded deeply, as if bowing to an appreciative audience.

I thought back again to the words I'd heard Tapio saying outside my window. '. . . *Spear, oh yes, I know you. I recognised you.*' I'd lost sight of the fact that there were two Spears on this trip. I'd let myself build a whole scenario around a snippet of conversation that I'd only partially heard. At the moment I'd cut in to their conversation, I'd heard the word 'Spear' but not what had gone before. It could very easily have been 'Mrs' or indeed 'Angela' that he'd said before. 'It was *Angela* Spear who was the person Tapio attempted to blackmail,' I said quietly. 'Wasn't it?'

My husband-to-be might well have already been drugged, perhaps even transported out here to this hut by then. But at that moment, I'd been so quick to assume he was the shady character Tapio knew more about and was attempting to blackmail. Tapio's greed had been his end and he'd not reckoned on the mild-mannered woman he was really talking to taking matters into her own bloody hands.

'Wait, it was you who killed my father and my mother?' Helmi sounded dazed, staring at Angela. Matthias was still gripping Helmi firmly by the arms. 'You . . . you killed them. You . . .' She was panting the words out, her breathing becoming more irregular. The tears were chasing down her face.

Angela merely shrugged. 'They were becoming too . . . unmanageable. I'd masked off the fact that Tapio and Onni recognised me. You fools hadn't realised. I only needed to stall for a little bit longer and we were away. But then Tapio got greedy. He had to be dealt with.'

Helmi let out a cry.

Angela looked surprised. 'Well, dear, you weren't very good at being a daughter, were you? Perhaps you should have thought about how much you loved them *before* they died.' She shook her head. 'You see, you children don't know what it is to be a mother. It is everything. *Everything.* And yet you give it so little respect. You save your outpourings of affection for after they have gone so all the world can see how much you profess to care. They had to die, I'm afraid.'

I took a step forward but she noticed and reminded me of the gun again. 'You're just the same, *Miss Smart*. You just see your mother as providing somewhere to live, food and vast quantities of booze.'

Mother cleared her throat. 'Perhaps we can talk about it. Motherhood.' Even with a gun held to her, this word seemed awkward in Mother's mouth.

Angela gave a simpering smile. 'Talk about motherhood with its number one enemy? Well, that could be interesting.'

'Oh.' Mother wasn't going to remain polite in the face of such unbridled criticism, even if a crazed woman covered in her own blood was threatening her life. 'So this little scheme of yours would be endorsed by Mumsnet, would it?'

No one spoke. No one dared to move, watching closely for Angela's reaction.

'Don't you question me!' Angela's voice shifted a gear. There was a rising tone of hysteria. '*He* started doing that. *He* would never have come out of the woodwork if it hadn't been for you and your stupid announcement. *Breffni Spear.* His father—' she looked down at her son — 'was a no-good waster of a man who dragged me on his ridiculous expeditions and ran off with his tail between his legs the minute I told him I was pregnant. He might as well have been dead. It was easier to tell my son that story.'

'You knew?' Aunt Charlotte said, aghast.

'Of course I knew! The only remarkable thing about that man was his name. Seeing it in your stupid announcement, Pandora, and all over social media . . . well, of course he saw it and he knew exactly who the Breffni Spear was who was getting married. He wanted to worm his way back into my son's life. Take a piece of him away that was mine. Just like your ridiculous daughter.'

Angela had the look of a storyteller who had reached the point where they were starting to relish the revelations and, most importantly, the audience's reaction. A cruel triumph spread across her mouth.

'Angela. Angel. Are you this @Angel_destroyer person?' Aunt Charlotte asked in confusion.

Angela laughed, shaking her head. 'I'm afraid not. Looks like there may be more than one person who hates you people.'

She coughed again. The ordeal had clearly taken its toll. Her face was badly injured but it didn't seem to concern her. It had provided the perfect smokescreen. None of us had thought the woman with all the injuries might actually have been in a fight . . . to the death. But the wounds didn't seem to bother her. The only thing that mattered was her son. All her emotions, all the pain, were very obviously entirely focused on the man she had drugged and strung up in an abandoned grain store.

'It had been a lifetime ago. Said he couldn't face the responsibility.' She looked down at Spear. 'His father left and agreed to never come back. And yet, when he chose to, he just thought he could come back into my life.' She used a darker voice now, one filled with consequences. 'When I heard that voice on the phone, it ran through my veins like poison. I'd not heard it for over thirty years, but I knew it from the first note. I was a young woman then, not drained of life. Not just the hanger-on in my son's life — the son I'd sacrificed my youth to.' She stared down at him, as if looking back into the past and seeing him there on the first day he'd come into her life. The first day she was alone as a mother.

One of the many things Mother resented about Dad dying when I was only thirteen was that she had to bring me up on her own. She always said she wasn't cut out for being a mother and a father. There were many times I could have shortened that sentence. But we'd stumbled through it and come out the other side with the workings of some sort of relationship. Not one the therapists approved of, but we'd survived. So far.

'His *father* said he was living out here in Finland under another name. He was proud of his *back-to-nature life*.' Angela gave a bitter laugh. 'Still, he'd seen the wedding announcement online. He used all sorts of meaningless words. He always did. Wanted to reconnect, form new links. He'd reassessed *his* life and felt he was now ready to be Breffni Spear again, ready to play a part in his son's life. Maybe they could even do some expeditions together. *Ready to play a part in his son's life*! His son—' she looked down and her face softened a little — 'His son is thirty-two years old! Where was he when that son was a tiny baby, screaming in the night and only me to answer? Every time he was sick, every birthday, school play, Christmas. Where was he?' She was almost shouting it out now as if it was a mantra. She looked around us all. 'Nowhere. That's where. *I* was his everything. There was no way I was going to let *that man* anywhere near us. I had to act and fast. So I went along with his little idea of meeting up.' Her eyes hardened.

'I suggested we meet here. It was isolated. I came out in October with no detailed plan, but I knew what had to be done.'

'Squirrels!' Aunt Charlotte announced.

Mother's face tightened in barely contained frustration. 'Not now, Charlotte!'

'No, Pandora. I will be heard. Squirrels are important.'

Mother's head fell into her hands.

'Look at the bloodied hare as well.' Aunt Charlotte searched our faces for some form of recognition. 'The squirrel we saw outside? They all change colour for winter. All the colours change here. When she—' Aunt Charlotte pointed at Angela in disgust — 'first described this place to us, she said we'd see red squirrels. They wouldn't put that in the winter excursion information. You wouldn't see red squirrels in winter. But you would in October, wouldn't you, Angela? When you'd been here!'

Angela gave her a little bow.

Aunt Charlotte narrowed her eyes and leaned forward. 'Red squirrels this time.' She dropped her voice to a whisper. '*Not* bloody herrings!'

She looked so pleased with herself I'd almost forgotten we were being held at gunpoint by a killer.

Angela looked momentarily bewildered, but a dark purpose soon spread through her eyes. She continued her story as if everything else had disappeared. 'I booked us a cabin by the lake. His father liked the idea of us *reconnecting*, as he so tactfully put it. It was easy enough. From the first moment I saw him, I was so repulsed that it just came naturally when the time was right. He was standing by the lake, preaching about life and meaningfulness.' She gave a little sharp jerk of her head. 'How ironic that his life ended right then. Ski shoe to the side of the head. That ridiculous look of surprise will stay with me for ever. It was all over very quickly and quietly. He just keeled over into the water. Down he went, a graceful plunge into oblivion.' She paused to admire her tale. 'I told that fool Tapio that he'd gone and left me. He didn't care. No one ever would. Breffni Spear, my husband, had died years ago.'

CHAPTER THIRTY-FIVE: A PLAN UNFOLDS

There was an unsettling silence, the wind keening through the gaps in the window. The loneliness of this place was all-consuming. We were completely at its mercy. I thought of Matthias telling us all about the ghosts and creatures that could spirit people away. '*People go missing out here,*' he'd warned. He was going to go further, tell us about something, an incident, saying, '*Only this autumn . . .*' but Angela had interrupted him then. No wonder. *She* was the reason the man had gone missing. But some man living alone under a false name would never be linked to her. She'd booked in with a man called Breffni Spear. Her own husband.

Spear groaned. Angela stared down at him, as if she was looking down into that lake again. 'It wasn't as deep as I'd imagined there at the edge. There was a very long, shallow shelf leading out.' She spoke in a neutral, detached voice, studying her son with a strange, dispassionate eye. 'He rested there in the murk and grime as peaceful as if he was just asleep, curled round on his side. He didn't look so vile any-more. He looked almost like he did when I first met him. When I loved him. He looked just like my son.' She looked at me narrowly. 'The next man I was about to lose.'

I didn't break from Angela's eyes. 'You're insane.'

She laughed. 'Maybe. Motherhood can do that to you. But I'd prevented my son from being stolen away by one man, and I was determined I wasn't ever going to lose him to some mad woman with her sideshow family.'

'Sideshow? Does she mean us?' Aunt Charlotte whispered.

'Just you,' Mother answered.

'Fate had shown me the way,' Angela continued, a sanctimonious tone creeping in now. 'It all opened out so beautifully to me in that moment. Yes, he looked just like my son. He always had. It had been hard for me to see my baby growing into the man who had abandoned us both. I'd told him his father was dead. He might as well have been. And now he was. All I had to do was use that to my advantage. Under all that dirt and weed, his face was so blurred out that it could easily pass for a younger man. It took only days to work it out. If I could lure everyone out here, into the darkness of winter, when he would be under the ice, I could create the illusion I needed. I just had to convince you.'

'But you couldn't know that you would.' Mother's voice was tentative. 'You couldn't know it would work.'

Angela raised an eyebrow. 'What murderer can? Taking a life is easy. It's just blood and guts, no different to an animal. Like that hare outside. The really messy stuff comes after that. There are a thousand ways it can go wrong. You have to trust to fate, manoeuvre the pieces into the right places. That's all you can do.' She paused, watching me. 'And you were so easy to deceive. You ran so quickly into the arms of catastrophe. Your obsession with death wasn't difficult to exploit. I even bought Spear the same coat his dead father had on. After I killed him, I just had to hope no one would discover his body for the next few weeks while the ice formed, but then Tapio had already told me they had no further bookings. He was closing the place up. So, I tethered the body down just far enough for it to be partially visible in the darkness. It looked so like my son, it was frightening. Brilliantly frightening.' She leered. 'And I hoped. That's all I had really. Hope.'

Helmi stifled her tears. There was hatred in her eyes. 'Which is more than you've left the rest of us with.'

Angela shrugged. Her cold nonchalance was so unnerving. The very real idea was developing that nothing was beyond her now. It was clear she was capable of doing anything in pursuit of her one goal.

'But it was Spear's idea to come here,' Aunt Charlotte said in confusion.

I shook my head, the truth dawning on me. 'No. No, that's not true, is it, Angela?'

She gave me a vicious smile.

I didn't break from her eyes. 'From the beginning, this has all been about the difference between what we were *told* and what was the truth, hasn't it, Angela?'

She smirked. 'Perhaps a little too late to realise that, but yes. It was a risk. It was *all* dependent on you *believing*. On the power of suggestion. But, like a child on Christmas Eve, you didn't disappoint. You believed it all.'

I looked to the others, unphased by her. 'Angela *told* us that she'd seen this place on Spear's computer, that he was keen on it. We just accepted that. When I asked Spear about it, I just said, "*Your mum saw this on the computer.*" She had, but not because Spear had been looking at it. We filled in the gaps she left for us. I never questioned it. None of us did. Because we *trusted* you.'

'Oh, yes, you're very trusting. Foolishly so. For instance, you easily believed that he would leave you.'

I looked down at Spear, so vulnerable at her feet. 'I just . . . he seemed so . . . distracted. I thought he was having doubts.'

She nodded. 'I'm afraid he'd started to suspect something wasn't right. He has a good radar for that. I was trying to act as normally as possible but luring a wedding party out to an isolated Arctic location so you can pass off the body of the groom's dead father as your son, well, you can imagine that took some planning.' She laughed again. 'Quite a high-wire act, I can tell you. I had to hold my nerve. So much could go wrong. I was trying to be as *normal* as possible but it wasn't the most natural situation, you understand.'

Aunt Charlotte sighed. 'I don't understand anything about this.'

'That's no surprise,' Mother said.

Angela ignored them. 'He'd started to ask questions and that was just getting worse when we arrived here. I had to act quickly. I drugged him with your zolpidem that night.' She nodded towards Mother, who managed to look irritated about the theft in spite of the fact that a killer was pointing a gun at her. 'In his prosecco.' She grinned. 'At your stupid *hen party*.'

Aunt Charlotte looked outraged.

Angela was suddenly contemplative. 'The drugs were so readily available! You know, that's the wonderful thing about travelling with the Smart Women. There's always a lot of self-medicating going on. You fill up the holes in your life with drugs, booze and—' she looked back to me — '*delusions*. If anybody was going to be fooled, it was you. All your therapy speak and musings on death. Your own mother has told the world about her mad, sad daughter.' She paused. 'And you *see* things, don't you?'

I felt my face flush.

'You're so *fragile*, so easy to convince that the worse thing imaginable has happened. All I had to do was set it all up and then lay it out in front of you. He'd disappeared. He'd *jilted* you. You were so ready to just soak it all up as if you'd been waiting for catastrophe. God, you *embraced* disaster. All *woe is me, everything goes wrong so why shouldn't this?* Her mouth turned cruel. 'You're pathetic. *You* were the reason it was going to work. You were the key element.'

Mother stepped forward. 'Now, wait a—'

'You can shut up, Pandora. The time to *care* about your daughter has passed.' Angela waved the gun at her again before refocusing on me.

'When I walked down that jetty, tempting you out to the lake where he was and you saw a man in the dark, beneath the ice, who looked like him and wore his clothes, well, you just leapt to believe that it was him. It was a beautiful moment to witness, as if you'd always believed it would end in tragedy. It was a self-fulfilling prophecy. You just couldn't allow yourself to be happy. Which was very useful to my scheme. All I had to do was gently guide you down that path and show you what you believed you'd see.'

I studied her for a moment with hard eyes, determined to give her no more satisfaction. 'Didn't quite work out how you'd imagined though, did it?'

CHAPTER THIRTY-SIX: A PLAN UNRAVELS

'It all started to get more complicated, didn't it?' I felt strangely calm. Her vicious words, designed to undermine and mock me, had provided the spur I needed. A stillness had settled over me. Spear wasn't dead. He hadn't abandoned me. That was all that mattered now. Everything was refocusing. I could see the end. I just had to concentrate on getting us all out alive. We were facing insanity. And that definitely *is* in my comfort zone. Ideas were starting to form. I felt a new surge of confidence. She might have the gun, but we had more control. We just had to use it.

I started in a firm, assertive voice. 'Being recognised was perhaps an occupational hazard of this particular endeavour. Although, like you said, it was definitely high risk, it was only two guys running this in the middle of nowhere. You could handle that. But then it started to get out of hand, didn't it? Perhaps your plan wasn't quite as wonderful as you thought.'

Angela attempted to narrow her eyes, but she flinched in pain. The raw skin was bulging and bloodied.

I sensed a gap in her armour. 'The odd comment was easy to ignore. But they were making it too obvious that they knew you and, more importantly, that there was another Mr Spear and he'd been here with you before. You'd thought it would be easy to dodge, mask it off, and you did, to start with. With *us*. But when Tapio took matters further and attempted to blackmail you, you had to act, didn't you? You hadn't foreseen that, had you?'

Angela shrugged nonchalantly. But she was rattled. 'Every endeavour has its obstacles. These things just have to be . . . dealt with and overcome.'

I heard Helmi take a sharp breath.

'Overcome. Hmm,' I mused. 'It was spiralling out of control, wasn't it? You had to act fast if the scheme wasn't going to derail. You'd already drugged your son and dragged him out on the *ahkio*, hadn't you?'

Angela gave a satisfied smile.

'You'd skied out here and then back again, hence there were no skis missing.'

'I was very careful,' Angela said, a hint of defensiveness creeping in now. 'I stayed inside the *ahkio* tracks.'

'Oh, there was no backing out when Tapio cornered you though, was there? You had to see it through, and if anyone attempted to stand in your way . . .'

'It was just one more person to kill.' There was a coldness in her voice that was disturbing.

She leaned her head to the side, contemplating her next move. But I'd hit my stride. And in my experience, one thing a killer doesn't like is having their story usurped. Or being stalled. But I knew time needed to slow down. I had to stretch things out if we were going to have a chance. 'Tapio was easy, wasn't he?'

I glanced over at Helmi, who had buried her head in Matthias's chest. The revelations were brutal for her, but if we were going to survive, this had to work.

I made my voice louder and clear. '*You* killed him so easily.'

Aunt Charlotte placed a hand on my arm. 'Ursula, I know you're excited, but try not to shout at the woman pointing a gun at us.'

Mother watched me for a moment, realisation creeping into her eyes. She suddenly exploded. 'Why shouldn't she? If *we are all going to die*, Angela might as well have her swansong. She's *gone insane and has a gun*!' She stressed those last words, almost shouting them into Aunt Charlotte's face.

'All right, all right.' Aunt Charlotte held out her hands. 'Let's just find some calm.'

'I'm not bloody calm, Charlotte.' Mother was still shouting. 'We are going to die and *soon*!'

Aunt Charlotte looked bewildered at this sudden display of hysteria.

Angela just laughed. 'Oh, you Smart Women. I have sat back and watched your toxic attempts to be a family. Your dysfunctional, needy relationships. You can't even die well together, let alone live in harmony. And you thought I'd let my only son marry into this horror show? There was no way I was going to let that happen.'

'Quite right, Angela.' I nodded. 'And you wouldn't let anything, or anyone, stand in your way, would you? The lily of the valley came from your garden.'

She grimaced. 'Tapio was such a disgusting pig of a man. Sitting there in his pants, drinking. Daring to try and black-mail *me*. I'd remembered the flowers were here.'

'Always such a keen gardener, you knew it was poisonous.'

She gave a contemptuous look. 'Of course I knew! It was easy to take a handful from your bouquet. How fitting,' she laughed. 'And then it was just as easy to flirt with him, drink with him and slip the dried flowers into his *pontikka*. When he was gasping and vomiting, I made sure I stuffed as many as I could down his filthy throat.'

Her face was so fierce with cruelty. There was a frighten-ing, crazed element to her now. We had to act soon.

Helmi let out a wounded sound. Matthias held her close. His face tight. Ready.

Angela sighed and shook her head. 'Then of course there was that fool of a man, Onni. He might as well go too if I'd done Tapio. No loose ends, you know?' She said it as if we would understand. 'He was more than easy. Opportunity opened its arms to me again. I just had to embrace it. And fast!'

She paused, contemplating our faces. 'Unlike your ridiculous blog tries to make out, murder isn't always intricately planned down to the last detail. If you're going to kill for a reason, and the plan is going to work, you need *opportunity*.'

'Motive versus opportunity,' I murmured.

Mother looked at me. 'What?'

'Just something I read.'

Angela didn't stop. She was rejoicing in her little sermon. 'Yes, you can plan it as much as possible but it needs that key element of coincidence, fate, call it what you will, to make the alchemy happen.' She spoke like a craftsman proud of his knowledge and work. 'All you can do is give it just the right conditions to flourish.

'I'd gone to the reception for matches, which by the way, I fortunately did find so I could burn the entry I saw in the reservations book while I was there. But what I also saw was your ridiculous show with the crossbow, Ursula.'

'Glad to be of service.' I laced my voice with sarcasm. 'In all the confusion I'm sure it must have been pretty easy to slip out. Through the door to the outside just behind the reception area, I presume? Matthias had appeared there when he'd gone in through the front door earlier.' I smiled. 'You were getting matches apparently and there were crossbows all over the walls. You grabbed another, ran to the car, killed Onni, then watched me come over. Thank you so much for the crack to my head.'

'My pleasure. I thought about killing you right there and then, but I thought it would be so much more poetic to have Ursula Smart as the murderer. Let's not forget, you'd been so quick to imagine my boy might have killed someone and then run off, hadn't you?'

My face reddened with shame. It was true. I'd even thought I'd smelled his familiar smell. Of course I had. His mother still washed his clothes, in the same washing powder as hers. She was the killer I'd smelled.

Even so, it had been far too easy for me to imagine it was the man I was supposed to marry who had smashed my head against that door. I'd thought everything I shouldn't think about the man I wanted to spend those remaining days of my life with. He'd abandoned me. He'd killed a man. He was dead. There were no more bad things left to think. But now wasn't the time for self-recriminations. It hadn't escaped me that Angela's plan had very much been revealed now and that she was entirely capable of preferring her son dead than seeing him live with me. The best way I could erase all those doubt-filled thoughts I'd had was to make sure he survived. That's what he'd asked of me in the first place.

I pushed on, working fast to stretch this moment out. '*You* took the crossbow bolt from me, and I looked so completely guilty. It was a gift. It was easy to slip back in through the side door as everyone else came out the front. I suspect that was when you saw the name Breffni Spear in the register and attempted to destroy it quickly.'

She shrugged. 'Just another of those loose ends. Then it was time to make sure you saw *my son* was dead and you'd never think to come looking for him. At least, not until they'd got the body out of the ice and realised you'd got it wrong. We'd be long gone by then.'

'Oh yes,' I interrupted. 'And, of course, Spear would never be able to resurface again, with Tapio's murder hanging over his head.'

She gave a cold laugh. 'Yes, I'd just imagined spiriting him away to a remote cabin I'd found and keeping him a little sedated and—' she smirked — 'chained up, for as long as I needed to.'

I stared at her in horror and then back at Spear. I couldn't bear to think of the horrific turn his life could have taken. A hostage. A prisoner for God knows how long.

'I would just have retreated to a life of solitude and grief. No doubt you would have quickly forgotten about me with Spear "dead". Why bother with the mother? Those new deaths I hadn't foreseen in advance were quite . . . advantageous.' Angela just continued as if she was walking through an everyday event. 'He'd never be able to return. And he'd never be able to come back to you, now you were quite obviously a killer too. You'd spend the rest of your days behind bars for Onni's murder.' She paused to smile. 'Or in the padded cell you really deserve.'

I felt Mother bristle next to me. 'You're the insane one here, *Angela*.' She spoke so loudly, almost yelling. 'How could you think that would work?'

Angela fixed her eyes on Mother. 'Oh, but it was working, wasn't it? Everyone was very quick to think of the bride and groom as potential murderers. To think that they killed Tapio and Onni. Were you not yourselves considering the Bonnie and Clyde scenario?'

'Rubbish,' Mother snapped. 'You're insane and a killer, Angela.'

'Pandora.' Aunt Charlotte dramatically shoved her finger in her ear and wiggled it. 'I may be about to die, but I'd sooner do so without being deaf. Please, don't shout!'

Mother took on the challenge. She raised her voice again. 'I don't care! I will shout if I want! This woman is a lunatic with a gun and she is going to kill us all.'

Aunt Charlotte tutted and edged away, but then looked back at her with a glimmer of understanding.

Angela was wistful. 'Sadly, I fear she is right. I've come this far. I almost died myself fending off Aino.' She shook her head. 'She was tougher than I thought. She'd seen me at the window when I left to check on Spear.'

I thought of the silhouette I'd seen at the window through my haze, the devil I had so easily formed from it. I looked at Angela in front of us now. The idea had not been so far from the truth.

'While you thought I was in shock, sleeping in my bedroom, I skied out here to check on my son and restoke the fire . . .'

'A little careless with your tracks that time though,' I interrupted again.

She was starting to look irritated. 'My plan had worked. I'd been resourceful enough to seize those *opportunities*! You were so busy with your ridiculous theories,' she laughed. 'You were caught up in the fantasy that murders are planned perfectly like some puzzle game. But they are gory, difficult, spontaneous, and whatever plans the killer has, they still have to stumble through each moment, adapting and making the best of what they're thrown. The plan is just the skeleton. You have to take the *opportunity* when it comes and make it work.' She gave us a patronising look. 'I know that's not quite as *romantic* or clever for your *blogs*. But that's not how it happens. I had to work hard and fast.'

She gathered herself, focusing in. 'It was almost time to go. But I couldn't take my boy yet. The storm was coming. I'd have to wait. I knew once I disappeared the balloon would go up and you'd start hunting for me.' She shook her head. 'I didn't know until I came back that it already had. When I returned to the cabin, you'd all left and there was only Aino. She was waiting for me in the bedroom. She knew. She was ready.' She looked rueful. 'The woman put up a good fight but she was no match for my gun in her big fat mouth.'

Angela started laughing manically and stroked a finger along the barrel of the gun. She was increasingly looking like a woman capable of something very drastic.

Time had run out. There were no more revelations to stall her with. We had to act fast.

Fortunately, Helmi chose that moment to lose her mind. She broke free from Matthias and hurled herself towards Angela, screaming indistinct words in Finnish. I may not have been able to understand the words, but her intention was very clear. I had been wrong. There was still more blood left to spill.

CHAPTER THIRTY-SEVEN: IT'S RESCUING TIME

I felt strangely still, detached from it all inside my shell as the chaos reigned around me. The opening note came from Mother, who pushed me back against the wall and shouted, 'Now!'

Aunt Charlotte ran for the door and opened it.

Helmi threw herself across the room in front of us, straight into the path of Angela's gun as it fired. Matthias grabbed Helmi's coat and dragged her down. He recoiled as the bullet thudded into him. He hit the ground behind Helmi.

The floor started to vibrate with a rhythmic thudding sound that was growing louder. Closer. A sound like hooves. A long pike with a sharpened end was the first thing to appear through the door, followed quickly by the antlers.

The call was clear. 'Rescuing time!'

Bridget came through the door on the back of a reindeer, the lance held out in front of her as proud as a medieval knight. Angela froze, the gun shaking in her outstretched hand, her mouth falling open.

'Lay down your weapon!' Bridget commanded, a fierce look of determination on her face as she crossed the room. 'And put your hands in the air.'

Aunt Charlotte looked on in awe. 'You *can* ride a reindeer!'

'Why the hell is she on a reindeer?' Mother's question seemed to be lost in the confusion.

'Thank God,' I breathed. Bridget's enthusiasm for listening at doors had finally found a purpose.

She nodded in a slightly military way. 'Had to unfasten this baby from the sleigh.'

Angela's wild eyes went round us all before she turned the gun on Spear. 'I think it might be time for goodbye.'

'No!' I shouted and began to move towards him.

She swung round and pointed the gun at me. 'I'll make sure you'll never have him.'

The lance drove home into Angela's shoulder just as she fired. Mother veered in front of me. Angela's arm jolted suddenly with the impact.

I felt Mother's body shift unexpectedly against me. She jerked unnaturally and turned to look at me in confusion before slipping to the ground.

'Oh my God, Mother!' I dropped to the floor, kneeling beside her, and instantly pulled back her coat. There was an emerging circle of blood blooming out fast across her cream-coloured jumper. The bullet had gone into the top left of her chest. I looked up at Aunt Charlotte, who was running across the room. 'She's been shot. Mother has been shot.'

The blood was quick to spread and started to pool on the wooden floor.

I couldn't think. My thoughts failed. I stared at her in disbelief, my mind unable to process or accept what I was seeing.

I was aware of movement elsewhere in the room. Angela was on the ground, the lance sticking up straight out of her. Helmi had run forward and grabbed the gun. She held it out firmly at Angela.

'Don't shoot!' Bridget ordered as she climbed off the animal.

But it was too late. Helmi stared down at Angela and said in a flat voice, 'I'm taking the *opportunity*.'

The single sound echoed round the walls of the tiny hut and into the frozen wilderness. Helmi stood perfectly calm, a detached look on her face, the gun in her outstretched hand. A perfect circle of red burned through the front of Angela's head.

My eyes quickly went to Spear lying beside her, unaware his mother, a murderer, was dead next to him. He looked so peaceful. So oblivious.

At my side, on the floor, Mother let out a long, laboured breath.

'Mother.' I held her hand. There was blood streaming down her arm, over her skin in thick trails. 'Please, Mother, don't leave me. Please. You can't die. I can't . . .'

Aunt Charlotte was on the other side of her. 'We need to compress the wound,' she said, her face taut and eyes bulging as she pushed hard into Mother's body. 'Pandora! Pandora, listen to me. You will stay with us. You cannot leave.'

Mother gave a weak smile that fell into a grimace, her face creasing in pain.

'It's going to be OK,' I gasped. 'It's going to be OK. Isn't it, Aunt Charlotte?'

Aunt Charlotte looked at me with fearfully resigned eyes. Her hands were covered in her sister's blood.

Mother groaned again and her eyes began to close.

'No!' I shouted. I stared in horror. 'No!' I held the sides of her coat and lifted her up. 'Mother, come back! Come back.' I held her to me and felt her body wilt. She grew limp in my arms. 'Please.' I threw my head back and screwed my eyes shut. 'Please don't die, Mother. You can't die. You can't ever die.'

But she could.

CHAPTER THIRTY-EIGHT:
THE WRECKAGE OF LIFE

All the averages and numbers of life mean nothing in the end. Nobody knows when it will be over. We just have the day we wake up to. There might be more. There might not. When I look back at that final moment, there were so many lives in the balance all clustered in that small, isolated room. Not everyone made it out. Death had been waiting outside ever since we arrived. He wasn't about to walk away from that hut empty-handed.

He'd already gathered in some souls back at the lodge. The bodies of Aino, Tapio, Onni and Spear's father all waited there. But out here in the woods, there were more lives ripe for the taking. Matthias had managed to drag himself to the side of the cabin and was half sitting, his arm hanging loose beside him, his face draining fast of colour.

Angela was skewered to the ground with the long lance jutting out of her, blood making its way to the floor. The simple spot where the bullet had entered scorched into her head. Helmi stood over her, holding out the gun, doubt and confusion deep in her eyes. She was rigid. So many possibilities making their way into her mind.

Bridget moved cautiously towards her. The reindeer grunted out a breath.

'Shh, now, girl.' It was hard to know if Bridget was talking to the animal or the woman with the gun. 'You can put that down now.'

Helmi looked at her as if she didn't understand.

Spear still lay beside Angela, his mother. He was so unaware of the enormous loss he'd just suffered, to the grief that would roll out from this moment. But it would be a twisted suffering. He would be forced to lament a woman he did not yet know anything about, a woman capable of inflicting so much pain. Of killing. And all for him, to protect their bond that was now so inextricably cut. All the pain and disbelief was waiting for him, waiting for him to discover who she really was. How many times is the truth only revealed by death? It strips off all the layers of life. All the veneer and surface of falsehoods we build fall away to leave the core of who we are.

For now, he was as immobile and as senseless as he had been from that first moment when we'd found him. Safe and innocent of all this horror that he would soon be born into. I wished I could save him from that. For now, he wouldn't be conscious for quite some time. Angela had given him a lot of the drugs, and I more than anyone knew how strong they were. I'd administered them to Mother enough times to know I had to be precise with the dose.

Still, that dark figure of Death waited out there in the black night, patiently looking at the window. Waiting to see if there'd be another soul to gather in. I held Mother's body close to me.

Helmi seemed to flicker into life. She lowered the gun and frowned at Bridget then back at the executed woman at her feet. She stared as if to question what had just happened here while she had been absent from her own mind.

'What . . .' Helmi was emerging from her trance.

'You shot and killed the murderer.' Bridget didn't feel the need to sweeten the news. 'You killed Angela.'

Helmi stood over the body in stunned silence until a look of confirmation took her face. Affirmation.

Bridget quickly took the gun from her and nodded.

Mother lay in my arms, her skin as smooth and pale as candle wax. I could still feel the faint whisper of a pulse in her neck but it was failing. Aunt Charlotte kept up the compression but there was an air of increasing futility to it.

I rocked Mother like I was soothing a child. She seemed so guileless, so peaceful resting there. Would I know the exact moment when it came? Would I feel her leave? Or is it as indistinct as thoughts? When we are born, there is an instant declaration of life, a howl, a scream into the world. Our exit is often much more vague. A time of death is given, but when did life leave? I remembered holding Dad just the same. His body so precious, so fragile with the remains of life. The final note of his existence fell with no symphony.

'Oh, Mum, we had so many more adventures left. You were meant to be old and irritable with me. I was supposed to *despair* of your antics. We were going to go on for ever. Together.' My voice failed. I leaned down to kiss her forehead. It was cold. All the pieces of her were there, eyebrows, lips, nose, but something was disappearing. Falling from her.

I felt Aunt Charlotte's arms around me. Warm and full of life. They were so different to the body I held. Aunt Charlotte didn't speak but I could feel the tears shuddering inside her. She knew she would have to be strong.

Bridget had shuffled in next to us, her eyes already gleaming with tears. 'It's going to be all right.' She gave us both a keen, expectant look. 'I know it is. It always is.'

Only it always wasn't. Death doesn't care what happens before it comes or about the person it takes. It doesn't care for fairness or other people's expectations. It doesn't care for averages and numbers. It just takes. Randomly, when it sees the opportunity.

Mother's thin, ruckled breath was barely moving her chest. She had a serene look as if she was settled to it.

'They'll be here soon,' Bridget said through her tears. 'Just hold on.'

But there seemed to be so little for Mother to hold on to. So little life left. I held her closer, as though she could absorb some of my life and let it sink through her, rejuvenating her, filling her up with years.

'Wait, who'll be here?' Aunt Charlotte sniffed.

'I saw their lights moving,' Bridget said, wide-eyed. 'There was some movement through the trees.'

'Tree spirits,' Matthias wheezed.

Bridget gave him a dismissive look. 'Don't be ridiculous. These were car headlights.'

'Oh, then hunters.' He nodded.

Bridget frowned. 'Would that not have been the first guess?' She shook her head. 'I found some flares in a kit bag on the *ahkio*. I sent them all up and I saw the lights start to move. I don't know how far away they were. You were all shouting about an insane woman with a gun who was going to kill everyone so I thought I'd better get in here and rescue you all first.' She looked very pleased with herself for a moment before her eyes resettled on Mother.

A silence fell over us as sudden and shocking as cold water. The thin rasp of Mother's breathing was now the only sound I could hear. I concentrated on every breath, each one so quiet. A weak sound that seemed so wrong. Weak was not a word meant for her. The only sound I'd ever known come from Mother, *her* sound, was strong. But now her breath started to fade. There was a defeated tone to it.

'No,' I whispered. 'No, please don't leave me. Stay. Stay with me.' I pulled her in tight. 'Please don't go away. Just hold on. Bridget thinks help is coming.'

Mother's eyes lifted a little and she tried to speak. I leaned my ear close to her mouth and she whispered, 'It will all be all right.' Then she fell limp in my arms.

I stared with no understanding. 'No?' It could have been a question.

I looked over to the window and to the dark shadow standing there in its frame. It eyed me for a moment, considering me. Waiting.

I shook my head. 'No.' This time I said it in hard defiance. 'No.'

I paused and looked at Mother. 'Not today.'

I turned my face to Aunt Charlotte and pushed down hard on her hand where it was still resting over the wound. She frowned but I felt the pressure increase from her hand into Mother's body.

Gently, I tilted Mother's head back and pinched her nose. I placed my mouth over hers. She was still warm. I blew steadily. Her chest rose in response. I started to pump her chest with the heel of my hand. I tried desperately to focus on what I knew of CPR, only what I'd seen online, but it's all we had. With so many near-death encounters, it had seemed like a good idea to have some rudimentary knowledge, but remembering now, in the heat of it, was so hard. I gave two more sharp rescue breaths but there was no response this time.

'Keep up the compression,' I said to Aunt Charlotte.

I don't know how long we tried for. There was too much blood. Every second, every breath was so long. Dragging her back to the world. *Our* world with every moment.

The sound of that first small cough will never leave me. Her eyes squeezed tight in pain and confusion, as if somehow this was not where she was supposed to be.

She filled her chest with new air, holding it there. I looked at Aunt Charlotte and we listened to the sound of Mother taking those first few breaths. To the sound of her being alive.

I must have cried out, I think, or made some noise. A desperate sound of relief. Aunt Charlotte looked stunned.

'Oh God.' I rested my head on Mother's chest, listening to the growing pulse.

With my head turned to the side, I saw that shape again at the window. It paused. There was a brief moment of hesitation before it turned and drifted into the night.

It was gone. Aunt Charlotte looked over at the empty window and then back at me.

There would be no more soul gathering tonight.

A white beam travelled across the wall opposite the window. Then another. A slash of light filled the room. Distant noises grew closer. The rip of engines bore down on us. Voices gathered.

'They're here!' Bridget announced and ran for the door.

'Hold on, Mother,' I breathed into her ear. 'Hold on to me. Don't let go.'

I felt her hand grip mine. 'I won't.'

CHAPTER THIRTY-NINE:
THE ANATOMY OF LOVE

Love is not a word I use very often. I don't feel comfortable with the sound of it. It feels gauche, silly almost. Trite. Just to say 'I love you' is almost like cheating, something to fill the space when you can't find any other words. It had, until then, often seemed so meaningless. So empty. There were a thousand other ways of saying it. Showing it. But that was before.

The Lapland Central Hospital back in Rovaniemi provided plenty of moments for me to make up for lost words. The hunters who'd found us had been able to snowmobile to the nearest house and call for help. FinnHEMS, the helicopter emergency services, came fast, claiming the sky with their lights and noise. The police weren't far behind, using snowmobiles and Border Guard helicopters to reach us.

The medics took Mother and Spear out first. I travelled with them, as did Aunt Charlotte and Bridget. Matthias was reluctant to leave Helmi alone with the police, but they insisted given that he'd been shot and was losing blood.

I'd said goodbye to Mother on a lightless night in December that should have been my wedding night. But now, somehow, we lifted through the darkness into the stars, high above the grey-white trees. Spear would be fine, they said. He'd live. They stayed silent about Mother. She lay as still as death. I tuned my hearing to listen to her gentle, quiet breathing.

Those livid green Northern Lights marked out our departure, flickering round us like spirits travelling over the land. From up high, it looked so calm, that snow-globe world. My mind fell to all those bodies. Tapio, his wife Aino, Onni impaled to his car, and Angela, a woman I had trusted so implicitly that I couldn't see how she'd choreographed everything to fake her son's death.

I pictured that man under the ice. Spear's father. I would never stop imagining his face cast in that green light.

But we would not see him again, although his picture would be in the papers many times, the one I'd seen so many times on Angela's sideboard. So like his son in so many ways except those still, grey eyes. I wondered if Spear was capable of doing what his father had done. Running. Leaving for ever. Disappearing into the night. I looked at him now, so peaceful in that helicopter as we flew out into the darkness. No, he would stay. For now. And that was enough.

The Mokki Murderer was what they dubbed Angela. Helmi's fate was yet to be decided but the court of the press had already decreed she was a Finnish hero and had saved many lives from the British housewife serial killer of Lapland.

Spear's father was excavated from the ice. All the bodies were accounted for. We waited to see if Mother would add to the tally. Her condition was serious. But in the end, that's all you can do. Wait.

There were moments we felt she was rallying, only to be told she'd gone back down again.

Spear was eventually dragged from his delirium. He was groggy but alive. I'd thought the worst part would be the explanation of what had happened. He had very little recollection and had seen so little through his comatose sleep. I tried to piece together the broken mosaic of what had played out. I couldn't capture every moment, string it together in a coherent way that made any sense. But I was wrong. It wasn't the description of the events that was the difficult part, it was how he received them.

He looked at me in disbelief. His father had been alive for a few moments in my tale. He'd been alive for all of Spear's life. It had been so easy for Angela to tell Spear his father had been lost at sea. Spear called himself stupid for not asking her for proof, but why would he? Why would he think his mother lied about such a thing? Who would? Some perhaps. Some not.

I thought of Angela and her *opportunities*. She'd been relying on fate for so long it had become second nature.

But now Spear's father was dead again, without Spear ever getting the chance to meet him. His mother was dead too. And she was a multiple murderer. It was as if each stage in the story had to be the pinnacle of the horror but then there was even more. I think the hardest thing for him to accept was that it was all for him, all because Angela couldn't let him go, couldn't bear to see him marry me.

'It's all my fault.' His voice was raw from the drugs. 'I tried to change everything. I should have known. She'd started to act strangely, asking me questions about where we would live, how often she'd see me, did I think it was really a good idea, given what happened last time I was married. I even found her with all my old baby photos and clothes.'

I gave a low smile. 'Mine too. A mother thing.'

'I was concerned. I should have said something. Told you my worries. I tried to tell you a few times. I just . . . I couldn't find the right moment, or the words.'

'I thought you were having doubts.'

'Doubts?'

'About me . . . us . . . this.'

He paused as if deciding whether to speak. 'You're the one thing I never doubt.'

I stared at him, not knowing how to respond.

'I should have talked to you about her. She was getting really strange. She'd said I'd always be her baby, which was kind of . . . kind of . . .' He looked down.

'Like a mother?'

'I was going to say disturbing.' He smiled but there was no joy in it. This would take a long time to settle into the heart of him, for him to work out some way to understanding.

He looked up at me. 'How is your mother?' he asked gently.

I squeezed my lips between my teeth and bit down. The words were stuck.

'It's OK. If you don't . . .'

'She's going to make it through, they say.' My voice broke and I felt the familiar warmth of the tears. 'It's been . . . there've been some . . .' I paused to refocus. 'There have been some moments when . . .' I cleared my throat. 'We've been very lucky.' My voice petered out.

He gripped my hand. 'Ursula.' Leaning forward, he winced. 'She's going to live. She's strong,' he whispered. 'Like you.' I saw the rueful look. It was more than he'd been granted for his mother.

Now all he had left was me and I was worried he might see that as the consolation prize at the end of it all. Or worse, partly to blame. Perhaps Angela wouldn't have been driven to such madness if it hadn't been for me. Or maybe it was always there just under the surface, waiting patiently, dormant, until the right conditions came along for it to germinate.

Our wedding was that catalyst. That, or Spear's father returning. It would have been enough to keep a lot of therapists busy contemplating all those *physical manifestations of trauma*. But for now, all I could see was that we were alive, however many ghosts we had between us.

The daily minutiae were returning so fast that it was already making the past few days seem improbable. Bridget had taken over Mother's blog, *Death Smarts*, for the time being while Mother was incapacitated. She'd already written a piece on how she'd come to the rescue of the Smart Women, riding in on a reindeer armed with a fishing harpoon. The first comment was querying whether this was a spoof post. No one informed Mother of the temporary alterations to the editorial team or the new slant on content. We'd just have to wait for that bombshell to drop later.

The media, however, had exploded with our names again. Theories abounded about malicious mother syndrome, domineering mothers, possessive mothers, lawnmower mothers, helicopter mothers, elephant mums, tiger, jellyfish, dolphin and plain old neurotic mums. There seemed to be no end to the ways in which mothers could be classified and criticised. One for every mother that ever lived. Angela was just another example to hold up and say she got it wrong. To be fair, she'd done that in very bloody style. The four deaths she'd been responsible for had technically afforded her serial killer status according to some commentators. Others disagreed on the time frame. It was being hotly debated on various true crime podcasts from the minute the story broke. There was no let-up in it.

Spear had a permanent hunted look in his eyes. He didn't speak about his experiences in the grain hut with his mother, if indeed he remembered anything of being taken there and strung up. But when I watched him, increasingly, there was that distant look of recollection. I wondered if it was worse that it was only half-remembered? Did the doubt leave a hole that could be filled by the very worst his imagination could conjure? I was falling into the therapy speak again. I had to be careful not to over-analyse him but, as a survivor of therapy, it's hard not to see it as the first port when the storm comes in.

But all that mattered in that moment was that we'd survived. Again.

There was a knock at the door.

'Hello?' Spear rasped. He was instantly alert. There was a constant nervous edge about him now, as if anything could happen. He'd even seemed anxious in his sleep.

The door cracked open. Aunt Charlotte and Bridget's faces peered round the edge.

'We're getting coffees if you'd like one.' Aunt Charlotte looked drawn, weary from the strain, but her smile had started to resurface with news that Mother was going to survive.

Bridget, however, remained inquisitive in that slightly over-enthusiastic way she had when jeopardy was close at hand.

'How's the patient?' she asked eagerly, hopeful for some new medical detail.

I could see a quick glimpse of that notebook and fluffy topped pen through the crack in the door.

'Genuinely? Or is this for the blog, Bridget?' I asked.

She looked overly affronted. 'How can you say such a thing?'

I leaned back and folded my arms. 'Oh, I don't know, perhaps it's the detailed daily revelations.' I raised an eyebrow. 'Does Mother know about her stand-in yet?'

'Stand-in? I'm on the team!' She lifted her chin defiantly. 'Your mother has always expressed the view that there should be full and frank exposure of the Smart Women's exploits. I'm merely abiding by her wishes.'

'You've made it sound like she did actually die, Bridget.'

She laughed a little too self-consciously. 'No need to worry. I am a grateful caretaker and will perform my duties to the utmost of my abilities.'

I pictured Mother's face on hearing this news.

'Caretaker! It's funny that.' Aunt Charlotte turned to look at Bridget. 'I can really see you in the role of the creepy caretaker in the basement, surrounded by a strange menagerie of stuffed animals.'

Bridget looked concerned. 'I've told you before that none of my pets are available for your distasteful taxidermy hobby.'

Aunt Charlotte shrugged. 'I can wait.'

Spear made a guttural sound and sank back into the pillows. He looked exhausted.

'OK, ladies, enough of the dead pets society. Didn't you say you were off to get coffees?'

Bridget looked blank for a moment, glancing down at the notebook before slipping it back into her bag. 'Of course.'

'We'll bring you something, Ursula.' Aunt Charlotte nodded as the door was closing. 'Maybe even a . . .' Her voice was muffled by the door.

I could hear them chuntering away down the corridor.

The room fell back into some form of peace, punctuated by beeps from the various machines.

Spear looked at me as if he was deciding whether or not to speak. Finally, he began in a tentative voice. 'So, what happens now?'

I widened my eyes as if I was surprised. I wasn't. I knew exactly what he meant. I'd been waiting for it. But I wasn't about to start making any decisions here. Although there was one thing I was already sure of.

'I don't want to get married.' I said it with the kind of quiet assurance I imagined sounded like authority.

But when his face crumpled, I lost all semblance of calm. I reached for his hand. 'Listen to me. I don't want to be the one responsible for whether or not you survive. My name is too dangerous to live with. Too close to all this death.'

'I . . .'

I held a finger to my lips and for some innate reason glanced at the door. 'That's why I'm not going to marry you.'

He let out a long sigh.

'And I'm not going to be Ursula Smart anymore.'

A shadow of concern was quick to spread over his face.

'It's not my real name. It never has been. Smart is just a pseudonym. Mother liked it for her blog and it just stuck. And let me tell you, that's not the only fictional content in her true crime.' I smiled. 'I'm someone else. Someone who wants to be with you for the rest of the days they have left. In peace. With no more drama or death.'

He shook his head slowly. 'I don't understand. What are you saying?'

'I'm saying that I'm hanging up my Smart Woman outfit.'

'Are there outfits?' He raised an eyebrow.

'Metaphorically, of course. Although . . .' I leaned closer.

The rest is . . . Well, I'm going to use a word that Mother and her blog have never been too familiar with.

Private.

CHAPTER FORTY: THE DIFFICULT
ENGLISH PATIENT

Mother was not a good patient. I felt sure they'd discharged her far too early but the staff at the hospital assured me she'd be better off at home in another country. I got the impression that they wanted to add, 'Just anywhere else other than here.' But, in fairness, they're nurses, not actual angels.

Back home, Mother was somehow more demanding and irascible than when we were surrounded by bodies with a murderer on the loose. But she'd been so close to death and I held on to that thought. I might not have got the chance to see her irritated face again. Although, after the fifth week of her ringing the little bell she'd found in a bedside drawer, it was a thought that I returned to with different sentiments occasionally. But over the weeks, she rallied. She was much stronger than any of us had imagined. The wound healed surprisingly quickly and she was soon back at her laptop, albeit still propped up in bed and wearing the latest Gucci pyjamas, a gift to herself to celebrate that she didn't die. There are cheaper ways to do that but, as Mother explained, she 'doesn't do cheap'. That's for people like Bridget who like feeding the birds.

She spent the days tapping away at *Death Smarts*, which she said needed emergency attention after Bridget's caretaker role. She ignored the very obvious point that subscriber numbers had gone up twenty per cent during Bridget's brief tenancy of the site. And also the fact that people loved the new section Aunt Charlotte had created called *Favourite Deaths*.

Mother's bedroom became headquarters for the Smart Women brand, as she so beautifully styled our family. She gave interviews from bed, wrote articles, appeared on podcasts and was even in talks for a book deal that involved her reimagining the near-death experiences we'd gone through in a more 'cosy' whodunnit crime scenario. I objected to this on the basis that it might appear disrespectful to the families who had lost loved ones to use their murders and write something that amounted to no more than a glorified puzzle or game. She assured me she'd consulted those people who might be affected and they were on board. Also, the projected sales revenues were huge. There was plenty of meat left on our Finnish adventures to keep her occupied for long enough. That was good. She would need a pretty big distraction from what I was about to tell her.

Mother had so many commitments and work that she seemed in her element. It would be a shame to disrupt this, but every chapter must come to an end. For now, we continued in the same vein and I was happy to deliver tea trays and comfort, even though she clearly didn't need to be confined to the bed anymore.

It felt like a necessary duty, a penance to take Mother her coffee and biscuits that particular morning. I could give her that at least, but I couldn't wait any longer. She had to know.

The front door opened just as I was heading upstairs.

'God, Bridget,' I gasped, 'you've got to stop just letting yourself in like that. I could be doing anything.'

'I hope not.' She'd brought Dupin with her and the monkey squealed in approval.

'Mother will freak out if she sees the monkey here again.'

Bridget bustled in and tapped the side of her nose. 'What her majesty doesn't know won't hurt her.'

Over the past few weeks though, I knew that wasn't true. There were a lot of things Mother didn't know and I felt sure I was about to hurt her with at least one of them.

Bridget watched me closely as if she knew my plans. 'Everything all right here?'

By here, I'm sure she meant with me, but I batted it away.

The sound of a key turning in the lock was distraction enough. As it opened, Aunt Charlotte was already making her excuses.

'I just saw this one coming in and I thought, bugger me, they're not having a meeting without me!'

'Meeting?' I looked at her in confusion. 'Of what?'

'The Smart Women, of course, Ursula. Where is your head these days?'

Not here, was the real answer. It was far away. It had been for a while.

I looked at Aunt Charlotte's warm, open face. I would miss seeing it every day. But it was time. They needed to know.

'I'm glad you're here.' My voice was solemn.

Bridget paused in her fussing with gloves and coats. She eyed me suspiciously. 'Why?'

'I just think I might need a wingman or two for what I've got to say.'

Aunt Charlotte glanced up suddenly. She'd been around the house enough to know where this was going. To most people it would have seemed like a natural progression. But then, Mother isn't most people.

'Right.' Aunt Charlotte sounded determined. She reached inside her tweed jacket and pulled out her hip flask. 'Just a nip or two of Dutch courage, I think.' She took a couple of big mouthfuls before offering the flask to me. I obliged.

Bridget looked between us and a moment of realisation passed over her. She intercepted the hip flask as I handed it back to Aunt Charlotte. 'Three's company,' she said as she downed the remaining whisky. It seemed like a fitting motto for her.

We climbed the stairs slowly, that Wednesday morning at ten o'clock, with the heavy scent of Scotch following in our wake. Mother heard us before we'd even reached the top step.

'Come on then,' she shouted from behind the closed door.

She was busy behind her bed table, the kind used in hospitals, but Mother had turned it into a truly mobile office. The array of laptop, mobiles, landline, papers, lipsticks, tea-cups and chocolates could be wheeled around to any location she chose. By me usually.

Her bedroom, or inner sanctum as I called it, had become a shrine to her recovery. Every surface was littered with cards and vases of flowers, balloons and handmade craft objects people had poured hours into making for her. There was no questioning the obvious devotion people had for her. A fan of the blog had even knitted a doll of each of the Smart Women. Somehow, seeing ourselves in miniature, toylike form was slightly disturbing and macabre. However big or overwhelming life felt, we were really only something so irrelevant and inconsequential that we could be held in the palm of a stranger's hands as she created us stitch by stitch. Mother's take was slightly different. She said I needed to stop analysing them too closely. She was actually inspired to start selling kits on the website, with knitting patterns available for each of them.

There was all kind of merchandise Mother wanted to start monetising. There was even a Smart Woman game someone had created that involved being one of us and collecting clues while attempting to avoid being the next victim. Working title: Smartuedo.

Arrayed along the top of Mother's dressing table was the most disturbing gift of all from an avid fan and amateur sculptor who had created clay replicas of all the murder weapons we'd encountered, including a broken chandelier, mushrooms, vape pens, cannonballs, a bracelet, a ducking stool, fish, and even a small replica of a priest hole which Aunt Charlotte had unfortunately reported on the website as a priest's hole. There had been comments.

But the overwhelming part of it all was that the whole room was testament to the fact that Mother had definitely given out our home address to more than the handful of people she'd assured me it was. '*Just the diehard fans*,' she'd insisted. It was a troubling word to use with all this new mania.

She seemed to ignore our entrance to the room, but I've learned from bitter experience never to underestimate Mother's ability to see everything. She was watching all right. I could tell by the random shifting of items across her tray table, the pretend texting and lack of eye contact, that she was analysing our entry. She had an innate ability to know when something was brewing. She was right. It had been.

CHAPTER FORTY-ONE: A TIME TO CAST AWAY STONES

'What the hell are you talking about?' Mother pushed herself up on her elbows. She locked her eyes on me with the piercing precision of a sniper.

'It's time, Mother. We both know that.' I put the coffee down on her tray table and attempted to plump her pillows.

She waved me away and turned to the other two who were standing guiltily still. 'Did you know about this?'

Neither of them made a sound or a movement. Aunt Charlotte flashed a look at me.

'You should be resting.' Bridget moved towards the bed and started tucking in the sheet. 'Doctor said—'

'Doctor said. Doctor said.' Mother's frustration was rising. 'Stop doing that, Bridget.'

I sighed and sat on the edge of the bed. 'It's very beautiful and you'd love it. If you gave it a chance.'

She folded her arms petulantly.

'It's in a very quiet wood. There's a stream. It's peaceful.' I looked at her with appealing eyes. 'I need to find some peace now, Mother.'

She looked astonished. 'With a man who's nearly got you killed twice?'

'Mother, if we're counting who I've had more near-death experiences with, the people in this room would probably top the leader board.'

Aunt Charlotte made a little noise in announcement. 'It sounds idyllic to me,' she offered.

'What? Setting herself up in a stalker's paradise?' Mother threw herself back into the pillows dramatically.

'I don't have a stalker.' Which is unbelievable but true, unless I included my own family.

'Ursula, it's dangerous. You could be killed.'

'That is not the usual reaction a daughter receives when she tells her mother she's found her first home.'

Aunt Charlotte and Bridget had plucked up enough courage to approach and perch on the edge of the bed. Somehow, we'd made this look like a deathbed scene rather than a joyous moment where I embarked on the next chapter of my life.

'Look, Mother.' I tempered my voice. 'No one wants to kill me. I just keep stumbling across murderers and that won't happen when I'm living peacefully with Spear in a little cottage, far from all this drama.'

She looked dramatically aghast. 'Oh, so it's *drama* is it here?'

We all looked around the strange, theatrical dressing room she'd created and then back to Mother.

'You can always come and visit,' I offered meekly.

'In the countryside? Me?' She was even more dramatic.

I looked at Aunt Charlotte and then Bridget. 'You'll have these two here to keep you company.'

'And that's supposed to make me feel better about it all?' She leaned forward. 'Abandoning me to the Tweedle-Dumbs?'

Bridget cleared her throat pointedly. 'I think we make a very good team on *Death Smarts*.'

I hadn't imagined anything that could have made the situation worse. I was losing any chance of convincing her.

I felt in my pocket and pulled out the folded piece of paper with the cottage details on it. I handed it to her like a child offering up a disappointing school report. 'We're completing this week.'

'What?' She took the paper. 'I . . . How long has . . .' She looked down in dismay before dropping the sheet to the bed. 'It's lovely.' Her voice was flat, shutting down.

I held her hand. It still felt weak and thin. My heart sank in my chest, and I sensed that familiar anxiety and doubt rise up again to fill the space. I'd felt it a lot through the whole process but, when I contemplated *not* doing this, I felt worse. When I even thought of abandoning our scheme, our little cottage in the woods, a sadness started to invade, a sense of lost opportunities. I'd had so many of those it was time to be what I could, not just what I was left with. My head was so full of conflicting thoughts that it didn't seem like most of them were mine anymore. They were random and scattered like dreams.

'I need to do this, Mother.' I kept my eyes on her. 'I need to find a life.'

'But you have a life. Here. With me.'

I could feel the tears starting to pool. She'd turned into that innocent child, the one who very rarely surfaced but was always there, the person she was always trying to push away and deny. For all her sharpness, she was so undeniably vulnerable. I had to tread carefully.

'Mother, I would like . . .' I sniffed and looked away. 'I would like to live a normal life.'

She shook her head and sniffed deeply. 'It's very overrated.'

I gave a small smile. 'But I'd at least like to try it out once.'

She pressed her lips together. Even Mother knows when she's facing defeat. She looked over at Aunt Charlotte, who simply nodded once.

Bridget had adopted a very grave look. 'It sounds reasonable to me, Pandora.'

We still hadn't entirely escaped the deathbed scene look of it all. I'd not expected bunting and champagne but this was a fairly dour tableau. I tried to inject some joy.

I leaned towards Mother. 'You can help me choose furnishings and curtains and . . . that sort of thing.'

Mother paused. We waited. Finally, she blew out heavily, as if accepting some great burden. 'I'll have to get to the mothership immediately.' This is her name for Peter Jones. She pushed the tray table away but then paused. 'Do you even have a colour scheme or design style in mind?'

I looked at her blankly.

She closed her eyes in faux dismay. 'We'll have to do something *rustic*, I suppose.' She pronounced the word like she'd trodden in it.

'Mother.' I held both her hands. 'This is not the end. This is a beginning. We're going to try out being happy.'

Her head fell and I bent and looked up into her face. 'Does that sound like a plan?'

She sighed. 'Well, I suppose it will have to, won't it?'

Aunt Charlotte rose to her feet and announced, 'I'll get the champagne.'

Mother frowned. 'Not the good stuff. That's for a sp—' She looked at me. 'Better bring the good stuff.'

Aunt Charlotte walked to the door and paused. She looked back. 'I've unpacked.'

Mother closed her eyes. 'Well, this day just keeps getting better.'

'Me too!' Bridget wasn't lightening the mood. 'We'll make such a happy little crew at the Smart Towers, won't we?' She was attempting a smile that looked more like a grimace. 'Dupin is so excited.'

Mother's eyes clicked open and I could have sworn a murderous look crossed them.

'Bridget,' Aunt Charlotte said as if she was calling her to heel. 'Downstairs, now.'

Bridget puckered her mouth and stuck out her chin. 'Very well. I go where I'm needed.' She rose with matronly style, smoothing down her brown skirt. 'When I get back, we'll talk about my new ideas for the podcast.'

'Bridget!' Even Aunt Charlotte could tell now wasn't the time.

When they'd both gone, I spoke carefully to Mother. 'Thank you,' I whispered.

I glanced over to the corner of the room to where Dad's shadow was lingering. He gave a warm smile that could almost have said, 'Don't worry, I'll take care of her,' if ghosts could look after the living. Although, in my experience, they can if you let them.

Mother wiped her hands down her face and reached for her phone.

I frowned a question.

'I need to message Bob. He'll be able to guide me through.' I saw Bob the Therapist's contact pop up on her phone and she started texting frantically like a teenager who's just discovered a secret.

'I thought you'd still not heard from him.'

'I see him more as my spirit guide now.' She didn't look up from the phone.

I smiled and watched her eagerness. She'd adjust, of that I had no doubt. The only doubts I had were my own.

It was going to be a hard road to our cottage, but I was determined. The Smart family would endure. None of us can leave our past behind that easily. I looked again for Dad. He was fading. Would he be coming with me, that *physical manifestation* of whatever it was? Perhaps.

One thing I was about to learn as we set out on this new life together, was that our ghosts are never far behind us. We would never be entirely alone. But even though we'd not managed the wedding, I was determined to have a honeymoon period or at least some space to breathe and just be.

As I started to leave the room, I looked back at all the chaos, with Mother right at the centre in her nest. I would miss all this. I would miss her. I gave her a smile but she'd distracted herself already, absorbed in texting Bob, or at least she wanted it to look like that. It was time to leave her to this maelstrom she'd created and find another path, one of my own creation for once.

I was about to say goodbye but thought better of it. For now, I left quietly. Mother doesn't do goodbyes.

I edged out into the hallway and softly closed the door. Downstairs, I could hear Aunt Charlotte and Bridget bickering over how best to remove a champagne cork, before the inevitable bang and a disconcerting scream.

'I told you not to point it there!' Bridget shouted.

I took out my phone and read the text. It was from Spear. I smiled. A simple three words and there were no more questions. I was getting used to the sound of them.

I heard the doorbell and he sent another text. *I'm outside. Is it OK to come in or do I need a flak jacket?*

I laughed. Aunt Charlotte was already opening the door and throwing her arms around Spear. I watched them through the banister.

'Dear boy, come in!' she announced. 'Bridget's been shot in the arse.'

He pulled back and frowned.

'Champagne cork, deary. No need to look so worried. We don't have murders every single day.' She laughed. 'Just some.'

I would miss this turmoil. Mother, texting in a frenzy to a therapist who would never respond; Bridget lying on the floor having been shot by a champagne cork, her pet monkey squawking in glee; Aunt Charlotte extolling the virtues of a sporran to Spear as she led him through into the kitchen. Who wouldn't miss this? But it was time to go and leave the discussion of Ursula Smart to the podcasts and interviews, the hysteria and circus of it all. I knew the @Angel_destroyers of the world were still out there but I was leaving all that behind. I was going to live peacefully in the forest, far away from all the madness. It was a new kind of dream to follow.

And it would be, until the day when danger found me again. Until I was standing alone at the doorway of my little cottage, so perfectly isolated in the woods, looking right into Death's face again. But that's not for now. That can wait. For now, this was enough.

THE END

ACKNOWLEDGEMENTS

It's still hard to believe that the seed of an idea can ever grow into a real book. There are so many people along the way who make that happen. Thank you to the wonderful publishing team who have always championed the Smart Women from the very first day. To Jasper, Emma and Laurel, thank you. Thank you to all the rest of the team at Joffe Books. A massive thank you to James Wills for believing in me and for being the best agent I could wish for. Thank you also to Helena for all your help, support and kindness.

This book was inspired by a wonderful winter trip to see our dear friends in Finland. After appearing on the news as the beleaguered family attempting to fly out of a Gatwick plagued by drones, we embarked on the most incredible adventure. You welcomed us into your home and showed us the unbelievable beauty of this extraordinary land. Thank you. I could not have written this book without your wonderful hospitality. Thank you also to Holly for organising a vital Murder Consultation group with your Finnish friends. Much of the research I gained from these lovely women is in this book, particularly their knowledge of Finnish folklore, customs, strong liquor, and all manner of floral, arboreal and dark matters. Thank you, Emma Tessier, Liisa, Maiski, Paula and Petra for devoting your time and being so free with your advice and help.

Writers are nothing without readers. Huge thanks to all the bloggers, reviewers and book groups whose enthusiasm and generosity keeps this all alive and thriving. I hope you approve of *Death Smarts*.

Writers also need other writers for the mutual love and tears — thank you D20s. Thanks also to everyone at the CWA for all the fun and support. Also, thanks to Venetia and the team at the Barnes Bookshop and to Matt Steele at Ivybridge Bookshop for your endless support. Indie bookshops are the best!

Finally, a huge thank you to my family. You are my constant support. To my Sarah, always an inspiration, always our books, my love. To my Delilah, for all our collaborations and getting me on that Dagger shortlist! To my Jimmy, for the models and endless ideas on how to kill people. And, finally, to the light of my life, my gorgeous husband. It is nothing without you.

THE JOFFE BOOKS STORY

We began in 2014 when Jasper agreed to publish his mum's much-rejected romance novel and it became a bestseller.

Since then we've grown into the largest independent publisher in the UK. We're extremely proud to publish some of the very best writers in the world, including Joy Ellis, Faith Martin, Caro Ramsay, Helen Forrester, Simon Brett and Robert Goddard. Everyone at Joffe Books loves reading and we never forget that it all begins with the magic of an author telling a story.

We are proud to publish talented first-time authors, as well as established writers whose books we love introducing to a new generation of readers.

We have been shortlisted for Independent Publisher of the Year at the British Book Awards three times, in 2020, 2021 and 2022, and for the Diversity and Inclusivity Award at the Independent Publishing Awards in 2022.

We built this company with your help, and we love to hear from you, so please email us about absolutely anything bookish at: feedback@joffebooks.com.

If you want to receive free books every Friday and hear about all our new releases, join our mailing list: www.joffebooks.com/contact

And when you tell your friends about us, just remember: it's pronounced Joffe as in coffee or toffee!

9 781835 262313